To MATTHEW,

SMOKE IN THE WIND

....

BY TONY MAY

....

Tony May

Published by:

FriesenPress

Suite 300 – 852 Fort Street
Victoria, BC, Canada V8W 1H8

www.friesenpress.com

Distributed to the trade by The Ingram Book Company

For THUMPER

ALASKA

CHAPTER 1

I could hear the cold north wind whistling in the darkness outside the double glazed window of my assigned accommodation. It was one of many rooms built into a bunch of pre-fabricated, heavy duty insulated double-wide trailers joined together with internal connecting hallways. The structure also contained a common TV lounge and mess hall. The blizzard from the High Arctic was ripping down the northeast slope of the Brooks Range and slamming into the small settlement of Deadhorse, Prudhoe Bay, Alaska. It was a treeless patch of muskeg and permafrost desolation approximately 1200 miles south of the North Pole and 250 miles inside the Arctic Circle. Swirling snow and a wind chill factor dragged the temperature down to minus 60 degrees Fahrenheit. Winter in Alaska, one cold son-of-a-bitch!

It's almost mystifying how the breathtaking beauty of the Alaskan summer cruelly and quickly dissipates as those cold Arctic winds begin to blow. Long time workers on the North Slope told me with a grin on their face that there was four seasons: June, July, August and winter. Fortunately for me most of the work I was involved in was done in heated workshops and offices or enclosed heated environments. Heavy duty equipment required electrically heated insulation blankets surrounding the hydraulic systems or the oil would freeze up, ultimately causing failure. Machinery that wasn't being utilized twenty-four hours a day was stored in centrally heated Quonset buildings. The pick-up trucks we used on the project when parked in unheated locations were usually kept with their engines idle. When they were shut off the electric block heater was plugged into an outlet to stop the engine oil turning solid. Most times it worked, but when it didn't the pick-up truck would be towed into a heated workshop where, hours later, it was thawed out.

Human skin exposed to the brutal elements for more than a minute would be frost bitten. We dressed in multiple layers of clothing starting with insulated underwear and finishing off with Arctic work gear rated to at least minus 46 degrees Fahrenheit, which included insulated coveralls, fleece lined gloves, socks, boots, hooded parkers, glasses, and face masks that left no exposed skin. Some guys had heated boots that they would plug into an electric socket for eight hours to charge the small batteries. When fully charged and switched on the inner soles would heat up. The boots came with three different heat settings and would last from 8 to 12 hours depending on the setting. Some guys liked them while some said they felt uncomfortable. I stayed with the pull-on Red Wing, felt lined, good to minus 40 degrees Fahrenheit steel toed boot along with heavy duty, sweat-proof, insulated socks.

It had been six months since my arrival in Alaska, the only state in the union that does not collect state sales tax or levies an individual income tax. I had taken a flight north, leaving behind the hot and dusty West Texas town of Odessa to work on the North Slope oil installations. The oil giant ConocoPhillips had hired me out of its Houston, Texas office. However, upon arrival at its Anchorage, Alaska office I had been informed I would be seconded to the Alyeska Pipeline Services Company as they required the services of a mechanical engineer due to the undertaking of a $250 million project to modernize and upgrade several of the pipeline pump stations.

The flight had lasted eight hours and that included an airline change at the SeaTac Airport in Seattle, Washington from Delta Airlines to Alaskan Airlines. Knowing my destination, I could not clear my head of the lyrics that kept pounding my brain from that Johnny Horton classic, "North to Alaska, Going north the rush is on." The only difference was this rush was not for the yellow gold, it was for the black.

After my initial two weeks in The Great White North, which were spent in Alyeska's Fairbanks office, I flew to the oilfield settlement of Deadhorse on the North Slope. Fairbanks is the second largest city in Alaska. Founded in 1901 it straddles the Chena River and was named after the twenty-sixth vice president of the United States, Charles W. Fairbanks, who had served in Theodore Roosevelt's second term. Additionally, the city of Fairbanks is home to the oldest college in the state, the University of Alaska. It's mostly a blue-collar town with a population of approximately thirty thousand and includes its share of Alaskan natives, some of whom I often noticed waddling along the downtown streets loaded on some shit that clearly wasn't doing them much good.

Alyeska is a service company owned by the same three oil companies that own and operate the Trans-Alaska pipeline: ConocoPhillips, ExxonMobil, and British Petroleum. Its main purpose is maintenance of the pipeline and pumping stations as well as guaranteed continuous oil flow of more than 2 million barrels per day. The pipeline itself, approximately half of which is above ground, stretches from Pump

Station No. 1, located in Prudhoe Bay on the East Coast, and zig-zags its way across eight hundred odd miles of Alaskan landscape to the Port of Valdez on the West Coast.

A total of twelve pumping stations along the route are utilized to push the crude oil through a forty-eight inch diameter pipeline over some of the roughest terrain in North America, which includes the Brooks Range, the mighty Yukon River, and the Alaska Range. The Alaska Range is the home of the highest peak in North America, Mount McKinley, or as the Alaskan natives recognize it, Denali–the "Great One". In total the pipeline crosses 34 major rivers and nearly 500 minor streams. It reaches its highest point of 4,739 feet above sea level at the Atigun Pass in the Brooks Range. The pipeline was built to withstand earthquakes, forest fires, and other natural disasters. It was a true engineering marvel.

The first barrel of crude oil flowed through the pipeline in 1977. Although it has resisted several gunshots, a drunken gunman armed with a high velocity rifle shot a hole through one of the welds causing a huge spill with approximately 6,200 barrels squirting from the bullet hole resulting in several acres of tundra being soaked in oil, which was removed during the cleanup. The shooter was sentenced to sixteen years in prison and ordered to pay the $17 million cleanup cost. It took a total of sixty hours to repair and restart the oil flow.

My job involved working on several of the pump stations that were being reconfigured from manual to automatic operation. I was stationed in Deadhorse, which meant that I would have to travel the gravel surfaced Alaska Pipeline "haul road", a.k.a. "The Dalton Highway", to reach my destinations. After I had officially signed up at the Alyeska office in Fairbanks and been issued with photo identification card I was also issued another official card that indicated the time allotted to travel from one pumping station to the next pumping station, commencing from Fairbanks and heading east to pump station number one or the other direction west to Valdez. The allotted time was based on 50 miles per hour and I had been informed this was for two reasons, speeding and safety.

Arriving at your destination too early indicated the obvious that 50 miles per hour had been surpassed and if you were overdue then the possibility an accident had occurred and search and rescue were dispatched. The pick-up trucks we utilized were fitted with two-way radios when driving over and through the twisting mountainous terrain of the Brooks Range, however reception was not always possible.

Before leaving each location it was mandatory to register the departure time with each security gate at each pumping station. Security personnel would then radio ahead with the names of those who were travelling, the type of vehicle, and its tag number and the time of departure. For example, I would register at Pump Station No. 1 before heading to Pump Station No. 2. According to the card I would have 74 minutes of travelling time to get from the first station to the second. On my arrival at Pump Station No. 2, I would check in with gate security and explain I was heading to Pump Station No. 3. That would give me fifty-seven minutes of travel time. On several trips I was tempted to put the pedal to the metal but I had heard several guys had been fired for cutting the travel times by half.

Devoid of horses, no one could really tell me how the settlement of Deadhorse got its name, although several stories were told. Some theorized that a miner rode his horse into the area many moons ago and when the brutal, merciless winter hit, the poor old horse went belly-up, hence the name Deadhorse. Another theory that circulated was about how a newcomer had found a caribou skull and, thinking it was the skull of a horse, decided the settlement should be named Deadhorse. The most likely story I was told relates back to when the airstrip had to be built for the Prudhoe Bay oil activities. The contract was given to Burgess Construction Company in Anchorage and they in turn hired a trucking firm in Fairbanks to haul the required gravel to build the airstrip. The trucking company was called Deadhorse Haulers, and they had got their name from a summertime contract they had to haul away horses that died during the frigid Fairbanks winters and most folk in Prudhoe Bay began calling the airstrip "Deadhorse." As time went on pilots flying into Prudhoe Bay and requesting landing clearance would radio "Deadhorse Tower".

In June 1982 Prudhoe Bay became an "Official Place" with the granting of its own Zip code, however the new Zip code directory listed "Deadhorse, Alaska, 99734", not Prudhoe Bay.

Deadhorse sits adjacent to the Arctic Ocean and consists of facilities for the oilfield workers and companies that support the operations for the largest oil field in North America in Prudhoe Bay. Although there are limited accommodations for the odd tourist in trailer hotels with such names as Arctic Oil Field Hotel and Arctic Caribou Inn, they are few and far between. This isn't too surprising considering Prudhoe Bay's longest stretch of daylight lasted for sixty-three days, twenty-three hours and forty minutes and the shortest day was sixty-three minutes. Furthermore, males out number females a couple of hundred to one, and drugs and alcohol are forbidden. If apprehended with either substance, it's cause for instant dismissal.

However there is one magical phenomenon to be witnessed in Deadhorse, as energy particles from the sun collide with the Earth's magnetic field to create the mesmerizing "Northern Lights" glowing with dancing waves of blue, green, yellow, orange, and sometimes dark red light up the evening sky. Eskimo legends claim that the Northern Lights are spirits playing ball in the sky with a walrus skull, or they are flaming torches being carried by departed souls guiding travellers to the afterlife.

Apparently an intense display of the Northern Lights has, in the past, caused many problems on the ground, such as intense electrical currents along electric power lines causing blackouts and enhancing corrosion in the pipelines. For me the Northern Lights are one of the most amazing sights I have ever seen and far more interesting than a roving heard of caribou.

Alaska, which is often referred to as "The Last Frontier", has a remarkable and very different history. The state's most popular sporting event is the Iditarod Trail Sled Dog Race, which begins each year on the first Saturday of March in Anchorage and covers more than 1,050 miles. Racers frequently face blizzards in whiteout conditions, sub-zero temperatures, and gale force winds that can create a wind chill factor of minus 100 degrees Fahrenheit.

The trail runs through passes in the Alaska Range with its sparsely populated interior, harsh tundra landscape, spice tree forests, hills, and frozen rivers and then along the shore of the Bering Sea and finally to the finish line in Nome. The race, which lasts between eight to ten days, consists of thirty to forty dog teams with the person in control of each team known as a "musher". Each team is made up of twelve to sixteen dogs, mostly Alaskan Malamutes and Siberian Huskies.

The most famous event in the history of dog sled racing in Alaska is the 1925 Serum Run to Nome, also known as the Great Race of Mercy. A diphtheria epidemic threatened the settlement of Nome, especially the Eskimo kids who had no immunity to the "white man's disease," and the nearest quantity of antitoxin was in Anchorage. The only two aircraft available were broken down and had never been flown in the harsh winters. It was decided to transport the twenty pound cylinder of serum by train from the southern port of Seward the 298 miles to Nenana where it was then passed to the first of twenty mushers who showed up around midnight in January. The mushers and their dog teams – more than one hundred dogs in all - then relayed the cylinder 675 miles from Nenana to Nome. The dogs ran in relays with no dog running more than one hundred miles. The delivery of the serum prevented the epidemic from spreading and saved hundreds of lives.

My contract called for a twelve hour day and I would work for fourteen days without a break and then I would get fourteen days off. The oil companies utilized charter flights that flew out of Deadhorse each day, weather permitting, with a stop in Fairbanks. This allowed folks to disembark and take their two weeks break while picking up returning workers then off to Anchorage for the same turnaround. The flights were free and once in Fairbanks or Anchorage you were on your own until it was time to fly back to work. During my time there I was only delayed once for six hours due to heavy fog, however some folks had up to a three day delay when those winter blizzards came howling, which also meant their relief could not return. They continued with their duties and collected overtime pay winding up with a shorter leave. Some were a little pissed off.

"But hey, it is what it is," they would say.

I alternated my time off in Fairbanks, Anchorage, and Seattle with a couple of trips to Odessa and then I'd head back to Deadhorse. During one of my winter breaks in Fairbanks I got to see the finish of the one-thousand-mile Yukon Quest International Sled Dog Race, which is the biggest long-distance race of the year in Alaska. The trail ran from Whitehorse, Yukon, Canada, to Fairbanks, Alaska. After seeing the enthusiasm of the locals it wasn't difficult to understand why dog mushing is the official Alaska state sport.

Upon returning from one of my harsh winter leaves the latest buzz around the mess hall was the mauling of a driller working on an oil rig in an area north of Prudhoe known as The Kuparuk Oil Field. Around 2:30 am on the graveyard shift the driller apparently left the rig floor, telling his boss, the Rig Superintendent, he was going to the parked emergency vehicle, a crew-cab pickup truck, to get a package of beef jerky. The vehicle was parked some twenty feet from the rig with the engine set on idle and all lights burning so as to prevent freeze-up and for a fast get-away to the camp and first aid if there was an injury or well blow-out. The rig camp was only a ten minute drive away in good weather, however on this occasion the weather was winter mean, almost a white out, with blowing snow and temperature down around minus thirty degrees Fahrenheit. Twenty minutes rolled by and the driller had not returned. In these conditions the Superintendent became concerned and hollered at one of the rig floor hands to go check. Less than a minute later the floor hand came running back, screaming. He had found the driller lying next to the emergency vehicle in a patch of red snow with half his head torn off and bear tracks all around.

The official report concluded the deceased driller had retrieved the package of beef jerky from the truck, opened it, and withdrew a stick. No doubt started to chew on it; a section of the jerky was clenched in his still-gloved right hand. Unknown to the rig personnel at the time, a polar bear had been lurking in and around the vicinity, and had most certainly caught the aroma of the jerky and attacked the unwary driller, smacking him with a huge paw and tearing off half the poor bastards melon. An empty, torn cellophane package that had contained several pounds of Klondike Kate's Hot Golden Nugget Beef Jerky was found next to the body. The North Slope Borough Police and the Alaskan Fish and Wildlife authorities were immediately notified and they in turn contacted their affiliated Alaskan native hunter who would shoot and kill the polar bear if it was located (It is illegal for a polar bear to be killed by a non-native Alaskan.).

The facilities I was housed in were occupied by a mixture of approximately eighty employees from the three oil companies, several oilwell drilling and service companies, and five folk from Alyeska including myself. The other four Alyeska guys were older than me, much older. The youngest was seventy one years of age and the oldest was seventy six. Here's the kicker: these guys were as physically fit and mentally alert as the average person. They all had engineering degrees and all had worked on the construction of the pipeline in the mid 1970s. When construction was completed they signed on with Alyeska and had been doing their two weeks on and two weeks off ever since. Obviously there wasn't much about the pipeline and pumping stations that they weren't aware of. All four of these old farts had many a tale to tell of the boom days of the pipeline construction, which had caused a massive economic boom in towns and villages up and down the pipeline route.

They told me that in 1974 the residents of Fairbanks strongly supported the pipeline but by the end of 1976 they had endured a massive influx of people, resulting in a spike in crime. House prices had skyrocketed and the infrastructure was hugely overstressed. However there was no turning back the clock. The large sums of cash being earned and spent by the construction workers caused an upsurge in illicit activity in the towns. Dozens of bars operated throughout the pipeline route. Hundreds of prostitutes were selling poontang and along with the hookers came the pimps who engaged in turf war shootouts. A huge police issue was dealing with the almost continuous drunken brawls. Many police officers and state troopers said piss on it and quit in large groups and became pipeline security guards at wages far in excess of that being paid by the public sector.

On the pipeline project itself, thievery was a huge problem. Record keeping was rat shit and allowed for large quantities of tools and equipment to be stolen. Reports showed half way through the project that as many as two hundred of Alyeska's pick-up trucks went missing from Alaska and were scatted from Miami to Mexico City. All four of those old timers told me that the building of the pipeline had been one hell of a wild ride.

I often wondered if after all the years of working in that frigid Arctic environment, with ice and snow covering the North Slope for approximately eight months of each year, had actually helped preserve those old farts.

Several of the pump stations were already in full automation but those that weren't were operated manually from a control room located at each pump station. The control rooms were operated 24 hours a day, 7 days a week, thus requiring two shifts of operators. Each pump station was equipped with living quarters sufficient to house 24 people including the security personnel and full mess hall facilities with two kitchen crews.

Before anyone could enter the mess hall or living quarters we had to pass through what was called the Mud Room. All living quarters throughout the pipeline facilities had a mud room. They were all located just inside the entrance door. It was a room with a bunch of bench seats where we would sit and remove our dirty outer boots. The room also contained shelves where boots could be placed. Some of the guys stored their bedroom slippers on the shelves and would slip them on after removing their work boots. I, like the majority of others, simply walked around in my non-sweat insulated socks, taking care not to step in any mud or snow that may have fallen to the floor from the dirty work boots as I exited the mud room.

The mess halls were all cafeteria style. We lined up with a food tray and the cooks served up whatever dish we chose. They always prepared several choices per meal, and there was always several delectable desserts to top off the meal. On this particular freezing cold January evening, in what is referred to as the "polar night", which occurs between November through to February as the sun does not show above the horizon, I sat with my tray of food at a table where several engineering inspectors who worked for British Petroleum were already seated and eating and they were pissed. From their conversation it was evident their facilities were going to hell in a hand basket and the onsite British Petroleum management folk were disregarding all reports these guys were submitting in reference to the crumbling and corroding pumping and piping systems of the BP facilities. These guys figured if repairs didn't occur soon, pipelines would rupture and crude oil would flow over the tundra.

After I finished the meal I headed to the common TV lounge and watched the half hour news telecast from Anchorage. When it was over I went to my room and cranked up the central heat as far as the wall control instrument would go, striped off the multi layers of clothes, showered, and stretched out on the bunk. I flipped the ON switch of the tape deck and listened to Randy Travis sing his country music through the Walkman's two mini speakers.

A half hour later I was dozing off to sleep when the ringing of the room telephone jolted me back to consciousness.

"Hello," I answered, confused as to who would be calling me in Prudhoe Bay. Some old coot from an employment agency in Houston, Texas, was on the line asking me if I was interested in going to work on an oil field project in Sumatra, Indonesia. He reminded me I had sent him a resume looking for overseas work a couple of months prior to his telephone call. As he was speaking I could see the icy snow crystals smashing against the double glazing of my bunk-room window.

"You bet," I told him without any hesitation, as visions of a country with hot sunny days, lush green jungles loaded with palm trees, white sandy beaches, and brown skinned beauties swaying in the tropical breeze bounced around inside my melon.

***

After growing up in Odessa, graduating from high school, and fully realizing I could not sing like that other West Texan, Roy Orbison, there really wasn't much else to do but go to work in the West Texas Permian Basin oil patch, so I hired on as a roustabout with an oil drilling company. I had noticed the local oil rig worker's, or rig pigs, as they were often called, driving around town in their shiny polished up Ford F130, Dodge Ram, or Chevy Silverado pick-up trucks, so I figured I'd give it a try.

After a year of dirty heavy duty rig labor I decided to hell with that shit and went to night school and learned how to weld and steel fabricate. The pay was better and the work was more appealing. Plus, I had seen a rig pig lose his thumb when he was working on the rig floor. Apparently he had put his hand on a moving half inch cable that well service company, Halliburton, was running through a sheave with a logging tool on the end as they logged the hole we had been drilling. His hand just rode along the cable for a foot or so and through the sheave, chopping off his thumb, which remained encased in his glove. The guy should have known better but shit happens. Anyhow they just carried him off like a broken wrench. Production didn't stop and next morning a new hire was there to replace the now nine-fingered man. As the old tobacco chewing driller told me between spits,

"Ain't no sympathy in the oil patch, Bubba."

I figured he most likely knew what he was talking about as he had two half fingers missing off his left hand and the pinkie on his right hand was down to a stub.

My first overseas assignment on the rigs was in Libya, North Africa with Loffland Brothers Drilling out of Oklahoma. Looking back, what a catastrophe that had been! Originally the company had twelve rigs drilling in Libya, but after the old Libyan king had been booted out by Colonel Muammar Gaddaffi, new rules were applied. Specifically, no oil field equipment could be removed from Libya, and Loffland Brothers Drilling sure as hell wasn't bringing in any spare parts. By the time I arrived in the country, only two rigs were capable of making hole and the only way the company had kept two rigs drilling was to cannibalize parts from the remaining ten. This was the original rusted and busted oil drilling company; it had been a welder's nightmare in that northern Sahara Desert.

I spent several years working overseas. Sometimes the positions I took were offshore other times onshore, but always on oil drilling rigs. During those years I found myself working in some nasty countries: Nigeria, Bahrain, Iran to name a few, but there were a few good ones too, such as Singapore. Eventually I went back to school when I was in my early twenties and graduated with a mechanical engineering degree from the University of Texas in El Paso. The next ten years were spent going from oil field construction project to project, an oil field nomad, so to speak. Finally I wound up in Deadhorse, Alaska, which was beginning to look like a dead end for my career. So when the sudden opportunity presented itself to leave the Land of the Midnight Sun and head back to Southeast Asia, it was a no brainier.

SUMATRA, INDONESIA

CHAPTER 2

Two weeks after the job offer I was on board the Cathay Pacific flight from Los Angles, California to Singapore where I had to hang around until PT. Petrochem, the American owned, Indonesian registered company that had hired me, processed the documentation required for a three month temporary work visa. After arrival in Indonesia there would be further processing for a two year work visa, which was the length of my contract.

I figured I'd stay a couple of years in Indonesia, save some cash, and then head back to the United States, hook up with that lovely little blonde gal out in Odessa and maybe we could open up a bar close to the beach somewhere south of Galveston and be our own bosses. Well it sounded like a great idea. I had an uncle living in Beaumont, East Texas, and he had gone to work overseas and came back with his ass national full and bought a bar. Sad thing was he had done that several times and always wound up broke. I guess he consumed more product than he sold.

I had been in Singapore several weeks after the fall of Saigon, Vietnam in 1975, bringing that so-called police action, as some called it, or the American war, to an end. It had been during my rig pig days when I worked on an offshore oil drilling rig in the south China sea, but that was fourteen years ago. I was curious if any of the bars I used to party in were still in business.

I walked along Orchard Road and turned onto Claymore Hill. Yep, there it was, just the way I remembered it: the Tropicana, lit up like a Christmas tree. It used to be one of the best bars in Singapore if you were looking to do a little drinking or needing some wacky tabacky, and there were always lots of lovely little brown ladies looking for some cash lovin'.

The Tropicana hadn't changed. It still had its U-shaped bar, a dance area in front of the bandstand surrounded by a bunch of tables and chairs occupied by occidental men and oriental women from all over Southeast Asia. I guess the noticeable difference from my rig pig days was the age and attitude of the male patrons. They were mostly older and quieter now and many wore neck ties.

Back in the 1970s it was rig pigs who were working the very active oil fields of Indonesia and the South China Sea and war crazed Vietnam vets who had taken their military discharge in Asia and never gone home. Most were from the United States with a sprinkling from Australia and New Zealand and the drunker they got the louder they became. Then the more you would hear how they were pissed off with the ending of the war and how they were ready to go back and kill every "motherfucken commie gook" in Vietnam.

I never forgot one army vet in particular. He was from San Antonio, Texas. We were revamping a World War II Landing Ship Transport (LST) that had been converted into an offshore oil-drilling platform tender in a local Singapore shipyard. Tex had come directly from Saigon to Singapore and had been hired on as a crane operator. One day Tex was busy manipulating a load that weighed several tons. He had raised the load approximately fifteen feet in the air when without warning it crashed to the deck of the LST, narrowly missing several Singaporean shipyard workers.

He claimed the brake on the crane had malfunctioned, but the same shit happened twice within a couple of days. Each time the load smashed down on the deck, almost splattering the local workers below. The drilling superintendent had the mechanic check out the crane but nothing could be found that would cause brake failure. Tex was fired.

As he walked down the gang plank he looked in my direction and winked, saying,

"See y'all at the Tropicana tonight, Bubba."

That evening I joined Tex as he was telling a couple of his buddies about what had happened.

"Three fucking times I tried to waste those fucking gooks. Damn near got 'em too," he had said.

"If I hadn't been run off I would've got 'em the next time."

Holy shit, I thought. This crazy son-of-a-bitch deliberately dropped those loads from the crane trying to kill gooks, as he had called them. I guessed the war may have twisted his melon. I often wonder if Tex had ever found his way back home to Texas.

I ordered a Tiger beer and checked out the female clientele. I caught the eye of a pretty face standing by the bar talking to a short fat pencil pusher. Each time our eyes met she smiled. I figured what the hell and beckoned her over. She ditched fat gut and came to my table and sat down. She was from Sri Lanka. After a little chit chat, a couple of glasses of wine, and an exchange of local currency we left for my hotel room.

Three days after my arrival in Singapore I flew out of Changi International airport on Indonesia's national airline, Garuda, for the forty-five minute flight across the Malacca Straits. We flew over the eastern seaboard of Sumatra, the largest island of the 17,508 islands that make up Indonesia, the world's largest archipelago. We passed over hundreds of acres of lush green palm trees and looking down on the jungle reminded me of the Jonny Cash song, Forty Shades of Green. It was hard to believe that green came in so many shades. Then we were landing in the dirty garbage riddled city of Pekanbaru, the capital city of Riau province.

I was met at the airport by an Indonesian representative of PT. Petrochem, who assisted me with my luggage and the required paper work, which included an immigration official taking finger prints of all ten fingers and palm prints of both hands. The PT. Petrochem representative then informed me in heavy accented English that we had a two hour drive to the oil field base at some place he called Duri, which apparently was PT. Petrochem and Caltex Pacific Indonesian operation headquarters for central Sumatra.

A few months later I learned that Duri had derived its name from the durian fruit that grows in abundance in Sumatra. The durian, or "king of fruits" as it is sometimes called in Southeast Asia, comes in several different sizes. On average it is about the same size and weight as a ten-pin bowling ball. The yellowish-green outside skin has sharp spikes, making it a bitch to carry directly in the hands. Inside the fruit is white and creamy with a taste that's hard to describe. I tried it several times but it was not a turn on for me, however most of the local Sumatrans love it. The smell is overwhelming and stinks like a combination of rotting cheese, decayed onion, and a splash of kerosene. The Durian has been banned on public transportation and in most hotels in Singapore because of the odour. When it comes to eating durian, locals advise people not to consume alcohol, however several South Koreans working in Sumatra ignored the warnings. One evening, tanked on whisky, they devoured several helpings of the durian and never saw the sun rise again.

The PT Petrochem representative and I left the airport in a Toyota crew cab pick-up that had seen better days and travelled through the streets of Pekanbru, which were loaded with rotting, stinking garbage and piles of coconut husk. Some of it was smoldering and fouling up the air quality in the sweltering 90 degrees Fahrenheit temperature. Still, the heat was a change in the right direction after having suffered the cold in Alaska.

When we reached the outskirts of the city, home to approximately half a million people, we crossed over the Siak River by way of a humped-back bridge, which allowed the passage of black smoke-belching fishing boats and tugboats pulling lumber-laden barges to pass under it. After crossing the bridge, on each side of the road among the coconut palm trees and slum dwellings were small shop type buildings with front porches that displayed rattan furniture for sale. Local craftsmen sat cross legged amidst their finished products, weaving what was on sale.

As we continued I realized the road we were travelling was one narrow son-of-a-bitch and twisted and turned its way over a low mountain range, which had a wall of mountain on one side and a sheer drop of hundreds of feet on the other. There were no safety guardrails anywhere. If you messed up with your driving or some dickhead ran you off the road you were going on a fast trip, straight down through the big leaf banana trees, palm trees, jungle growth, and whatever else until you hit that full stop and that's when the pain would begin.

We shared the two-lane road with countless beat-up six-wheeled trucks that were way overloaded with freshly cut logs from the jungles that were being cleared to make way for President Suharto's government-forced immigration of people from the overpopulated island of Java into the sparsely populated island of Sumatra.

Wherever possible along the mountainous terrain, small culti-vated areas of tapioca crops were growing on different size flat top plateaus. It was evident by the height and ruggedness of the hills and lack of roads that no mobile farm equipment could have been utilized. The only access to these locations would have been by foot, meaning all cultivation from planting to harvesting was by hand and that would mean a lot of hard backbone aching labor.

After crossing the mountains the land levelled out to where the jungle had been cleared, exposing rich red-colored soil that supported more tapioca crops and large palm oil plantations. Dotted amongst the fields were what looked like two or maybe three roomed houses with rusting corrugated tin roofs and their outside walls painted a bright turquoise with white trim. I could smell the wood smoke that was billowing from their rusting tin chimneys.

As we passed one of these houses, which was set back several hundred feet from the roadside, I noticed a young woman, probably in her twenties, run out the front door, followed by a bare chested man wearing only a sarong. As he exited the door he grabbed her by the arm, swung her around, and slapped her up along side of her head. Then he pushed her against the side of the building and raised his fist as though he was going to lay a beating on her.

I was in the rear seat of the crew cab and glanced forward at the driver who had also seen the incident. He did nothing, just kept on driving. After a few moments of silence I realized that there was nothing either of us could do. What the hell, I thought. Domestic violence is worldwide. The only other buildings that appeared every two or three miles were quaint little light blue colored one room Islamic mosques. Apparently the locals didn't have too far to walk when called to prayer.

Indonesia is the world's most populous Muslim nation, although not all follow the Islamic religion. About ten percent of the Indonesian people are Christians, Hindus, and Chinese Indonesian who mostly follow Buddhism.

Finally we reached a small village. The driver told me it was called Sompomadong. Man, what a shit hole. It was nothing but a bunch of one storey slum dwellings with a few little shops along the red-dirt roadside, all of which had rusting corrugated tin roofs, garbage strewn everywhere, and half naked brown skinned kids running in between and around the buildings. I noticed what was at least a ten foot high chain-link fence with three strands of barbed wire on the forty-five degree angled top, which faced outward along one side of the road we travelled. The fence had appeared as we reached the edge of the village. Curious, I asked the driver what it was all about and he told me it was part of the boundary fence around the Duri Caltex oilfield base. We stopped at a break in the fence, which was a security gate manned by dark blue uniformed Indonesian security cops. They promptly checked the drivers identification, looked me over, asked the driver a few questions in a language I didn't understand, which were without a doubt about my identification, as I was being stared at while the driver answered. Finally the security barrier was raised and we were waved through the gate.

I was delivered to the PT. Petrochem base office and introduced to Bill Bass, the area manager, who was from Tennessee. He in turn introduced me to several other field superintendents. One of these guys, a Californian named Dan, was built like a brick shithouse. He sported a crew cut and had chest and arm muscle that equalled anything Arnold Schwarzenegger could display. He also wore a Masonic ring on his right pinkie. Later I learned that he had been in the United States Marine Special Forces. He had fought with the British Special Air Service in Aden during the Suez Crisis in the late 1950s and had been an advisor in country to the South Vietnam military in the early 1960s.

The Duri base camp consisted of company housing for both ex-pats and local hired Indonesians who worked for Caltex. PT. Petrochem housed most of us ex-pats in totally worn out two bedroom trailers with common bathroom facilities in the middle separating the two bedrooms. Three floor brick and mortar motel style accommodation was being built to replace the worn out trailers, however it would be months before we could actually move in. We did have air conditioning, however, even though the systems were old and made an incredible amount of noise. You could hardly hear yourself think, but they made it comfortable to sleep. The night temperature in Duri never dipped much below 75 degrees Fahrenheit except when an electrical storm ripped through, cooling down the atmosphere. After all we were only three degrees north of the equator.

Indonesia's oil fields are some of the oldest on the planet. The first oil well was drilled in Sumatra back in 1884. In 1936 two American oil companies, Texaco Inc. and Chevron Corporation, formed a joint venture and became known in Southeast Asia as Caltex Pacific Indonesia. It has been reported to be the world's largest and most successful joint venture in business history. Caltex discovered the Duri and adjacent Minas oil fields in Sumatra only months prior to World War II. Today they are Indonesia's most productive oil fields.

Several weeks after my arrival the skinny electrical engineer from the state of Maine that I shared the trailer with was sitting on the toilet taking a crap when the rotted out floor and rusted piping gave way and he and the commode plummeted several feet to the ground below. He didn't get hurt but he was not amused. I was, I mean, Hi Ho Shitter, away!

The ex-pats I worked with at PT. Petrochem were a mixture of nationalities who mostly came from the English speaking nations of the world with the odd German and Italian thrown in for a bit of flavour. At any given time there were approximately six thousand Indonesians and one hundred and twenty ex-pats employed by PT. Petrochem throughout the Sumatra oil fields. Most of the ex-pats came from the United States and many of them had served in the military in Vietnam. Others had worked for United States construction companies involved with the building of the bases in support of that Asian conflict.

The head honchos for Caltex were all from the United States and here is where discrimination kicked in: the housing for those guys was top shelf. PT. Petrochem had three managers and their houses were second shelf. The local Indonesians who worked for Caltex in some kind of position of authority were given bottom shelf houses, and then there were the peons like myself who shared rat holes.

The vehicles we were given ran pretty much parallel with the housing. Caltex management and the PT. Petrochem chiefs had new four-wheel drive crew-cab trucks while the rest of us drove worn out rear-wheel driven Isuzu or Toyota models. I quickly learned it rains a lot in the tropical jungles of Sumatra and those red-dirt roads became as slippery as Alaskan ice trails in no time at all. With our rear-wheel-drive Isuzu and Toyotas, it wasn't hard to wind up in the ditch.

I had to drive ten miles through the jungle every morning and again at night to get to and from the steel fabrication shop that I managed and some of those trips were a challenge. To ease the tension I would insert a tape into the vehicle's cassette deck and listen to Ricky Van Shelton belt out some good old country music or that long legged beauty Cher singing from her album "Heart of Stone."

The fabrication shop produced items to support the ever expanding oil field activities and we worked it six days a week, ten hours a day with around eighty Indonesian workers.

Almost half of all oil produced in Indonesia comes from the island of Sumatra, which equates to the population of Sumatra having the highest per capita income in Indonesia. The little brown folk who worked in the fabrication shop averaged around fifty bucks a week for sixty hours of work, which means Indonesian workers in other parts of the country earned chicken shit and the poverty of the nation is a human tragedy. Indonesia, once referred to as the Spice Islands, had suffered 350 years of Dutch colonialism. In fact one of the local elders told me most Indonesians had a better life during the Japanese occupation of World War II than they had when the Dutch ruled.

I had been in Sumatra a couple of weeks when I met Charlie Blackcloud. He was part Seminole Indian from Florida and had been in the country for several months working as a piping superintendent. Blackcloud's main responsibility was supervising several crews of Indonesians who were involved in laying pipelines from the multiple wellheads across the oil fields to the storage tank facilities.

The Caltex base had a television lounge room, pool table, and booze bar. Before you could drive yourself around the local highways or to work you had to obtain an Indonesian driving licence. An international driving licence, which I had, was not recognized by the local authorities and as yet I had not had the opportunity of returning to Pekanbaru to obtain an Indonesian licence.

PT. Petrochem provided a driver during working hours but after that you were on your own. It was a Saturday night, which meant

Sunday was a sleep in day, our only day off, if we were lucky. I was drinking a local Bintang beer at the bar when Blackcloud walked over to me and asked if I wanted to go to the whorehouse with him later and check out the local LBFMs.

Surprised by the question, but without hesitation I told him,

"Sure,"

"I will be staying all night," he added.

"No problem," I told him.

About three Bintag's later Blackcloud said, "Let's go."

I didn't need to be told twice. Singapore seemed like a long time ago and I was hornier than a three peckered owl.

***

As we drove off the base heading along the same highway I had came in on from Pekanbaru, it became evident Blackcloud had his beer goggles on and his eyes had that Bintag focus from the way he was driving.

"Charlie, you are getting mighty close to the edge of the road and there is one hell of a drop-off," I said.

I was thinking that any second now we were going to go tits up over the edge.

"No," he said. "Just looks like that from where you are sitting."

I decided to change the subject and asked Blackcloud where the whorehouse was and what was the meaning of LBFM. He told me the whorehouse is about five miles along this road and then we turn right and into the Bali Rajah District and it's a couple of hundred yards back in the jungle.

"LBFM," he said. "Well that means Little Brown Fucking Machine and that's just what they are Bubba, so hold onto your balls."

The establishment consisted of one large room with a booze bar that could seat maybe fifteen people. About half a dozen smaller rooms were located all around the main room. Later I learned these rooms were bedrooms. Approximately a dozen little brown ladies ranging from their late teens to late forties were either sitting at tables with other ex-pats or were seated on stools at the bar. I checked them out; shit what a bunch, they all looked like they had been whopped with the ugly stick. Cruellest bunch you ever laid eyes on. One had a huge belly full of baby and she was still selling pussy.

I sat on a stool at the bar and ordered a Bintang. As I observed the action of couples going and coming from the bedrooms I also noticed a cute little five-foot-nothing lady standing by herself at the back of the room. Without a doubt she had the prettiest face of the whole bunch. I beckoned her over to the empty stool beside me and told her my name was Bubba. She responded in broken English that she was Anna. I bought her a Bintang. She took a slow sip, looked at me, smiled, and then asked me if I wanted to go "pom pom".

I had no idea what she was talking about so I hollered at Blackcloud, who already had a little brown girl draped over him.

"Charlie, what's a pom pom?" laughter broke out all over the bar room.

"It's what we came here for," he answered.

I got the message. I turned back to Anna and told her,

"Sure I do, let's go."

The bedroom, if you could call it that, had a bare concrete floor, no ceiling with only a corrugated tin roof, a single wide bed, and a side table with a light on it. The bed was rock hard; no bounce there. I paid Anna two thousand Indonesian rupiah, which amounted to maybe a couple of American dollars, and we both undressed.

Once we were both naked, Anna went to automatic pilot. First she sat on the bed. Next, without a word, she twisted herself around and lay on her back, closed her beautiful dark almond shaped eyes and drew her knees up to her breasts. Then she slowly spread them exceptionally wide, exposing what had been paid for. I turned out the light and stayed with her all night.

The next morning I doubled Anna's fee, kissed her good bye, and left with Blackcloud, arriving back at base a half hour before they quit serving breakfast.

During breakfast we were joined by the light vehicle fleet superintendent, Roger Riddle. Riddle by name and riddle by nature and the more I got to know him the bigger riddle he became.

Roger looked at me and said,

"You are a rookie here Bubba, so you may not have heard, but if you have family at home that you don't want to know about you going down to the Bali Rajah, be careful, because there are assbags with cameras snapping shots and they mail the photographs to your family."

I thanked him and said,

"No problem Roger, there's no one back home." I thought how I wouldn't like some prick to mail pictures of me and some LBFM to that little blonde lady in Odessa. Now that I had an address for the foreseeable future I decided I would write her a letter.

A couple of weeks later, on our Sunday off, I had another outing with Charlie Blackcloud. This time we drove twenty-odd miles back in the jungle along what was basically a logging road until we came to a small camp used by the local loggers. I immediately noticed there were several elephants next to a clump of trees, each one was anchored to a tree by a heavy-duty chain around one foot, the other end wrapped around a tree. The elephants were used to drag trees that had been cut out of the jungle to the waiting trucks and loading equipment.

"Come on," Blackcloud hollered. "We are going for an elephant ride."

One elephant was wandering around with the mahout, or driver, on its back and they were headed in our direction. The elephant had a large chain wrapped around it's girth. Once the mahout and the elephant were close to me and Blackcloud the mahout brought the elephant to its knees. He indicated to me with his hand, as neither of us knew each others language, to climb on and sit behind him. He then motioned for Blackcloud to climb on behind me. When we were both sitting firmly on the elephant's back he had the animal slowly stand up. Instinctively I hung onto the girth chain with one hand as firmly as I could and grabbed a hold of the mahout with the other. Blackcloud wrapped his left arm around my waist and we both hung on for dear life. With that, the mahout tickled the elephant's ear with a stick and we took off along a jungle path.

Ten minutes later we came to a small flowing stream. A fallen tree trunk spanned the stream which, at a guess, was about six feet across. The mahout steered the elephant up on to the tree trunk to get across the stream. Without hesitation the elephant slowly stepped up on the tree trunk placing one foot in front of the other as it walked across the stream. We all moved forward without a hitch. However, when it was time to step off the tree trunk it was at least an eighteen-inch step down to the red dirt bank. The elephant managed to get its two front feet onto the ground without a problem but when the beast plonked that rear left foot on the ground its spine twisted down to the left, Blackcloud started to slip slide.

"I am falling off," he hollered. "For Christ sake hold on Bubba!"

At that point he was holding on to me so tight that I didn't have a snow ball's chance in hell of staying on. I could feel myself slowly starting to descend with him.

"I am fucking trying Charlie but you ain't making it easy," I shouted back at him.

Seconds later, my sweating hand that had been holding onto the girth chain, slipped loose. Blackcloud continued his slow slip slid off the elephant's back and pulling me with him. Even though I had a death grip on the mahout's sweat-stained shirt I knew there was no chance in hell I could stay on as we slipped further down. When I heard the rotting sweat-stained shirt start to rip I knew it was game over and within seconds Blackcloud, me, and the mahout's sweaty shirt were in a pile in the dirt. All I could hear was Blackcloud hollering.

"God damned son-of-a-bitch, that's the last time I ride a god damned elephant."

By then I was laughing as I waved the mahout's ripped shirt at Charlie and told him,

"Well, I guess I better give him a couple of rupiah for his stinky old shirt before he calls his buddies and we get the shit kicked out of us."

I paid the mahout a little extra for the destroyed shirt. He was laughing and mumbling in his dialect and pointing at where we had bit the red dusty dirt.

Five months into my contract Caltex decided to double the capacity of the fabrication shop. Basically this meant that the Indonesian shop supervisors and I would need to hire an additional forty to fifty workers with skills such as welding, pipefitting, and crane operating as well as laborers. However, I was in for a big surprise when I learned of the restrictions that governed whom we could and could not hire because of Indonesian history.

In late 1965 a small group of junior army officers in the Indonesian capital city, Jakarta, kidnapped and killed six top army generals and tossed their bodies into a deep water well in a coup attempt to overthrow President Sukarno. Within days the rebel junior army officers were slaughtered by the Indonesian army under the supervision of General Suharto and his close associate General Nasution. Both generals claimed the Partai Komunis Indonesia (PKI), also known as the Communist Party Indonesia, was behind the attempted coup and that the PKI, the largest communist party in the world outside of the Soviet block nations and mainland China and at that time, was supported by Communist China.

General Suharto and the armed forces moved quickly to grab the reins of power. They curbed President Sukarno's authority, reducing him to little more than a figurehead and later exiling him to his Java plantation. A blood bath then ensued to eliminate any and all suspected PKI. Estimates of Indonesians murdered over the next couple of years rose to the millions. Anti-communist organizations, particularly Muslims, were encouraged to join in the mass killings of anyone suspected of being PKI or a PKI sympathizer.

Indonesians of Chinese descent were instantly butchered. Muslim bands crept into homes at night, massacring entire families with their large heavy-bladed machetes. Some of the victims were buried in shallow graves but many had their heads severed and then placed on fence posts or paraded through villages on sticks by the Muslim bands. In the North Sumatra province of Aceh, small rivers and streams were literally clogged with bodies. Many rivers throughout Indonesia ran red with the blood of slaughtered suspects. General Suharto assumed the powers of the president and wielded uncontrolled power riddled with massive corruption and brutality, which was clearly demonstrated in 1975 when the Indonesian forces invaded East Timor.

The Portuguese had colonized the island of Timor in the mid sixteenth century. Skirmishes with the Dutch in that region eventually resulted in an 1859 treaty in which Portugal ceded the western portion of the island. In 1949 the Netherlands gave up its colonies in the Dutch East Indies, including West Timor, and the nation of Indonesia was born. East Timor remained under Portuguese control until 1975 when they abruptly pulled out after 455 years of colonial rule. Several months after the Portuguese left, the Democratic Republic of East Timor was declared an independent nation. Nine days later President Suharto ordered his military into East Timor and annexed it.

The Indonesian occupation of East Timor was initially characterized by a pogrom of brutal military repression that lasted for the next twenty-four years. During the occupation a campaign of pacification ensued, and an estimated 103,000 conflict-related deaths from killings, hunger, and illness occurred. In August of 1999, in a UN-sponsored referendum, an overwhelming majority of East Timorese voted for independence from Indonesia.

During massive street protests and riots President Suharto was run out of office in 1998, taking with him over 40 billion dollars he had cheated out of his nation.

When it came to hiring new workers for the fabrication shop, the laws that governed hiring stated that any person whose family history dating back to their grandparents that may have had any form of PKI connection could not be hired. Investigations into the backgrounds of each candidate was carried out by the local authorities who were either police, village chiefs, or their henchmen. Of course corruption played a huge role and records were often lost or altered depending on bribes or tribal connections. One thing was certain: absolutely no Indonesian of Chinese decent was to be considered for employment.

After I finally finished hiring the new shop crews I had a conversation with Dan the Marine Special Forces man and I mentioned the rules regarding new hires and the shit about the PKI that had occurred some twenty five years earlier. I wondered how on earth a twenty or thirty-year-old in 1989 could be held responsible for something his grandparents may or may not have done. I mean, how in the hell could someone be held responsible for some shit that happened before he was even born?

Dan agreed it was a total fuck up. He then went on to tell me he had been in Vietnam in 1965, training South Vietnam Rangers in the fine art of killing, when the word came down from Marine Headquarters in Saigon that a contingent of United States Marines Special Forces was to be dispatched to Indonesia to assist the Indonesian military with the annihilation of communist insurgents.

He also told me that the United States government, through the Central Intelligence Agency (CIA), had heavy-duty involvement with the whole shiteroo. The CIA had systematically compiled names of possible communist operatives from top government echelons down to village chiefs and their councils. Then they turned the list of names over to the Indonesian army, who hunted them down one by one and murdered them.

I immediately felt anger and sadness after Dan told me about my country's involvement in what was basically mass murder, mostly because of the fact that it was never exposed in the United States media to any great extent. It's because of shit like that that America, as a nation, and American citizens in general, get fucked over by assbags who never consider the consequences of their actions. It made me think of the Gulf of Tonkin reports about attacks on United States naval destroyers by North Vietnam forces that never occurred. These lies were told to appease those who had dollar signs in their eyes.

President Sukarno had nationalized the mining and petroleum industries and when General Suharto took control he returned all the offshore and onshore oil fields and the ore mines back to the United States and European developers. Maybe that was reason enough not to publicize the shit that had occurred, however if Suharto had not done that I most likely would not have been working in Sumatra enjoying the climate, palm trees, jungle, and the little brown ladies down in the Bali Rajah. As they say in West Texas, a man's gotta do what a man's gotta do.

CHAPTER 3

It was hard not to get somewhat involved in the personal lives of some of the Indonesian guys working in the fabrication shop. One of the supervisors, Efendi, a Muslim from Medan, North Sumatra, confided to me that he was having financial problems regarding his sixteen year old daughter. She had finished her primary schooling and had been accepted for nursing school but first she had to pay for a medical exam, tuition fees, and a truck load of books for her studies.

Efendi had worked for PT. Petrochem for six years. Although he played a significant role in the Muslim community he was no extremist and was well respected by the other shop employees and a fine human being and very difficult not to like. Islam was his religion and he practiced it as such. When he told me about the costs regarding his daughter he was on the verge of tears. I asked him how much all that shit would cost and he figured it would be around eight thousand rupiah, converting to about four hundred American dollars. Unfortunately that amounted to several months salary for the poor guy. I am not really a soft touch, but piss on it, what could I do? I gave him the cash.

Indonesia, which is not much different in many ways to other Southeast Asian nations, is ruled by a very small, very wealthy, and very powerful group of individuals. To ensure they retain their power they rule with the support of an iron military fist, so to speak. To guarantee the status quo the price of education beyond primary school is kept at a premium, out of reach of the majority of their citizens. In other words, no higher education for the multitudes means no threat for the ruling few.

Primary schools in Indonesia cannot cope with the amount of students the country has. Because of this, most students must attend half-day schools – half of the local kids attend school from early morning to noon, the other half attends school from early afternoon to 5:00 p.m. With no evidence of government concerns, and no new schools being constructed, Islamic fundamentalists saw an opportunity and exploited it, realizing this made an excellent breeding ground for radical Islamic teaching. Schools were set up with money from leading Muslim countries of the Middle East. Saudi Arabia plays a huge role in the teachings of Islam in Indonesia and scoops up many young males and ships them off for indoctrination by the mullahs in Saudi. Then the young Indonesians are returned to their country with their melons totally twisted against Western civilization, and what they perceive as infidels. At that point they are brain-washed and well prepared to take up arms and bombs in the name of Islam.

No matter where you are in Indonesia, there is always the constant aroma of burning clove cigarettes. Ninety percent of smokers usually smoke the brand Kretek, which is a blend of tobacco and cloves. The word kretek is a term that describes the crackling sound of the burning cloves. I tried smoking one of these mean mothers but I coughed and spit for hours after that. My lungs hurt and I wound up with black circles under my eyes. The little brown guys in my shop laughed their asses off when they realized what I had done and how my body handled it.

I learned about another popular brand of cigarettes called State Express 333. Some of the little brown guys would smoke them in the fabrication shop. They told me they are actually manufactured with one pound of marijuana to every ten pound of tobacco. After hearing that, I had to try one of them for myself. Shit it was just like smoking an old Joe Camel; no buzz, only a headache.

There are hundreds of billboards across Indonesia that show the Marlboro Man in his signature Stetson cowboy hat, carrying his saddle, smoking a Marlboro, and encouraging the young to fire up. Well, that's exactly what they are doing in Indonesia. In fact the Philip Morris tobacco company is constantly targeting the youth there and it doesn't help that the tobacco industry in Indonesia employs more than ten million people. Needless to say there is definitely an absence of regulation. Unfortunately, in an over populated nation with a huge unemployment rate, nothing is going to change any time soon. It doesn't seem to matter that an estimated two million people die annually in Indonesia, either directly or indirectly from cigarette smoke.

The head office for PT. Petrochem was in an area of Jakarta called Blok M. It was owned by an American who had worked in Vietnam during that ten thousand day conflict. He had two very close associates who were also from the United States.

All three of them had been in Vietnam together working for the United States construction company Brown & Root, and the general consensus was that all three were associated with the CIA. Furthermore, all three were gay.

One of the guys was the manager of an engineering company in Bangkok, Thailand. Rumor had it that he owned a house that was always stocked with young Thai males. The third individual, who was known as California Ken, had been the resident manager on the Duri site for PT. Petrochem. However, he left a couple of months prior to my arrival to join the international construction company Canham and was currently the project manager on a Canham project in Iraq.

The Indonesians in the shop I worked with told me California Ken had an Indonesian boyfriend who shared his house on base and they would often be seen together driving around the Duri oil fields. They told me Ken had taken his lover to California and put him through computer school. California Ken, they said, came from a very rich family and was loaded. In fact, he owned and flew his own aircraft. Most of the ex-pats I spoke to about California Ken seemed to be in awe of the guy. On one occasion when the PT. Petrochem owner visited the Duri oil field site he was accompanied by a young Indonesian male who was extremely effeminate. They were both dressed immaculately in identical white suits. I really didn't give a shit about their personal lives, but I guessed the rumours were most likely true.

Among the wide variety of ex-pat personnel working for PT. Petrochem were several American managers who were mean moth-erfuckers. They dedicated their time to trying to fire as many employ-ees as possible. They would line some poor sucker up and keep him in their sights until they could run him off. In my first ten months on the job I witnessed at least twenty ex-pats go down the road, two-thirds were run off for whatever chicken shit reasons the managers could think up. The rest just up and quit. They either got sick of the man-ager's bullshit or found another job somewhere else. A few of them simply got drunk and punched someone out, or took a little brown girl to their room on base. It was okay to have an Indonesian male visit an employee in his room, as some of the ex-pats did, but to have an Indonesian female visit was immediate grounds for dismissal. The managers made sure you were like a wild goose in winter – gone! Day and night there were a thousand eyes watching, waiting for anyone to fuck-up. It was like living in a fish bowl.

Oil patch work was scarce in the 1980s. The deal with PT. Petrochem was that each individual had to get himself to Singapore at his own expense from wherever. The airfare from Singapore to Indonesia was covered by PT. Petrochem, a measly fifty bucks, but if you wanted the job that was the deal.

There was a big old boy from Muskogee, Oklahoma, who had been on the oil field site for approximately eighteen months. He had fallen head over heels in love with a little brown lady who had been selling her body down in the Bali Rajah District. He went and rented a house in Sompomadong village, obtained contract marriage papers from the local village chief, and moved his sweetheart out of the bar and into his rented house. However, she didn't come alone. She had her very close female friend move in with her and apparently they were lesbian lovers.

If the Okie from Muskogee suspected anything between his lady and her lady, it didn't seem to bother him. He just spent every dime on the love of his life, living from pay check to pay check. About six months into the arrangement the shit hit the fan. Apparently one evening a loud argument erupted over whom was sleeping with whom. One of the manager's spies immediately ratted out the Okie and the following day he was rounded up by PT. Petrochem security cops, fired, and flown out to Singapore.

I heard he was crying as he was being escorted onto the aircraft. Not only was he being separated from his soul mate but he was flat broke. PT. Petrochem managers didn't give a fat rat's ass, they were grinning. The Okie from Muskogee was like a fart in a fan factory – gone!

Under Indonesian labor law, three warning letters had to be issued to an individual before he could be terminated. This did not happen with Okie. Instead the managers said he was an embarrassment to the company and he was upsetting the harmony of his Indonesian neighbors. The general consensus around the base was that the previous resident manager, California Ken, had instilled in the brains of the managers that warning letters were to be utilized as a tool for obedience. Those fuck heads used and abused them to satisfy their own egos.

Many of the ex-pats were required to work seven days a week for weeks on end. The Sunday they worked was to be counted as an extra day when they went on leave. Some got run-off before they had taken any leave and were never paid. On one particular Sunday morning a field supervisor had slept in and showed up for work an hour-and-a-half late. The guy had not had a single day off in more than six weeks. When he arrived at his work station, one of the shit-for-brains managers handed him a warning letter for being late. The guy accepted it, went directly to the shitter, dropped a turd, wiped his ass with the letter, and then returned and handed it to the manager telling him to stick it and the job up his fucking ass.

On another day the heavy lift crane superintendent was out in the oil field checking the equipment. He exited his shitty little worn-out Toyota pick-up truck to speak with one of his crane operators. Out of nowhere, along came one of the assbag managers, who wrote a warning letter then and there because the superintendent had left the keys in the pick-up trucks ignition. This same prick manager also had a hard on for the local Indonesians and had two of them fired after he found a three foot length of garden hose behind the seat of a company ten-ton truck they were using to perform their daily duties. He claimed the piece of hose was used to siphon gas from the truck's fuel tank. There was no evidence to support the claim, only suspicion. The Indonesians didn't have a hope in hell of proving their innocence, especially since they had been issued two previous warning letters. They were terminated.

That same manager was later confronted by a knife-wielding Indonesian out in the field. Fortunately for him, Dan, the Special Forces man, was on the scene and disarmed the attacker before any damage could be done. I was told that while they waited for security to arrive and take the offender into custody, Dan proceeded to instruct the bad guy on the correct method of how to utilize a knife when in attack mode.

It has been said that what goes around comes around and that manager eventually got his. He had been on a single status contract, which means that his wife and family were left back in his home country. Well, during his absence, his wife decided to take him to the cleaners. She sold everything they owned in the United States and then cleaned out their joint bank account, leaving him flat broke. That manager left Sumatra with his tail between his legs like the mongrel dog that he was.

When I mentioned what had happened to the manager to several of the local supervisors in the fabrication shop, they instantly applauded the news. They told me how that manager was hated by all the Indonesians for all the sadness and pain he had caused many of them over the years he had worked there. After hearing their stories, I was glad he was finally gone.

All the PT. Petrochem managers on the Duri base used the local women for their maid service and anything and everything that happened within an ex-pat's household spread through the local jungle telegraph like wild fire. The little brown fellas in my fabrication shop would tell me all the latest gossip. Apparently one hot and steamy Sumatra morning the wife of the current resident manager went a little loopy. She took an axe and hacked up the household furniture, screaming at her husband the entire time. She told him he could write her as many warning letters as he wanted and he could stick them all up his hairy ass. She added that she was leaving Sumatra and all the bullshit forever and going back to the United States.

***

The oil fields of Sumatra continued to expand. Massive Caterpillar D9's were let loose and square mile after square mile of jungle was decimated with reckless abandonment. It seemed like nobody gave a shit how much was destroyed. One morning a herd of wild elephants was disturbed during the destruction of their natural habitat. Word spread and half a dozen ex-pat dickheads from PT. Petrochem's field office rushed out with their cameras for a photo shoot. The elephants became pissed off and charged the camera goofs, who scattered like leaves in the wind. One of them in his haste fell and broke his arm, a minor casualty considering what could have happened.

Throughout the oil field, waste oil from well blowouts corroded pipelines and discarded engine oil was left to lie and contaminate the jungle floor. There was never any clean up of any kind. As bad as it was, I could understand why the Indonesians didn't raise any hell about it, because they didn't know any better. All anyone had to do was look around the villages, towns, and cities to see how pollution had no importance in Indonesia. In fact it was on the same level as poverty. It was there and that was the way it was. Caltex ex-pats did know the difference, however I guess clean up costs were not in the budget.

The slash-and-burn activity of the indigenous folks in their endeavour to clear the land for tapioca crops and palm oil plantations also contributed to the destruction of the jungles. The fires the natives set were unbelievable. The smoke was so intense that the Pekanbaru Airport would be forced to close for several days. The prevailing smoke in the wind was blown across the Malacca Straits and hundreds of miles north into southern Thailand. It covered Malaysia, forcing many people to wear dust masks to avoid respiratory problems or even death. Flight schedules in and out of Kuala Lumpur's International Airport were also disrupted.

Singapore suffered the same consequences. Even though government officials of the impacted countries complain about this, the jungles still burn each year to the detriment of neighboring countries, wild animals, and their habitats.

About forty miles north of the Duri oil field base is the town of Dumai. With a population of about half a million, Dumai sits on the eastern seaboard facing the Malacca Straits. It is Indonesia's largest palm oil export port, and the oil company, Chevron, owns and operates an oil refinery with pipelines bringing the raw crude from the Minas and Duri oilfields for refining and export.

Three miles south of the city limits, back along a winding gravel road that twists and turns its way through the jungle until it ends, there is a small open valley where there is a gathering of run-down buildings on both sides of the road for several hundred yards. In daylight it looks like a shit hole but at night it is lit up like a Christmas tree. The dilapidated buildings transform into colorful bars and the aroma of clove cigarettes and American music would blare from the outside speakers. Hundreds of scantily dressed little brown ladies, lounging and sitting on the front porches, would beckon passers-by to come in and sample what they had to offer other than the Bintang beer. This little slice of Indonesia was known locally as The Valley of the Dolls and was a popular destination for many Duri ex-pats, especially on Saturday nights.

On one fateful Saturday night Big Joe Puderay from Baton Rouge, Louisiana, decided it was time to go get him some little brown poontang. After swallowing a bunch of Bintang beers at the Duri base bar, he headed his old Toyota pick-up truck in the direction of the valley of the dolls. Unfortunately, he never made it.

The beat-up, mechanically unsound, ten-ton trucks that hauled the cut-down jungle trees along the single lane highways of central Sumatra very rarely had tail lights or reflectors of any kind. If a driver of one of these rigs needed to take a piss he would simply stop his truck, leaving it parked on the road without any lights, no warning, nothing, and if you happened to be driving in the dark of night it was an accident just waiting to happen.

Big Joe obviously did not see the truck that was stopped in his path and he just drove right up under the deck that was loaded with logs. The force of the impact ripped off everything that was higher than the hood of the pick-up, including Big Joe's melon. After the accident, the pick-up was hauled back to the Sompomadong police storage yard. The following day, Dan and I went to check it out. Everything level with the hood was peeled back as though a can opener had been used. Bits of Big Joe's gray matter and other flesh pieces, along with blood splatter and broken windshield shards, covered the seat. The stench was strong in the 95 degree heat but that did not bother the flies that were already having a feast on Big Joe's remains.

It took five hours to have Big Joe's body removed from the pick-up. The Muslim police and emergency personnel would not touch the remains of a deceased Christian. PT. Petrochem had to locate an Indonesian of the Christian faith to retrieve the remains. The truck driver just took off and was never apprehendred.

Another road tragedy involving an ex-pat occurred at the fifty-mile road marker heading between Duri and Pekanbaru. Once a month, all ex-pats from the Minas oil field, which is close to Pekanbaru, were required to make the two hour drive to Duri for a meeting. It was after one of these meetings that Sam, who came from Alberta,

Canada, was slammed head-on by another one of those fucked-up log carrying trucks.

The PT. Petrochem report said that two trucks had been racing each other and went round a bend in the road, neck and neck. Sam, coming from the other direction, had nowhere to go other than a several hundred foot drop off the road. Unfortunately he didn't have time to do much of anything.

One truck kept going after Sam and his chicken shit Toyota pick-up had been pushed backward some twenty yards along the road, pinning Sam inside his cab. The other unhurt truck driver jumped out of his vehicle and took off, never to be seen again. By the time the Caltex emergency crew and local cops arrived on the scene, Sam was already deceased. Furthermore, his body had been stripped down to his underwear. His clothing, watch, wedding ring, wallet, and boots were all gone. Sam left behind a wife and four kids back in Calgary.

Several days later I spoke to one of the supervisors in the fabrication shop. He told me that Sam hadn't died instantly. His friend who understood English and lived near the scene of the accident said that he and other Indonesians living close by had heard Sam yelling, "Help me, help me." His friend had also seen local poverty-stricken jungle dwellers emerge from the dense growth and strip Sam of his belongings.

While Bahasa Indonesia is Indonesia's national language, millions of the people still cannot speak it because of the thousands of different tribal dialects. One word that is common throughout the country is the term used when Indonesians reference white skinned foreigners and that word is Boolay. I asked both Indonesians and ex-pats about the word's origin, and the most common answer I got was that it referred to foreigners' blue eyes. I never came across an Indonesian with blue eyes; theirs are almost black. The term had been used for hundreds of years and had specifically been a reference to the Dutch colonists. Great, I thought. I guess I was stuck with being a fucking Boolay as long as I was in Indonesia.

The Batak tribe of North Sumatra were savage headhunters until the end of World War II. They have a much larger and bigger bone structure than most other Indonesians, and ninety per cent of Bataks follow the Christian faith. At the fabrication shop I had approximately twenty Bataks working for me. As the months rolled by, I noticed how they displayed an aggressive attitude towards their work. Their presence almost seemed to scare the other smaller workers, but if nothing else, they made good supervisors. It was a PT. Petrochem Christian Batak security chief that was called upon to actually collect the bodies of Sam and Big Joe.

Dan the Special Forces man was divorced when he arrived in Sumatra. Within a year he had found himself a little brown girl, fell in love with her, and remarried. He was on a single status contract, which meant that no married housing on base was forthcoming. Dan and his new wife ended up renting a house on the outskirts of the village that belonged to a corrupt police superintendent. It was of a higher standard than most village housing and was surrounded by a six-foot-high brick and concrete security wall with broken glass embedded along the top.

Because of the extreme poverty in the area, break-ins and theft were ever prevalent. Freshly washed clothes that were hung out to dry would often be stolen while they were still wet. Therefore it was necessary to hire local village security to patrol to scare off the bad guys.

The Islamic religion makes a huge deal out of stoning the devil. In some of the less modernized Islamic countries of the Middle East and Africa people are literally stoned to death. A hole is dug and the condemned person is half buried with a sack placed over his or her head. After that anyone and everyone stands around in a circle and throws stones at the poor bastard until death.

I heard stories from several ex-pats who were living off base who claimed they had been woken up at night by stones raining down on their roof.

Indonesia has a different temperament when it comes to unmarried cohabitation. If an ex-pat found a little brown girl that turned his crank down in the Bali Rajah District or in the Valley of the Dolls, as did the Okie from Muskogee, and he wanted to shack up with her, the procedure was to go to the village chief and apply for a contract. The man would have to pay the chief a fee somewhere around fifty bucks and then a contract bearing his photo and the woman's photo, along with their identification particulars, would be typed up. The couple could then live together legally. The contract was renewable on a yearly basis. When the ex-pat ultimately left Indonesia, the contract became null and void regardless if any kids had resulted from the union. Although the contract allowed legal cohabitation, the head honcho down at the mosque didn't always agree with the arrangement. He would have some of his followers go throw stones at the house where the Boolay devil slept with his whore.

Dan had a legal government marriage and it was registered with the United States Embassy in Jakarta, however, the old fools in the mosque didn't believe that Boolays should have the right to live with or be legally married to Indonesian women and he sent his lackies to stone Dan's house. This occurred regularly, sometimes several nights in a row. Finally Dan was pissed enough and decided to eliminate the problem his own way. Thick jungle foliage grew all the way to the security wall that surrounded Dan's house, affording him total concealment as he lay in wait for three nights with a baseball bat. Sure enough, late on the fourth night, around one a.m., three lackies started throwing stones from different quadrants around the house. One by one Dan stealthily approached each lackey and, using the baseball bat, smacked their motherfucken' Muslim melons, instantly rendering them unconscious. Once they were out cold, he picked up each body and tossed it over a neighbors fence. Needless to say, stones never rained down on Dan's house again.

From an American's point of view, the interpretation of the Islamic religion by the Muslim extremists in Indonesia is so unreal that one has to wonder why so many of the believers actually accept it. After several visits to the Bali Rajah District and many conversations with the little brown girls, a picture started to form in my melon about how cruel their society truly was.

Anna, my first encounter in the Bali Rajah District, explained that she had been married with two children. She had been born and raised in the largest city in Sumatra, Medan. One morning her husband was walking to work when he was suddenly struck by a truck and killed. She received no government assistance and no insurance from the truck company. She didn't get any financial assistance to help support her kids and no widow benefits or help from the mosque she attended. Basically she was left to fend for herself and her kids. Her parents were as poverty stricken as she and millions like her are to this day. She told me she found work in a biscuit factory that was owned and operated by the hated Chinese Indonesians. The wages were chicken shit and the owners controlled their employees like slaves. She explained that by the time she paid for public transport to and from her home to work six days a week, which was the standard work week, with no overtime payments, she was almost broke. After several months she and her kids were beginning to go hungry.

A neighbour friend of hers returned to Medan from the Bali Rajah District for a family visit and told her about the Boolays and the cash that could be earned for pom pom. She decided to give it a try; at least she would be able to send money home to her mother, who would take care of her kids while she was gone. All she ever got from the mosque was shit and abuse. She was totally condemned for her lifestyle. But here's the kicker, as a previously married woman there was no chance for Anna to remarry because the male Muslim fuckwits won't have anything to do with a non-virgin woman. In their eyes, Anna was considered a "dirty woman" because she had spread her legs for her husband. Without a husband and not being a virgin deemed her an outcast and, to be blunt, totally fucked.

All the little brown girls selling their bodies in the Bali Rajah District came from the poverty stricken ranks of Indonesia. It is a fact that some families in Indonesia sell their daughters into prostitution for a few rupiah to buy a little rice for survival with no consequence regarding the law. Sadly, the selling of women and young children into the sex industry is rampant throughout Asia.

One of the ex-pats working for PT. Petrochem, a pock-marked piece of shit from Louisiana, came back to Duri after a week of rest and relaxation in Medan. He began boasting about how he had gotten himself liquored up and had the mama-san of a whorehouse in Medan procure an eleven-year-old virgin girl for him to mess with. He took great pleasure in describing how he deflowered her. It was sickening to hear and it made me wonder just how twisted that poor child's melon would be for the rest of her life having been brutalized by this ugly stinking drunk low-life son-of-a-bitch.

A couple of days later Dan, "The Dude from Dallas" (as he was known), and I were talking about what should happen to that disgusting child-molesting bastard. Dan of course wanted to kill him, dump his body out in the jungle, and let the beasts devour it. I almost agreed with him, but the Dude from Dallas came up with the idea of planting marijuana in the pedophile mongrel's pick-up truck. Once that was done, we'd make an anonymous phone call to PT. Petrochem security. The guy would at least be run out of the country. If the local cops were called then he would most likely do hard Indonesian jail time.

Dan and I looked at each other and then at the Dude.

"Where the hell are we gonna get our hands on some weed?" I asked.

The Dude from Dallas just smiled."Leave that to me," was all he said.

Three days later, the pock faced piece of shit was escorted by four PT. Petrochem security guards to the Pekanbaru Airport, never to be seen again.

The Dude from Dallas was okay in my book. He was in his late twenties and said that he had once tried out for the Dallas Cowboys football team but didn't quite make it so decided to travel and work overseas. This project was his first outside of the United States and he seemed to be enjoying himself. He had rented a house on the edge of Sompomadong village where he and his little brown lover (whom he had pulled out of the Bali Rajah District after obtaining a marriage contract) had set up house and installed a pool table, a full surround-sound system, and a beer bar that was lit up with multiple colored lights.

There was a group of ex-pats and Caltex Indonesian employees who visited with the Dude regularly and many of them partied until dawn. I had been invited to visit and had every intention to do so but I just hadn't got around to it.

One afternoon the local cops came to our worksite, arrested the Dude, and escorted him to the local jail house. He was charged with trafficking marijuana. He had only been working with us for eight months.

Apparently the Indonesian narcotics cops had been investigating a drug cartel that stretched from northern Sumatra all the way down the archipelago to the southern island of Bali. The cartel's major drug was marijuana or "ganja", as it is known in Southeast Asia, but heroin was the big cash cow in the major cities such as Jakarta, Surabaya, and Medan.

The leader of the cartel was an elderly Indonesian Chinese lady with lieutenants spread throughout the archipelago. Her tentacles spread all the way to the Golden Triangle where the Thailand, Laos, and Chinese borders merge in a triangle and provide the world with tons of the powder including the highest quality, referred to as "China White". Somehow the Dude from Dallas had connected with a local member of the cartel and commenced supplying his house-guests with illegal drugs until he got busted.

A couple of days after the arrest, PT. Petrochem advised us that the Dude could have visitors. Naturally Dan and I went to see how he was doing. His cell was an eight-by-ten with a squat hole shitter in one corner and nothing else in it except a woven bamboo straw mat on the floor where he slept. The Dude told us that when it rained the water rushed in and he had to sleep standing up. Mosquitoes were his worst nightmare and we tried to give him several cans of Buzz Off repellent so that he could defend himself. However, his captors wouldn't allow it.

PT. Petrochem and his little brown lady supplied him with food, the cops would only supply the cell, no soap, no toothpaste, no ass-wipe nothing. This was hard time, Indonesian style. A week later he was transferred to the Dumai prison some forty miles from the Duri base, which made visiting more difficult.

The penalty for drug trafficking could have cost the Dude his life or at least a hard twenty-five to thirty years, but money, bribes, and politics (being what they were at the time) spared the Dude and he was deported, persona non-grata, after three months in jail. Lucky for him a few well-connected high-ranking Caltex employees and some of their offspring who had messed with the Dude's wacky tabacky would have been publicly exposed if the shit had gone to a court case. The so called "loss of face" is an extremely bad situation, something no Indonesian ever wants, so between the Indonesian authorities, PT. Petrochem, and Caltex, cash changed hands and all charges were dropped. The next time I saw the Dude from Dallas he was casually drinking a Tiger beer in a Singapore bar. Sitting beside him was his now legal Indonesian wife.

CHAPTER 4

Every now and then one of the guys I worked with would stop by the fabrication shop for a mug of coffee or a cool drink. I always kept a supply of assorted beverages handy for that reason. Not long after Dan the Special Forces man had whacked the muslims' melons, he visited and started to open up about some of his war stories from his service in Vietnam. I had been drafted for Vietnam but was ultimately rejected because of a busted kneecap I had received on my sixteenth birthday. I had drank several beers and got to where I wasn't feeling much pain, went for a motorcycle ride with a friend, and fell off the ass end of his Harley Davidson. After that mishap, I could never straighten my left leg all the way again.

Dan began by telling me how he was out on patrol in the Mekong Delta with several South Vietnam Rangers when they were suddenly ambushed by the Viet Cong. During the firefight he had somehow become separated from the Rangers and realized the enemy was hot on his trail. He hit the muddy Mekong water and quickly cut several hollow stemmed reeds, which he then used to breathe through after submerging in the brown river water and waiting for the Viet Cong to pass his location. He added that, for good measure, he took out the last member of the four man team that had been trailing him. Dan quietly stalked the old Charlie Congs and grabbed the last one in line, reaching around his face and covering the enemy's mouth with his left hand. In the same motion, he lifted and twisted the Congs head and slit his throat with the knife he had in his right hand.

"Ya know, the one thing they never teach you in basic training is about the stench that comes up from the guts out through the throat that has just been slit open," he muttered. "It's enough to make ya puke."

We each sipped a cold Coke and bullshitted for a while. When we both grew quiet, I looked over at Dan and said,

"There is one god damned thing I don't understand about the shit the United States gets itself into. It creates wars and then drafts its young men to go and get whacked."

Dan looked at me and didn't say anything. He just nodded and took another sip of his coke.

I continued, "Then there are those chicken shit right wing religious assbags who scream and holler about abortions, about pieces of nothing that can't even fart yet, but they don't say a word or raise any kind of hell about the draft or sending young healthy men who are not even twenty-one years old to get killed in some distant fucked-up country that we have invaded! These soldiers are just teenagers who have shared a life with their parents, their siblings, and their friends. They have loved; they have been loved; and they are loved. Still, all I hear is this shit about aborting a fetus that hasn't done a fukin' thing except make a woman's belly big!" I shook my head with disgust and confusion.

"Ya know Dan, I just don't understand why it seems so fucked up..."

Dan shrugged and looked at me.

"Well Bubba, I guess there are some things we just are not meant to understand," he said. He hesitated a moment before continuing.

"Let me tell you about some shit that has been twisting my melon ever since I left Vietnam and the Marines. During my time in that fucked up war, I witnessed my country use what can only be classified as chemical warfare against the Vietnamese. Between 1961 and 1971 our military used more than 19 million gallons of herbicides developed by Dow Chemical and the Monsanto Company for defoliation and rice crop destruction."

"Really?" I asked.

He nodded. "There was a military operation referred to as "Ranch Hand," where chemical compounds called Agent Pink, Agent Green, Agent Purple, Agent Blue, Agent White, and the most lethal one, Agent Orange, which included the deadly ingredient dioxin were sprayed from the air over thousands of acres of that country. Eventually all that shit has seeped into the soil and water supply and, therefore, into the food chain. Now it is being passed from expectant mothers to their foetuses. The dioxin remains in the soil and is now damaging the health of the grandchildren of the war's victims. So tell me Bubba, how fucked up is that for the American people to accept?"

***

There is a tribe of dark-skinned indigenous Sumatrans known as the Sakai tribe. To this day, the tribespeople live as they have for hundreds of years. They do not wear clothes but on occasion they will don sarongs. If they do have something covering their genitalia it's usually a piece of a banana leaf that hangs in front and is hooked onto a strip of jungle vine that is tied around their waists and bare butt crack at the back.

The Sakai follow along the many rivers and tributaries throughout the Sumatra jungle fishing and hunting in the local area around their camp. When a particular area runs dry of their food supply they simply pack their meager belongings into their small log dug-out canoes and move along the river to another area of abundance. Once they find a decent area, they set up another camp that consists of one-room huts made of bamboo with thatched roofs. These huts are perched on bamboo stilts that are at least eight feet above the ground with rickety looking bamboo ladders for entering and exiting the huts.

On one of my Sundays off, several months after my arrival in Sumatra, I decided to go for a drive along the two-lane black top road that led to Pekanbaru (I had finally gotten an Indonesian driver's license). Approximately ten miles from the Duri base camp the road crosses a river. As I approached the bridge, I noticed several of the Sakai stilt houses perched on the river bank and decided to take a few photos of them.

I pulled the little chicken shit pick-up truck I was driving onto the narrow gravel shoulder at the edge of the blacktop. I didn't bother to turn off the engine and I didn't get out either. Instead I just leaned out the window with the camera and started click- clicking away.

All of a sudden I heard screaming. Startled and confused I immediately lowered the camera and looked over in the direction of the screaming. That's when I saw a naked boy of about seven or eight years old. He was jumping up and down, and his right hand was raised with a clenched fist. I realized he was looking directly at me as he screamed. I simply smiled and clicked another picture. However, as soon as I pressed the shutter release button on my camera, four tall slender Sakai warriors ran up over the river bank and onto the road. They too were screaming and coming right at me! They were all carrying spears that looked to be about six feet long; two of the warriors carried machetes. The only thing they were wearing were those crazy banana leaves in front of their dicks, which kept bouncing up and down exposing their balls.

Holy shit, I thought. This is insane! I couldn't believe what I was seeing. They kept coming, screaming! Yea, they wanted my ass. Thank God the pick-up truck was still running. Without hesitation I slammed it into gear and took off, throwing bits of gravel in to the air behind me at the fast-approaching warriors. They retaliated by throwing their spears and machetes at the pick-up truck. I heard several of the weapons bounce off the pick-up's tail gate. Never again, I thought, trying to calm my nerves and keep my eyes on the winding road. Never again!

I just kept the pedal to the metal and a death grip on the steering wheel until I had put miles between those crazy bastards and myself. As I drove along I couldn't believe what had just happened; it didn't seem real. Then I got to thinking what could have happened to me if I had gotten out of the pick-up truck. It has been said that "Arrow" was the brand name of the shirt General Custer wore at little Big Horn. Well, we also know he wound up with a shirt full of arrows! I hate to think what kind of shirt I would have been wearing after those Sakai shithead warriors had finished with me. I can guarantee crimson would have been a dominant color.

The following day I had a meeting with Bill, the area manager. When our work business was completed, I decided to tell him about what had happened the previous day. The more I spoke, the wider his eyes became.

"Holy shit Bubba!" he exclaimed. "We should have told you about the Sakai. Never take photos of them. They believe photographs steal their spirits, and for that they will literally kill a man."

What an assbag, I thought to myself. I could have been whacked or badly injured by those spear chucking fuckers and I would never have known why.

***

Shit in the Middle East was beginning to hit the fan. The Wacky Iraqi, Saddam Hussein, was rattling his sabre and accusing Kuwait of stealing his oil by utilizing directional drilling. Saddam wanted payment. The emir of Kuwait basically told him to fuck off and, to add insult to injury, he also stated all Iraqi women were nothing but ten dollar whores. With that Saddam began to marshal his forces and line them up along the Kuwaiti border.

The Indonesian Muslims began to take notice when it became evident that the infidel United States was beginning to put pressure on the Wacky Iraqi to back off.

Around the same time, I noticed that the attitudes of several of the supervisors in the fabrication shop were changing. The men were becoming very vocal about their religion. In fact, they started making anti-American comments. I also noticed the same individuals were spending more time in the prayer room than usual, probably stirring up shit. Each department within PT. Petrochem had a prayer room enabling the Muslims to fulfill their daily obligation of praying five times a day. When I mentioned the shit stirring to a couple of the Batak Christians they told me that the more radical Muslims we had in the shop had come down from the northern province of Aceh. Intense fighting had been going on there for many years between President Suharto's army and the Acehnese rebels, who practiced the Sharia Law, or Islamic law. The Acehnese rebels were fighting for separation.

Aceh province encompasses the northern tip of the island, Sumatra. As far back as the thirteenth century it was one of the earliest centers of Muslim learning in Indonesia. Historically, Egyptians, Arabians, and Indians traded with Aceh, contributing to the province's wealth and influence. Aceh was independently governed by an Acehnese Sultanate and after a twenty-five-year war, the Sultanate surrendered to the Dutch and was forced from the country. After the communist uprising in 1966, Aceh was created as a separate province with autonomy in religious and cultural affairs.

Today, the Acehnese people are 98 percent Muslim and the province is loaded with oil and natural gas reserves. Additionally, there is a long history of separatist uprisings against outside rule. These uprisings tend to be fueled by human rights abuse by the Indonesian armed forces and feelings of economic exploitation. In fact, I had been told by Indonesians working in my fabrication shop that President Suharto had sent his military into Aceh villages and killed the entire population. Every man, woman, and child were slaughtered; the military showed no mercy.

One of the ex-pats, Known as Big Kev, who came from Darwin, Australia, had been working up in Aceh province on a liquefied natural gas plant that was being built by the international construction company, Canham, near the city of Lhokseumawe. Big Kev, who had only been on-site for a month, told me the situation for ex-pats was not good in Aceh. Apparently the ex-pat guys had to be very careful when it came to what they did and where they went after work. According to Big Kev, he went to his room after work one evening and found a printed flier on his bed, advising all Boolays to leave Aceh province or be killed. This was part of the struggle for liberation from the Suharto dictatorship. Big Kev figured, fuck it. Why take the chance? With that he relocated to PT. Petrochem. He was amazed how we could fraternize with the little brown girls. In Aceh, two Americans had actually been shot dead on a pipeline project for messing with the local ladies. Those poor women had their heads shaved and were paraded through the streets of Lhokseumawe, where they were insulted and garbage was hurled at them.

***

Six months had passed since my arrival in Sumatra and it was time for me to take two weeks' leave. After listening to the stories the guys in Sumatra had told me, I decided I would spend a week or so of my vacation time in Thailand. I took the forty-five-minute flight to Singapore and checked into the old Negara Hotel on Claymore Street next to the Thai Embassy. You could bring a herd of elephants into your room and nobody would bother you. In other words it was a good party hotel and a place where oil field workers from all over stayed when they were in town. A Denny's restaurant was next door, as well as a place called Genevieve's Bar, which always had a bunch of good-looking Asian ladies looking for a party. After dropping my suit case in my room I visited a travel agent on Orchard Road and arranged and paid for four days in Phuket and three days in Bangkok.

The next day I flew into Phuket and checked into a little hotel on Patong Beach. After a quick shower I decided to go for a walk and find something to eat as the sun was starting to sink into the Andaman Sea. It didn't take long to find a restaurant; the streets were loaded with little eating cafe's and beer bars. After I finished eating I decided it was time to check out some of those beer bars that lined both sides of the street, all of which were loaded with LBFMs. I wasn't really looking for any loving that night, and after an hour or so of bar hopping I decided to call it an early evening.

As I walked along the busy street back to the hotel, passing many bars, the little brown girls kept calling out to me "Come in here handsome man!" At first I was slightly flattered, but then I noticed they said that to every male who walked by. Finally I had just about reached my destination but right before I crossed the street back to the hotel I was drawn to a little open air bar called The Ducks Nuts. The Ducks Nuts? I thought. I had to grin at the Thai sense of humour. I figured I'd have a night cap before going to my hotel and located an empty bar stool to sit on. "The Power of Love" by Laura Branigan blasted from the loud speakers above me.

Sitting on the adjacent stool was a pretty Thai lady in her late twenties. Within a few minutes I learned that she spoke excellent English. She smiled and told me her name was Noi. After some small talk she agreed to spend the night with me. So much for an early evening.

The stories I had been told about Thailand were now beginning to make sense. Noi hung around with me for the next couple of days, showing me the sights around Old Phuket Town during the day and taking me to popular discos at night. When we grew tired of the night life we would simply head back to the my hotel room for a repeat performance of the previous evening.

Noi asked if she could come to Bangkok with me. I had no reason to leave her in Phuket, so I said "fuckin A." The next morning we caught an early flight into Don Muang International Airport in Bangkok. By noon we were checked into the Nana Hotel on Sukhumvit, Soi Nana, opposite the Nana Plaza, which had three floors of beer bars and hundreds of male and female sex workers. During the Vietnam war the Nana Hotel was known as the unofficial Bangkok CIA headquarters. By the look of many of the ex-pats sitting in the lobby with their LBFMs, it could very well still be.

Bangkok is a city of ten million plus people in the Land of Smiles. It is a city with hundreds of Buddhist temples and it straddles the mighty rapid-flowing Chao Phraya River. Simply put, it is a city that can supply anything and everything a man or woman could ever want and more. Personally, I believe it is a city that should be visited a least once in everyone's lifetime.

We visited Pat Pong, a district in central Bangkok that caters to the sexual fantasies of all comers. There were boxing rings set up along the streets where Muay Thai fighters kicked the living shit out of each other for the audience and a few local Thai baht. Transvestites, gays, and lesbians were abundant on the streets, offering their bodies for strangers' pleasure (or pain, if that's what one was looking for). There were street stalls that sold virtually anything one could want, and there were countless dishes of spicy Thai food for sale. The whole district was lit up with every imaginable neon sign and colored lights were strung in trees and where ever they could be hung. Pick-pockets roamed the crowded streets and plied their craft along with the drug dealers.

Unfortunately, all good things must come to an end and eventually it was time for me to head back to Singapore and Sumatra. Noi came to the airport with me and kissed me goodbye. I handed her a fistful of dollars and baht and vowed that I would be a boomerang and return. As soon as I handed her the cash, however, I briefly thought about my dreams back in Texas. Goddamn it! The way I was spending money I would never save enough to buy that bar in Texas. About all I would wind up with would be a six pack of beer and a television set.

***

Before I left for my two weeks' leave it had been arranged that old Buck, a likeable man from Utah who was in his late fifties, would look after the fabrication shop I had been managing.

Buck called himself a Jack Mormon, which meant that he was not practicing his religion anymore. Buck had actually been the one who told me the story about the Nana Hotel and how it was a good location to stay in Bangkok. He had also told me he had spent several years working in Saudi Arabia.

He said that on his way back to the United States he had decided to stop over in Bangkok for several days to unwind after the strict Islamic bullshit of Saudi Arabia. He checked into the Nana Hotel and, according to him, it took three months before he could extract himself from all those little brown lady legs that were like a 7-Eleven convenience store, they never closed, and loving arms that wouldn't let him go. Eventually he knew he had to go back to reality and boarded a plane to Utah.

On my return, Buck was no-where to be found. I was told he went and got himself all liquored up, took a little brown girl to his room on the base, and that was all she wrote. I guess P.T. Petrochem had found out about his guest and immediately ran him outa Duri. Of course, if it had been a little brown boy Buck had taken to his room, he would've still been in Duri when I returned. Although I was saddend to learn Buck was no more, I quickly got over it when I saw there was a scented letter waiting for me from that little blonde lady in Odessa.

After being in Sumatra a year, I had seen a lot of guys come and go. In fact, an old boy from Kansas arrived one afternoon, stayed the night, and quit the next morning. He approached the area manager, Bill, and simply said,

"This shit ain't for me." With that he was gone.

The following week a black guy from New Jersey arrived. He seemed like a nice enough fella, but it was clear he had a bad drinking problem. He stunk like a brewery every day. He had only been on the job a couple of days when he showed up at work wearing the Indonesian Islamic male head dress, a black skull cap. He wore it everywhere he went, including the workplace and when he went to the bars at night. This went over like a fart in church with the PT. Petrochem upper echelon.

The Indonesians working in the fabrication shop were confused by his appearance. They approached me and asked,

"Why he do like this?" Admittedly, I wasn't sure.

"Man, I don't know," I replied. "Maybe he is an American black Muslim."

Caltex had built a recreation center for its ex-pat employees that consisted of a tennis court, a swimming pool, and a small booze bar, and they allowed PT. Petrochem personnel to use the facilities. The Caltex folks had both Saturday and Sundays off and they would often gather for a Sunday poolside barbecue. The New Jersey piss tank made it through till his third Sunday. Rumor had it that he started drinking after he quit work at 5:00pm on Saturday and by noon the following day, Sunday, he was still at it. He staggered over to the recreation center and that's when the shit hit the fan. He waltzed right up to one of the blonde headed Caltex wives, a woman in her late forties, and took hold of her left breast. She screamed! Security was on him like white on rice. They grabbed him, cuffed him, and instantly escorted him to Pekanbaru, where he was held overnight in a lock-up till morning. By noon he was like the snow in the rain, gone!

Although PT. Petrochem hired its share of dildos, they also hired a bunch of good solid people too. Two guys who really knew their shit ran the Crane Department. Roy was from New Orleans, Louisiana, and his boss, Gerry, was from California. They would visit my shop on many occasions to shoot the breeze and have a cold Coke, which sure helped pass the time.

At the end of the Muslim month of fasting, Ramadan, comes the celebration, Edel Fitre, which, like Christmas is celebrated in Indonesia. We got several days off for both celebrations. During my first Christmas in Indonesia, Roy and I went to Pekanbaru for a couple of days. We were both amazed and entertained as we walked around, especially when we saw a bunch Indonesians nonchalantly gather in a circle and suddenly unleash two roosters they had stored under dome-shaped cane baskets. The roosters would be set on each other and start to fight. These cockfights lasted to the death or until one rooster received such bad injuries that it couldn't continue fighting anymore. The Indonesians worked themselves into a frenzy as the roosters ripped each other open with their spurs. The more the blood flowed the louder the screams of excitement grew.

The one prominent feature of Pekanbaru (besides the tons of rotting garbage and the stink of clove cigarettes) was the overwhelmingly visible poverty. It was so hard to believe that a government of any country could accept this reality for its people. One had to remember that the corruption of the dictatorial Suharto government actually caused that lifestyle and the abuse of power to guarantee the status quo.

The Suharto regime had become a family of corruption. It was commonly understood that Mrs. Tien Suharto, who had the nickname, "ten percent Tien," received ten percent of the cost of every contract that required government sanction, delivering millions and millions of dollars into the Suharto coffers. She was Suharto's most loyal aide as well as his closest and most influential advisor. She also openly expressed preferences as well as dislikes toward certain cabinet ministers. The practice of nepotism, which gave special favors to their children, relatives, and friends, dominated the Indonesian business world with their conglomerates and monopolies. The multi-million dollar manufacture of the Kretek clove cigarette was owned by one of the Suharto sons.

There was no social safety net in Indonesia for the population with regards to pensions; they just didn't exist. The only so-called social security older folk had was their offspring. People would have as many kids as possible, recognizing that maybe half would die but the other half could ultimately take care of them in their old age. There was no health care available. Basically, if someone didn't have cash and became ill, that person would more than likely die, regardless of gender or age. Like the Catholic religion in poverty-riddled South America, the Islamic religion in Indonesia did nothing to elevate or encourage the government to change its ways. Everybody had their hand out, begging. It sure made me feel very fortunate to be American.

As we wandered the streets and markets, we had to stay alert and dodge the countless small motorcycles that whizzed by. Occasionally we witnessed motorcycle accidents. Those little two-stroke smoke-belching modes of transportation were, in the majority of cases, the family automobile. It seemed like a contest to see how many bodies could fit on one machine. The most I ever counted was seven. Poppa would be the driver, momma and kids would pile on. Sometimes there would be two up front on the gas tank and the rest of the family would be stacked on momma's lap and on the rear fender, all hanging on for dear life. Amazingly momma sometimes rode side-saddle, holding on to a baby! I could only imagine what a mess would've occurred if they became entangled with a car or a log carrying truck. Unfortunately, that was a regular event.

In the middle of the dry season in Sumatra, the outside day temperature is always hovering around 100 degrees Fahrenheit. Most afternoons, an ex-pat would drop by to take a break from the intense heat. I had the office with air conditioning. The adjoining fabrication area of the shop was open on both ends with the side walls covered half way down from the roof. It also had a complete roof. During those hot dry seasons a cool breeze would often blow through to the delight of the little brown folk as they worked tediously. It was a whole bunch cooler than their compatriot's workplaces in the jungle.

On one particular steamy afternoon, Roy stopped by the fabrication shop. His shirt was saturated with sweat. I took one look at him and grinned.

"You want a chilled Coke, Roy?" I asked, already reaching for the door of the mini refrigerator I had purchased for my office.

"You bet," he hollered as he sat down on the chair in front of my desk and wiped sweat from his face with his red and white checked hanky.

He always spoke a couple of decibels above most folks. We shot the shit for ten minutes or so and then Roy casually asked if I had hung around much with that cracker, "Roger the Riddle."

"Not a lot," I shrugged, mostly just knowing that he was from somewhere in South Carolina.

"Why? What's up?"

Roy continued, "The other night, I was in the base bar having a beer with him, when he got to telling me how he flew Cobra helicopter gun ships during the Vietnam war."

"No shit," I answered.

Roy nodded. "The Riddle also told me on his last month-long leave he was involved in something he loved doing, a Black ops special mission, apparently down in Central America somewhere. He said he flew a helicopter at tree-top level in a battle situation."

"Shit Roy!" I exclaimed. "You think that's true?"

"Don't know," he shrugged. "But I asked him why he quit that shit if he liked doing it so much. He told me he couldn't handle the smell of human blood any more."

I shook my head slowly. "Son-of-a-bitch, Roy," I said quietly. "I guess you just never know."

It was January 1990 and my job was beginning to feel very monotonous. It was always the same shit but a different day. However, different characters kept arriving. Larry was a surveyor from San Diego, California. After a month or so in-country he took himself to the Bali Rajah District to find himself a LBFM. Well he found one, and he and the little brown girl did what he had been hoping to do. But when Larry left the whorehouse and got into his pick-up truck and was about to turn the key to leave, someone started punching him in the head through the open driver's side window.

Stunned, Larry turned to see a drunk, half-crazed New Zealander who was hollering and throwing punches at him.

"What the hell?" he cried, trying to protect his head.

"You just fucked my girlfriend, you dirty, rotten bastard," the New Zealander screamed.

As the punches continued to fly, Larry managed to fire up his truck and drive off. That crazy Kiwi should have realized his girlfriend was only doing her job.

One time we had a suicide on base. An Australian guy hanged himself with his belt from the rafters in one of the mechanical workshops. Seems his little brown sweetheart had tossed him for another lover and he just could not handle the pain of a broken heart. As they say, love and war do not follow the ordinary rules of life.

The PT. Petrochem field engineer was a Texan and I don't think I have ever met a dumber son-of-a-bitch within the engineering field. This turkey didn't even know how to turn on a computer. He was on a married-status contract, which gave him a company house on-base with his family. During the Christmas New Year season his wife and kids went back to the United States to spend a month or so with her family. The Texas dickhead went to the Bali Rajah District and started swallowing Bintang beer like it was going out of style. An hour or so later he had his beer goggles on and got it in his drunken brain to follow a little brown girl into the shitter where he grabbed her, brutally sodomized her, then just left her lying bleeding on the shithouse floor. The assbag went back to drinking as though nothing had happened.

Two days later Larry the surveyor dropped by the fabrication shop for a Coke. That's when he told me about the event that had taken place with the assbag Texan. He had heard that the victim was still bleeding and the other Bali Rajah District girls were getting worried about her.

Later that day I had to have a meeting with Bill, the area manager. When we finished our business conversation, I explained to him what I had been told noting that there would be hell to pay if the girl died. Bill sprang into immediate action. He had the PT. Petrochem security cops immediately visit the Bali Rajah District to gather evidence and, if required, get the girl to the local hospital for treatment. Security took her to the hospital where she was stitched up and the company also gave her a bunch of rupiah to keep quite. She accepted the money and was put on a bus for the ten-hour trip back to her home in Medan, Northern Sumatra. That poor girl would have had a painful trip. The Texas assbag was given five days to pack up his shit and get outta Duri. I don't know if his wife ever found out about what happened, but I assume questions would have been asked when he returned home before his contract had expired.

Crime and corruption go hand in hand in Indonesia. Late one afternoon the Duri oil field was suddenly swooped down on by half a dozen police pick-up trucks carrying armed cops escorted by PT. Petrochem security personnel. They hit several locations throughout the oil field, rounding up a couple dozen workers by the time they were done. The workers were quickly carried off to their headquarters in Sompomadong.

Apparently an organized ring of workers had been stealing pipefittings, flanges, wrenches, ball-peen hammers, and what ever else they could carry off without being seen. The stolen items were then transported to Medan City in northern Sumatra and sold in various stores. It wasn't hard to understand why the thefts occurred. All the poor little beggars were trying to do was get a little extra rupiah to feed, school, and house their families. They sure as hell weren't earning a liveable salary.

The office manager in my shop was from the Batak tribe, as were many of his police friends, and he visited with them after things had settled down a little to try and get the full story. He learned that one of the ringleaders would not talk or rat out his buddies so the cops broke a bunch of bones and all of his fingers on his right hand to persuade him to change his mind. After enduring all that pain, he talked.

The significance of breaking the bones and fingers of the right hand relates to Indonesian culture.

After a bowel movement the left hand is always used to clean the anus with water. Toilet paper is a luxury that poverty does not afford. Food is always eaten with the right hand. When any item is handed from one person to another, it is always given by the right hand. However, with the ringleader's right hand broken and unworkable, all of his actions – eating, ass cleaning, and the handling of anything – would have to be done with the unclean left hand. That was considered a huge loss of face for the poor bastard.

In the end eight of the workers were officially charged. A few more of them were rounded-up in Medan. All of them were incarcerated for their crimes. I never learned how long they were jailed for, but you can be sure it wasn't a short time. When it comes to stealing from one of the oil companies, a government cash cow, thieves who get caught can be assured they will be old men before they are ever released from prison.

KUWAIT FIRES

CHAPTER 5

December 1990 arrived and my contract was complete. I'd had enough jungle for a while and I was becoming concerned about the way events were evolving in Indonesia. There was just so much injustice in the nation. Furthermore, radical Islamists were gaining strength and hatred for the West and Westerners was on the rise. I figured it was just a matter of time until it exploded and when it finally did, there was going to be a lot of serious hurt. It was time to leave Sumatra and head back home to West Texas and Christmas.

Several weeks after arriving back in Odessa, I was startled awake by the 6:00am ringing of the telephone. It was January 14, 1991. The voice on the other end of the line was asking me how I was doing and then asked if I would be interested in going to Kuwait to organize and manage a steel fabrication shop for the "Kuwait re-build." I was now mentally awake and recognized the voice belonged to Bill Bass, whom I had recently been working with in Sumatra, Indonesia. I was also aware that the wacky Iraqi had invaded Kuwait. The only thing I didn't quite understand was Bill's reference to rebuilding Kuwait.

Without waiting for my response, Bill told me he had quit the project in Sumatra and was now in the London, England, office of the

United States construction company, Canham International. In his new role he was the Field Services Manager for Canham and he was looking for a crew to go to Kuwait for the rebuild project.

"So what do you think?" he asked.

I finally got off a few words and said.

"Bill, the war with Iraq hasn't started yet!"

"Don't worry about that," he replied. "In three days, on the seventeenth, the shit is going to hit the fan big time."

I thought for a bit, trying to logically weight my options. I had worked in the Middle East oil fields before and I really had no use for the desert or its people.

"Sure, I'll go," I said. Immediately I wondered what shit I was about to get myself into.

"Great! Hang by your phone," he said. "I already have a copy of your resume that I brought with me from Sumatra. Someone from Canham's human resources department will contact you."

I hung around the phone and Odessa for a week or so but no call ever came from Canham International and I never bothered to try and call Bill back. Honestly I wasn't all that interested in the job offer; as far as I was concerned the Middle East was only a sand box full of oil and Western civilization haters.

After Bill's phone call, however, I started thinking about travelling for work again. Finally I said piss on it, kissed the little blonde lady goodbye, and boarded an economy flight that took me back to Southeast Asia and that hot, stinky, polluted capital city of Indonesia,

Jakarta. It was as good as any place to start looking for employment, even though the country was headed down a path of religious turmoil.

I figured it would be a year or two before the shit really hit the Jihad fan, and if I was not successful by then I'd head across to Singapore, Kuala Lumpur, and then on up to Bangkok.

Jakarta is a city of ten to twelve million people – no one really knew for sure as there was never a census. A large percentage of its people couldn't read, write, or speak the national language. They came from all over the archipelago speaking only their own local dialect.

Sukarno–Hatta International Airport was over-crowded and sweaty with that familiar clove cigarette odor. Short brown Indonesian men were continually harassing the new arrivals in broken English. "Sir, you want taxi? Come with me, sir. Taxi sir?"

I picked up my suitcase and saw one of the men look directly at me.

"Sir, I am Christian, you want Taxi?" he asked.

"Okay Tuan (sir), please drive me to the Sari Pan Pacific Hotel on Jalan MH Thamrin Avenue, in Central Jakarta." I replied, speaking slowly so that the driver could understand me. I had stayed at the Sari Pan Pacific Hotel before and it was as good as any four-star hotel, plus it was only a hundred yards from the six-floor Sarinah department store. A MacDonald's restaurant, the Green Bottle Bar, and the Hard Rock Cafe' were close by as well.

Once at the hotel, I realized that the television sets in the hotel lobby and restaurants were continuously showing images of what Saddam Hussein was saying was going to be "the mother of all battles" and United States news programs were calling the Gulf

War, "Desert Storm." As Bill Bass had told me, the aerial bombardment of Bagdad and other parts of Iraq had commenced on January seventeenth in an effort to expel Iraqi troops from Kuwait. After the August 2, 1990, Iraqi invasion of Kuwait, it had taken only two days of intense combat for most of the Kuwaiti Armed Forces to be overrun by the Iraqi Republican Guard. Many of the Kuwaiti military personnel had thrown down their weapons and high-tailed it into Saudi Arabia, Bahrain, and Iran. The wacky Iraqi threatened to turn Kuwait City into a graveyard if any country was to challenge his take-over of Kuwait by military force.

The day after my arrival I decided to visit several haunts where I knew ex-pats hung out. There were a couple of bars located a good thirty minute taxi ride from the Sari Pan Pacific Hotel in a part of Jakarta known as Blok M. The Top Gun and Sports Page bars were on the same street, almost opposite each other. They were also just around the corner from the PT. Petrochem office.

As I got into a taxi to head toward Blok M, the cab driver turned to face me. Suddenly, his eyes grew wide.

"Are you American?" he asked. "America no good!"

"What the fuck are you talking about?" I asked incredulously.

"Bush and America make war on Muslim, kill Muslim. Bush and America no good!" he said adamantly.

I shook my head. "You have it wrong!" I replied. Then I explained myself in slow broken English that I thought he would understand. "Iraq crazy man, Saddam Hussein, go into Kuwait and Saddam's army kill many Kuwait Muslims. Bush and America go to Kuwait to stop Saddam from killing Muslims, so Bush and America must be a good friend to Muslims for stopping Saddam from killing them."

He looked at me for a moment. "Maybe," he finally said. "So where you want to go?"

We travelled in silence as the driver took me through the traffic congested streets of Jakarta. I guess he got lost in his twisted melon after what I had said to him. As we drove along, I noticed there were banners and posters hung and pasted everywhere with the slogan, "Visit Indonesia Year 1991." The tourist authority of Indonesia was earning its money by publicizing the attractions of their country.

The bars the driver dropped me off near, the Top Gun and the Sports Page, were owned and operated by ex-pats. Two Americans, who rotated from their offshore oil drilling rig employment, ran their bar, the Top Gun, when they were on leave. It was customary to make payoffs to corrupt police and local mafia. One of the American bar owners had refused an extra payment to a local mafia low life. Several days later, as he stepped from the toilet into the bar, the low life plunged a knife into his belly and ripped him open. He died on the floor of his bar.

The killer was later caught and sent to prison. Rumor has it that, for many months after the murder, a collection of Indonesian rupiah was taken up from the patrons of the Sports Page and Top Gun. Once there was a large enough sum, it was paid out for a prison hit on the killer. I have no idea if the hit was actually carried out. All I knew was that the bars were good places to pick up a job since guys were coming and going all the time. Solid information could be had from fellow drinkers. I walked into the Top Gun and ordered a Bintang.

I had been in Jakarta for a couple of weeks roaming around the different offices of the international construction and oil companies, trying to get job interviews without much luck. I would always leave a resume at each location, hoping it would get into the right hands, but I figured that most times it would no doubt end up in a waste paper basket.

Television sets all over Jakarta were tuned into CNN. On February 23, 1991, a ground assault by coalition forces invaded Kuwait and advanced all the way into Iraqi territory. The coalition completed its advance and a cease-fire was declared only one hundred hours after it began. The wacky Iraqi had been knocked on his ass. However, before Saddam Hussein had left Kuwait, he had his military employ a "scorched earth" policy. This included blowing up and setting fire to more than seven hundred producing-oil-wells – Kuwait's life blood.

I decided to stay in the Jakarta area for another few weeks, continuously smelling rotting garbage and clove cigarettes, watching CNN discuss the war in Kuwait coming to an end. One Saturday evening I was feeling particularly down on my luck. I considered heading out to maybe hook up with a little brown lady. I was stretched out on the bed in my hotel room watching an English television channel showing the latest American music videos. The female group, Wilson Phillips, were performing their latest hit and the lyrics were profound: "Hold on for one more day, things will change, things will go your way." Suddenly the phone in my hotel room rang. When I answered it, I was surprised to hear my sister, who was back in Texas. She said that some guy from London had telephoned. He was looking for me regarding a project in Kuwait. She hoped I didn't mind but she had given him my Jakarta hotel phone number.

Since I wasn't having any luck finding a job, I figured I would hang around and see if my telephone rang again. Sure enough, it did ring a half hour later. A British-accented guy said he was calling from Canham International and asked how soon I could be in London for company processing regarding the Kuwait rebuild project.

"I can be there just as soon as I can get a ticket." I replied.

After I hung up, I began to think about Kuwait all over again. I also thought about those Wilson Phillips lyrics! What the hell, I thought. At least I would get to see several hundred oil well fires and reload my bank account, even if I only stayed a month or two.

That Monday morning I bought a one-way ticket to London with a one night lay-over in Singapore, then on through Colombo, Sri Lanka, arriving in London the following Thursday morning. After passing through British customs without a hitch at Heathrow Airport, I caught a taxi to Canham's office in Grosvenor Square, close to the Novatel Hotel where Canham had booked me a room. Several hours after arrival, I was in my room, sleeping on and off, trying to get over my jet lag.

***

Early the next morning, I headed over to Canham's office and reported to the guy sitting in the field services manager's chair. I had met Homer in Sumatra before, but didn't really know the guy. He was filling in for Bill Bass, who had flown out to Kuwait some ten days prior to my arrival. Homer took me to meet the project manager for the Kuwait rebuild, who turned out to be California Ken, the guy I had heard about when I was in Sumatra.

Ken had been running a project for Canham in Iraq before the Kuwait invasion, but he had been in the United States when the wacky Iraqi went into Kuwait. Since there would be no returning to Iraq, Canham's top management had decided that California Ken should manage the project the company was referring to as "Kuwait Fires." As I shook his hand, memories of what I had been told regarding his sexual preferences came rushing into my melon. As long as he didn't put his hand on my ass I had no problem with him. I couldn't care less that he would rather hear a fat boy fart than a pretty girl sing.

I also met up with Butch, the heavy equipment manager for the Kuwait rebuild. I had known Butch in Sumatra. He had come into Indonesia from Atlanta, Georgia. I had seen him many times in the Duri base bar and down at the Bali Rajah District. He always had a smile on his face and a pleasant personality and would always say hello to everyone he encountered. He had learned his skills as a first class heavy-duty mechanic by serving a five-year apprenticeship at Caterpillar's Illinois factory. He then stayed on for another ten years with Caterpillar, eventually leaving with the rank of superintendent. There wasn't much the old fart didn't know about that company and its machines. Butch had told me the day he left Caterpillar, he signed an agreement with the company that he would not go to work for any of its competitors for a period of ten years.

But soon Butch ignored that contract, said to hell with 'em, and went to Japan on a lucrative contract. He spent the next five years with the Japanese manufacturer of Caterpillars main competitor, Komatsu.

After shooting the breeze with Butch for a while, he informed me that he was flying out to Dubai, United Arab Emirates, the following day.

It would take three days to complete the necessary documentation in London and then we would be flown to Dubai where we would have to hang around another two or three days for a permanent residence visa for the United Arab Emirates. Canham and the Kuwaitis had reached an agreement with the United Arab Emirates to utilize it as a marshalling point for all the ex-pats and equipment required for the rebuild. We would then be flown into Kuwait where we would spend six weeks working and then be entitled for two weeks' leave. We would be flown out of Kuwait by Canham to Dubai without having any visa problems and we were then on our own to go anywhere in the world we wished. However, we'd have to return to Dubai the night prior to our return into Kuwait. Canham paid for our accommodation in one of the many five-star hotels both going and coming from Kuwait if it was needed. The day before leaving Kuwait, each one of us would visit the Canham Accounts Department and receive the United States dollar equivalent of an economy class return ticket to our home port. I received $3,500 cash each leave.

The night before Butch left London for Dubai, he and I went out for dinner and were joined by the medical doctor Canham had hired for the Kuwait Fires project. He told us he was somewhat of a specialist when it came to flesh burns. It seemed appropriate that he would be going to Kuwait with that knowledge. During the meal we all chit chatted about the mess in Kuwait and Butch and I reminisced a bit about the Bali Rajah District and the little brown girls.

As the night wore on we noticed the doctor was getting after the booze big time during the meal and when it came time to get up and leave the table, the good doctor couldn't find his legs and fell flat on his ass. Butch and I looked at each other and I know we were both thinking the same thing. Later, when we were heading back to our hotel, Butch leaned over to me and said, "Looks like we have a doctor with a drinking problem on our hands."

Canham completed my documentation, which included a heavy-duty medical exam at one of London's Harley Street doctors, and then I received my visa. Finally I was ready to go. The night before I left London I decided to hit the fart sack early, but before sleep I watched a little local television.

The news channel was showing footage taken with a night vision camera mounted in the nose of a Black Hawk helicopter. The camera, with its eerie greenish night vision, was concentrated on a highway with bumper-to-bumper vehicles of all descriptions, some civilian, some military. All of the vehicles were stationary. Suddenly, the helicopter's guns opened up and the camera began shaking. I could see tracer bullets streaming from the gunship, smashing into the traffic jam. Other helicopters were firing into the vehicles too, which immediately exploded on impact. People could be seen running in every direction. Some would stop, turn, and run the other way to no avail; the tracers inevitably found their mark.

The whole thing was an extraordinary vision into the devastation of the "Highway of Death" at the end of Desert Storm in Kuwait. It was this massacre that induced General Powell to basically end hostilities with Iraq. I switched channels, trying to find a change of scenery. Eventually I came across three voluptuous, scantily dressed ladies with holes torn in the ass of their blue jeans singing, "I'm your Venus, I'm your fire at your desire." I watched until they finished their song, then turned off the television and fell asleep dreaming I was partying with Bananarama.

The next day I left London heading for Dubai. Don, a machine shop manager whom I had met in Canham's office, rode with me. He lived in Santa Barbara, California, and would be managing the machine shop in Kuwait. Don told me that he had been employed by Canham most of his working life. Our other traveling companion was the good doctor with the booze problem. After we passed through United Arab Emirates customs in Dubai, we were transported to the Chicago Beach Hotel. We were to stay there for a few days while we waited for the necessary documents for residence in the United Arab Emirates.

During those couple of days, Don and I wandered the shopping malls and gold markets. We also relaxed on the beaches of Dubai. The more I got to know Don, the more I liked him. On my second night I spotted the good doctor staggering around one of the beer gardens at the hotel. He was higher than a Georgia Pine! I sure hoped he would put the plug in the jug, so to speak, before he arrived in Kuwait.

Finally we were given our passports, stamped up with the residence visa and advised that tomorrow we would leave for Kuwait.

CHAPTER 6

The chartered Evergreen Airlines Boeing 727 departed Dubai for Kuwait at 12:20 p.m., on Monday, April 1, 1991. As the aircraft lifted off the tarmac I wondered if the date had any subliminal message. The flight lasted about an hour. As the aircraft advanced closer to the Kuwaiti coastline, the shining celestial blue canopy of the Persian Gulf became a radically different composition of brown-gray smoke through which the aircraft began to descend toward its goal.

As we lost altitude and flew over beaches, highways, and a fire-blackened storage tank farm containing absurdly distorted structures that had once held thousands of gallons of crude oil, I could see the orange-red flames of numerous oil well fires through the highly concentrated smoke. Needless to say, it was a profoundly somber vision. Fires could be seen in every direction as the aircraft turned for its final approach into the Kuwait International Airport. They rose up into the smoke, their highest points became lost in undulations of their own sooty product.

The airport was in shambles. The control tower had suffered intense war damage and was now a vacant burned-out blackened structure. The terminal buildings were in similar condition. The aircraft touched down on the only usable runway. I noticed that numerous bomb craters littered the entire airfield. During Desert Storm this had been the location of a severe military confrontation.

After landing, the aircraft taxied past several rows of military vehicles, Black Hawk helicopters, fighter jet aircraft, satellite dishes, and radar equipment. The radar equipment sported similar surface patterns in their paint work as General Schwarzkopf's desert fatigues.

The aircraft came to a halt in an open area that was encircled on three sides by warehouse-type structures. Several pick-up trucks and mini buses were parked along side one of the buildings. Four or five men with Evergreen Airlines embossed on their coveralls were standing by the vehicles. The rear door was opened and we disembarked out under the tail wing of the aircraft. As I made my way down the stairs, I saw an old Arabic man who had been a fellow passenger get down on his hands and knees to kiss the asphalt surface. Apparently he had been a long time resident of Kuwait and had been out of the country on business when the hostile entrance of the Iraqi forces occurred. He was finally returning home after an unwanted exile of almost a year.

The men wearing the Evergreen Airlines coveralls approached the aircraft and began to unload our suitcases and the airfreight. They advised us to wait by the mini buses and pick-up trucks, which were a couple of hundred yards from where the aircraft was parked. They also told us that Canham International representatives would be arriving shortly to meet and advise us of the situation.

While waiting I was awestruck at the devastation in and around the airport. The smoke from the oil well fires was blowing in our direction but it was maybe twenty feet above ground level. Several burned-out vehicles stood forlornly among the bombed-out buildings. After a short wait a new Chevrolet Caprice sedan appeared and two individuals in dress shirts and neck-ties got out of the vehicle. They approached us and introduced themselves. One was a vice president of Canham International; the other was California Ken. They shook our hands, welcomed us to Kuwait, and told us the mini buses would take us to the high-rise apartment buildings where we would be housed.

There had been approximately thirty passengers on the flight to Kuwait, all male. No one had been processed through Kuwaiti immigration or customs, as they were literally nonexistent. The airport was now under management of the French military as a member of the coalition occupation forces.

We boarded the mini-buses for the journey to the "Towers," as the British driver referred to our new accommodations. As the vehicle I was traveling in moved out of the airport and onto the highway, I looked out my window to see two Arab men clad in military desert camouflage uniforms holding an individual dressed in civilian attire. They had their victim bent backwards over the front end of a pick-up truck and were in the process of beating the shit out of him. Using the bus intercom system, the driver informed us that what we had just witnessed was the Kuwaiti militia enjoying a little revenge on a Palestinian whom they probably suspected had been a collaborator during the Iraqi occupation.

About a mile from the airport, on the edge of the highway, was the twisted burned hulk of an Iraqi Army tank. It had obviously taken a hit from a tank busting missile, most likely the armor piercing depleted-uranium penetrating type, and was disfigured almost beyond recognition. The poor bastards who had the misfortune of being inside at the moment of impact wouldn't have stood a snowball's chance in hell of surviving the hit.

As the bus continued its journey, the devastation was continuous with virtually no intermission. War damaged buildings, abandoned cars, trucks, and military tanks were scattered along both sides of the dual-lane highway. Some were twisted and burned, others were totally wrecked. Some of the automobiles were flattened and had obviously been run over by a military tank, but by which army was anybody's guess.

We exited onto an overpass that would take us to the Towers. Moments later we came to a standstill. The driver informed us this was an ideal location to view the burning oil fields and take photographs if we wanted to get off the bus and do so. Even though our range of vision was limited due to the pollution, it was still an incredible sight. Hearing and smelling hundreds of oil well fires roaring out of control and seeing the smoke twirling, rolling, and always moving in ever changing patterns with shades of grays, blues, whites, and blacks writhing together was absolutely mesmerizing.

As I looked around I noticed other remnants of the military conflict in the area. Sand bags were stacked along the retaining walls of the overpass, which crossed above one of the main arteries that led from Kuwait City south to the border shared with Saudi Arabia. Live rounds of fifty-millimeter ammunition, each round about six inches in length, were scattered among the sand bags. The overpass had been a fortified position used by the Iraqi military.

When we were done looking around and snapping pictures we reboarded the bus and, after a twenty minute drive through the continuous devastation, pulled up in front of twin high-rise buildings. Both were constructed of brown sandy colored bricks and contained approximately twenty floors. The sign above the lobby entrance read "Fintas Towers". I got off the bus and went inside to what I figured would be my new home for at least the next couple of months.

The camp boss welcomed us and issued us with room keys. Once I had my key, I took my suitcases to a suite on the sixteenth floor that I knew I would be sharing with two other Canham employees, a South African I hadn't met and the crane superintendent, whom I had worked with on the project in Sumatra.

Gerry was considered one of the good guys in Duri. He was a big man standing approximately six-foot-four inches tall and weighed in at over three hundred pounds. In the late 1960s he had been drafted into the United States National Football League and was in his rookie year when another draft notice from his California home town draft board put his ass in the army. He served in a construction battalion stationed in Da Nang, Vietnam. He said that one evening the base came under heavy mortar fire. The next day it was his duty to assist with the clearing of the destruction. He had to help removing dead bodies; some of them were in pieces. Most of the deceased had been Vietnamese people who had been working on the base. He was responsible for stacking the remains into pick-up trucks and unloading them at a makeshift morgue. The way he told it I believed he was still having nightmares about the whole experience.

The three-bedroom suite was huge with gray marble floors. There were two full bathrooms, a guest toilet, a spacious living room, and a full kitchen. There were even facilities for live-in domestic help. Clearly someone had been living high on the hog before the war had emptied out the building. A dual-lane highway separated Fintas Towers from the beach of the Persian Gulf. The window of the room I would occupy faced west toward the desert. I was afforded a spectacular view of the oil well fires. The furniture was minimal: a bed and a closet. The entire suite was virtually without furniture. The Iraqi soldiers had stolen almost everything and maliciously vandalized the entire building. In fact one of the full length floor-to-ceiling windows in the living room had been shattered and was creating problems for the air conditioning, allowing some of the outside 95 degree Fahrenheit heat to penetrate, even though it had been boarded up with a slab of plywood.

Mess room facilities had been established off the lobby area. Canham had hired a catering company from Britain to provide meals for the ex-pats and third-country national work force that would be required to kill the fires and rebuild Kuwait. I consumed a late lunch and hitched a ride with Robert, the camp boss, to Canham's office, which was located approximately twenty miles south of Fintas Towers at a location called Mina Abdula. Canham had acquired office space in one of the many deserted office buildings that were in abundance. Mina Abdula was also the site of the newest and largest of the three oil refineries in Kuwait. All of them had suffered damage during the Iraqi occupation and Desert Storm, and none of them were currently in production and wouldn't be for some months to come.

The highway systems of Kuwait compare favourably with any in the United States, and as we travelled the dual-system south, Robert explained that the extensive holes and fragmentations that appeared intermittently on the asphalt surface had been caused by cluster bombs the allies had used against the Iraqis. Considerable damage had also been caused by tracked vehicles used by both sides during the recent conflict. More bombed and burned-out pieces of military equipment littered both sides of the highway. Other objects were also scattered along the roadside: furniture, clothing, building materials, and countless dirty green and cream striped blankets. The blankets, according to Robert, had been Iraqi military issued. We were sharing the highway with United States army Humvees and other military vehicles. Robert told me United States Special Forces, British Special Air Service, and the French Foreign Legion were still engaged in rounding up Iraqi army stragglers who were mostly hiding out in the Palestinian section of Kuwait City.

When we arrived at the office building occupied by Canham, I noticed that the windshield of the vehicle we'd been traveling in was peppered with brown droplets of oil. The smoke density in

Mina Abdula was far greater than at the airport and totally obscured the sun.

I took the elevator to the third floor of the building and located the office with Field Services Manager marked on the door. I knocked and heard the response to enter.

Bill Bass stood up from behind his desk and extended his hand to welcome me to Kuwait. It had been several months since I last saw him in Sumatra and it had been Bill who telephoned me three days before Desert Storm had commenced and asked me if I was interested in managing a steel fabrication shop in support of the Kuwait rebuild. He quickly apologized for the delay in my being contacted after he had originally telephoned me.

He then went on to explain that after several weeks had gone by and he had received no response from a half dozen guys he had contacted for the Kuwait project, he visited Canham's Human Resources Department in the London office and discovered the Brits were in the process of filling his positions with locals. He got pissed off and raised his concerns with California Ken, who very smartly rearranged the thinking of the human resources department and also cancelled the North American candidates coming through the London office. From then on they would be processed through Canham's San Francisco, California, home office. He added that I was one of the last candidates from the United States to process through London.

Bill had already been in Kuwait for several weeks. By the look of his office staff he was doing okay for himself. He shared his office with a very attractive Philippine secretary who was in her early twenties. By the way Bill acted and kept looking in her direction there was no doubt he was dipping his dick. Bill was a philanderer. His third Indonesian wife, and I don't know how many kids, were all being housed in Dubai while Canham paid the bill and back charged the project.

After a few minutes of shooting the shit Bill explained the challenges that were faced to recover the oil fields. Kuwait had been devastated during the occupation. The Iraqi military, devoid of pity, had literally destroyed and looted most of the country both economically and physically. Electric power and water systems received heavy damage and the oil industry was in chaos. Kuwait had more than one thousand producing oil wells prior to the invasion. However, no one was sure just how many were damaged or on fire.

In the ensuing months we learned that a total of 749 were damaged, 727 were on fire, and 22 were damaged and violently discharging raw crude. Previously the largest number of fires in any field at one time had been in the Libyan Desert during the mid-1960s. Five oil wells situated very close together caught fire after the first well exploded in a fireball and the gusting Shamal desert winds pushed the flames into the four remaining wells causing them to ignite.

Bill also told me there was virtually no equipment present in the country to operate a steel fabrication shop. The next few days would have to be spent searching Kuwait City, rounding up what may have been left behind by the fleeing Iraqis. Additionally, a location for my fabrication shop had yet to be chosen. Just as Bill was ending his assessment of the situation, Butch, the heavy equipment manager, entered the office and asked if we were through. He was ready to head out to the field and there were no spare vehicles to use. He also needed to round up equipment. It made sense that I accompany him. Bill then informed us that another new arrival, Don, the machine shop superintendent, who was in the same situation, may as well ride around with us. Don had come in on the same flight from Dubai as me.

Butch had only been in Kuwait for a couple of days. As we headed back along the highway toward Fintas Towers, he told us that, to date, four fire fighting teams were in the country with very little equipment. Piece by piece, some equipment was slowly coming up from Saudi Arabia, but not without problems.

Just a couple of days earlier a convoy of approximately fifty trucks was held up at a border crossing where Saudi Arabia customs officials literally dismantled each vehicle before they crossed into Kuwait. No one knew why, but after cash was passed under the table, there were no more problems. I was told the term for the bribe was "tea money."

After travelling about ten miles, Butch pulled the Jeep Cherokee off the highway and headed in the direction of the fires. Several minutes later we passed by the partially twisted and burned out tank-farm I'd flown over earlier. Butch told us that it was this tank farm that Saddam Hussein's boys had blown up and dumped more than four hundred million gallons of crude oil into the Persian Gulf, causing the largest oil spill in history. The path the crude had taken on its journey of a couple of miles to the Gulf was down the road-side ditches and underground drainage system. Some of the crude had been on fire and a section of the black top road surface had melted and was now a layer of solidified tar.

A mile further down the road, as we neared a housing community, I noticed a sign leaning at an acute angle by the roadside. It read, CITY of AL AHMADI in both Arabic and English.

Situated some twenty five miles south of Kuwait City, Al Ahmadi was a virtual ghost town. Before the invasion it had been the center for vital support services to the oil sector and home to approximately five thousand oil field workers. During the conflict it had received significant damage by both Iraqi military and allied attacks. All drilling rigs, drill pipe, spare parts, and camp equipment had been dismantled and shipped into Iraq by its military. The closer we got to the fires, the more concentrated the smoke became. Butch had to turn on the vehicle's headlights; street lighting was nonexistent, owing to the damaged power system.

As we continued driving through the dimly lit deserted streets, it was hard to believe that we were still on the inhabited Earth and that mankind had actually created the catastrophe we were witnessing. We drove by hundreds of vacant vandalized houses and business. Broken office and household furniture, wrecked cars, abandoned military tanks and trucks, and countless oily green-and-cream-striped Iraqi Army blankets lined the edges of the streets. Meanwhile, crude oil continued to rain down from low rolling black smoke and the constant roaring sound of the oil well fires was ever present.

The Magwa oil field came all the way to the edge of Ahmadi. Its closest oil well was only a hundred yards from the abandoned houses. Its fire was furiously raging upward of fifty feet. I could feel the heat on the side of my face as it effortlessly penetrated the window of the Cherokee as we drove by. Canham earthworks crew had built detours around areas of the roadway where the desert had depressions and pools of black crude oil were beginning to form lakes. However, before any earthworks could begin, unexploded ordinance left by the Allies and any mines that may have been placed by the Iraqi's had to be cleared by Allied military specialists.

We drove another mile into the Magwa field, passing a few Iraqi Army tanks. Their hatch covers were open and turret guns with fully loaded bullet belts were hanging from the firing mechanisms. An Iraqi army Jeep stood covered with oil off in the distance, its four wheels were almost touching each other, its chassis bent in U-shape. Apparently it had been in a confrontation with a land mine.

Butch steered the Cherokee off the Magwa road and into a fenced yard. We could see flashing blue light and cascading sparks through the pitch-black darkness of smoke as Philippino welders worked. Several corrugated iron buildings, a couple of cranes, bulldozers, and pick-up trucks were in the yard. Men dressed in coveralls, hard hats, and dust masks were in the process of fabricating corrugated iron shields around Caterpillar D9 bulldozers that would be used in the battle to extinguish the fires. Peering through the smoke I was able to recognize the decals on the pick-up truck doors. It was the unmistakable insignia of oil well fire fighters; an oil derrick with fire billowing from its substructure. The insignia indicated this yard was being utilized by the crews of Joe Bowden Wild Well Control, based out of Spring, Texas.

In October of 1990, anticipating massive oil field destruction, the Kuwait Oil Company, operating from Washington, D.C., and London, England, established initial contact with four fire fighting companies, one from Canada, Safety Boss, and three from the United States, Boots & Coots, Joe Bowden Wild Well Control, and the Red Adair Company. Additionally, non-conventional fire fighting methods were explored, ranging from crushing or crimping the well heads, to doming and tunneling, to robotics and chemicals, and a variety of others. The Kuwait Oil Company received more than eight hundred proposals for non-conventional oil well fire control.

It was impossible to know if the sun had set or if it was still high in the heavens. Needless to say, it had been a long day. After cleaning the black and brown oil drops off the windshield that continuously rained down from the twisting, swirling overhead smoke with a diesel fuel-soaked cloth, and with no discord from me or Don, Butch turned the Cherokee around and we headed back to Fintas Towers.

***

After the evening meal and with the black rain that had fallen onto my arms and face from the dark smokey canopy washed down the shower drain I was pleasantly moved by the spectacular view from my bedroom window. The night skies blushed a brilliant orange filling the room with flickering color that was interlaced with the sound of live rounds of ammunition that contained red and green tracer bullets being fired into the night sky by crazy fucking Arabs who were shooting at their demons – a nightly occurrence. The brilliance of the night gave way to the morning, which was enveloped in pitch black darkness of smoke allowing only a faint glimpse of the fires glow to permeate along the horizon. There was no heaven, no moon, no stars, and no sunrise, only total blackness outside. The dense smoke skimmed lightly and rapidly across the desert surface, stinging our eyes, filling our nasal passages, causing headaches and fits of sneezing.

After our 4:30 a.m. breakfast, Don and I rode with Butch to Ahmadi, where the fire fighters were quartered in Ahmadi House, a complex of dormitories, offices, and a mess hall. Cars, pick-up trucks, and mini buses were parked among the dozen or so palm trees that grew in the parking lot. Their foliage was laden with oil, giving them a sheen that glistened when the sun's rays flashed through the twisting uneven smoke, striking them momentarily.

An estimated five million barrels of crude oil were being lost daily due to the oil well fires. The pressure of the escaping oil as it roared out of the damaged well heads was estimated to reach seven hundred miles per hour. At this speed it was unable to be totally consumed by the fire and the unburned crude would travel with the smoke in the wind and uninterruptedly shower down, creating black rain. The wells that weren't on fire were spewing their product and forming lakes in the desert.

The smoke billowed across the rooftops of the buildings around Ahmadi House. The three American fire fighting teams, Red Adair,

Boots & Coots, and Joe Bowden Wild Well Control were all present. Their team members dressed in individual team colors of white, red, and yellow coveralls with their fire fighter insignias on their backs. The lone Canadian team, Safety Boss, donned its beige colored coveralls with bright yellow reflective tape stitched around the arms and down the outside of each team member's leg. Some of the fire fighters had one pant leg tucked inside the top of their Wellington-style Red Wing safety boots (I guess they thought it looked cool).

The men all stood or sat on the large open porch of Ahmadi House discussing strategies and bullshitting each other. Some ranted about the equipment shortage, which without doubt was desperate, while most all were drinking coffee from styrofoam cups. Meanwhile, brown skinned women from India, Sri Lanka, and the Philippines walked between the buildings carrying linen and other household items that were required for cleaning the rooms. Some of them smiled when catching the attention of a fire fighter. During the Iraqi invasion, most of the women had been abandoned by fleeing Kuwaitis who had employed them as domestic help. Many of their compatriots had been murdered by the Iraqi forces.

Moments later, Bill came out of the mess hall picking his teeth with one hand and his coffee cup in the other. He was wearing a black baseball-type cap with the Canham insignia on it. He nodded good morning and then informed us that there was an equipment dealer in Kuwait City with some of his stock left even though the Iraqi soldiers had stolen most of it. He suggested that we should go check it out.

***

Downtown Kuwait City was akin to a disembodied soul. No pedestrians walked on the sidewalks. No police offers patrolled the streets. No stores were open for business. Most had been looted. Their plate-glass windows were shattered. Basically no infrastructure existed. Refuse of the war littered the streets. Traffic lights were bent and broken and devoid of power. We passed by the multi-floored Meridian Hotel. Several of its gold-tinted windows were now only blackened remnants, and the ground floor was burned out. Parliament and many other government buildings had also been badly damaged by fire and looting. During the occupation thousands of homes had been stripped of their contents and more than fifty thousand automobiles had been stolen. Saddam Hussein's scorched earth policy had blanketed Kuwait.

After locating the supplier, Boodai, both Don and I placed an order for machine and fabrication shop tools. It was anybody's guess as to when the order would be filled; everything had to be imported. Boodai's shelves were almost completely bare. At the Mohamed Abdulrahman Al-Bhar Caterpillar dealership, Butch inspected several used Caterpillar D8 bulldozers and explained to the dealer that he would have a couple of his heavy-duty mechanics test run them in the ensuing days. If they were in good operational condition the project would purchase them.

We made our way back toward Ahmadi. Along the coastal highway we could see that many of the apartment buildings facing the ocean had been remodeled by the Iraqi military. Windows and doors that once opened onto balconies had been removed and replaced with bricks leaving small openings that were adequate enough for aiming the barrel section of portable weapons. Obviously the invaders had anticipated a marine assault by the coalition forces. They had dug slit trenches for several miles along the beaches. However, the land assault had actually come from the south, crossing the Saudi Arabian border. Then it quickly moved north, fanning out over Kuwait. Yea! Kicking ass.

We decided to have lunch at Fintas Towers and during our conversation Butch explained that Canham was organizing a massive forward logistical base at Jebel Ali in the United Arab Emirates. The project would be receiving thousands of pieces of equipment by cargo ships and barges. One-hundred-ton cranes, cars, pick-up trucks, articulated vehicles, earth-moving equipment, helicopters, as well as communication equipment, portable camps, and hundreds of tons of bottled drinking water as the Iraqis' had sabotaged the desalination plants. Food and countless other items required to support thousands of people fighting oilwell fires in a desert environment would also have to be imported .

Canham expected to eventually import six-thousand manual workers from the Philippines, Thailand, and Indonesia to assist in rectifying the environmental terrorism of Saddam Hussein. The Kuwait officials also approached the United States Air Force, requesting the use of its giant C-5A cargo aircraft and the Russians with the world's largest aircraft, the Antonov, to transport oversized fire fighting equipment. Their roll-on, roll-off capability dispensed with the need for heavy cargo handling equipment, which had been stolen or destroyed. Without these huge aircraft, control operations would have been delayed several months. Soon more than nine thousand pieces of heavy oil field equipment would be flown into Kuwait by these massive flying machines.

After lunch the wind quit blowing and Mina Abdula was immersed in ground-level smoke, making visibility minimal. Our nasal passages were constantly aggravated by the black soot, which often induced nose bleeds. We were forever picking our noses trying to clear our air ways of the black shit that would congeal inside. The air inside Canham's office was more agreeable than the outside atmosphere.

Don and I went to speak with Bill in his office. We explained to him our unearthing of equipment in Kuwait City. He informed us that our respective shops would be established in the existing Kuwait Oil Company's facilities. Additionally, within the next couple of days

Philippine workers would be arriving by air to staff them. Meanwhile all we could do was familiarize ourselves with the location and meet the skeleton crew of local personnel who were currently manning the facilities. The next day a pick-up truck that was being conveyed from Saudi Arabia would be assigned to us. With that we left Mina Abdula with Butch and his Cherokee and headed north for Fintas Towers.

Back at Fintas Towers, I went to my room and noticed a memorandum on top of my pillow. I picked it up and saw it that it was from the project manager. It was addressed to all personnel and the subject was titled "E.O.D., Presentation at Fintas Towers".

Canham personnel were located on many work fronts throughout Kuwait. The most economical and efficient method of memorandum circulation was to have the camp boss utilize his staff for distribution purposes. At 7:00 p.m. the British Army Bomb Disposal team arrived in the lobby of Fintas Towers with an array of defused munitions, bomblets, mines, and booby-traps. They explained that the long-nose bomblets on display were capable of penetrating inches of solid steel and were called Rockeyes. The smaller mines looked like the top off a Thermos flask. However, if stepped on they had enough power to remove one's foot and maybe half of the person's leg. Additionally, a bicycle wheel that had been booby-trapped and rigged with an armed floatation device had been fabricated for use in oil storage tanks and pipelines causing untold havoc if detonated.

The army officer directing the presentation described the horror and mutilation that would be caused by the mishandling of live armaments. The oil fields, he stated, were littered with mines placed by the Iraqis and unexploded munitions, such as cluster bombs, dropped by the allied forces. Many of these existed under several inches of surface oil accumulation, making access to burning oil wells extremely hazardous. He added that the seaports and oil refineries were also booby-trapped and the huge quantities of hand grenades, ammunition, firearms, and rocket-propelled grenades that had been left behind by the Iraqis should not be handled by unauthorized personnel.

After the British Army Bomb Disposal team had completed its presentation, several of the team members passed around the defused munitions for our familiarization. California Ken announced that Canham's first priority was to establish a clear and safe working environment, as well as safety protection of all personnel. All areas would be certified clear and safe by an Explosive Ordnance Disposal contractor prior to any person entering the work area, thus eliminating potential mishaps. He then announced at the request of Kuwaiti officials that the Kuwait rebuild project would be designated the 'Al-Awda Project', which translated into "The Return," an apt title considering the desertion of the majority of most of the country's residents during the occupation and now the influx of thousands for the restoration.

CHAPTER 7

I woke at 4:00 A.M. to the dancing orange reflections ricocheting off the bedroom walls. The aroma of the burning wells emanated through the air conditioning system, which was now in full operating mode since the repair of the shattered window. Its orifices were surrounded by black soot stains. It was going to be another dark smoky day.

Don and I acquired a Chevrolet half-ton pick-up truck from Bill at Ahmadi House, which had become the early morning mustering zone during the project's infancy. We then located and checked out the Kuwait Oil Company shop amenities in a sequence of buildings abutting a one-hundred-square-yard asphalt courtyard. The facilities were extremely old and housed millwright, machine, and fabrication shops. In the ensuing months, the area would become a very crowded and busy environment.

The personnel manning the shops were mostly Kuwaitis with an array of twenty-odd Pakistanis, Philippinos, and Indians, who had remained in the country during the occupation. They greeted us receptively. Don and I annexed a vacant lunch room in the fabrication shop to use as an office. Canham's procurement personnel had gathered some of the abandoned office furniture and stored it in a warehouse that had been emptied of its contents by the Iraqis. We selected our requirements and converted the lunch room into a furnished office.

After I quit messing with the office, I decided to go for a stroll around the facilities. As I walked in the mid-morning darkness, I could hear what sounded like a departing jumbo jet with its four engines on full throttle. It was actually a massive oil well fire about a half-mile away, a raging inferno roaring its fire in opposite directions at ground level. Each orange-red flame stretched out several hundred yards from the well-head. Later that day, I learned it had been christened "The Long Horn", or "Moustache", depending on whom you were speaking with.

As I ambled through the murkiness, I looked up to where the sun should have been blinding my eyes with its desert brilliance. However, all I could see was a yellowish dimly lit orange ball. Immersed in the blackened madness, I could smell and taste the product of the oil wells that were spewing their souls skyward. They burned in all their glory, spreading their white, black, gray, and brown smoke over the land. Droplets of oil fell on my unprotected arms and face, leaving their soaking brown stains on my clothes.

The Kuwait desert was absolutely devoid of light. I could see some vehicles off in the distance, advancing slowly with their headlights stabbing into the darkness. There were no street lights to help guide drivers to their destinations. War machinery stood silent, abandoned by the fleeing losers. Devastation was everywhere. The smoke in the wind moved slowly overhead, never stopping. Day and night, it travelled onward over the desert, over destroyed buildings, and out to sea. It continued travelling hundreds of miles down the coast line of the Persian Gulf and over the island Sheikhdom of Bahrain, where freshly washed clothes hanging out to dry became soiled again by the falling black rain.

Oil-soaked sea gulls wandered in what seemed to be disillusion. When disturbed, they'd take flight for several feet and then land. Date palms sagged heavily, their foliage dripped with black crude. I came across a brown dog, its oil stained hide hugged its protruding ribs, sitting in a pool of dirty, oily water. The dog just looked at me through blood-shot eyes with an expression of emptiness, almost as though waiting to die. I felt sad for the poor bastard but there was nothing I could really do. Cats, with their fur coats also full of oil, scurried off whenever I got too close to them. Suddenly a faint ray of sun slipped through the black canopy, but then the twisting, swirling thick smoke quickly swallowed it up. At times I felt light headed and my eyes stung. There was no escaping the enveloping environment as the oil wells burned out of control.

As I walked past those deserted and broken buildings in that man-made madness, I began thinking to myself that I must have been mad to have left that beautiful fresh air and lush green jungles of Sumatra for this hell. But just as fast as that thought entered my melon, I remember that I was being paid three times more to be in the shit than I was being paid in Sumatra. In the end it all comes down to cash!

After a 12:30 p.m. meeting with Bill and other members of the Field Services Department I joined Don and Butch and together we drove to the Magwa oil field. Once there, I noticed that several European television crews and American military personnel were on the scene. We got to witness Red Adair's team kill a fire with four high-pressure hoses using a composite of water mixed with house-hold detergent. The mixture was aimed from several different angles at the base of the fire, which was shooting up a twenty foot length of pipe called a snuffer tube. The flames sucked the oxygen from the base of the snuffer tube, which was being held in place by a crane over the damaged wellhead. The water and detergent mixture eliminated the oxygen, causing emulsification and snuffed out the flame.

The light colored crude continued to ascend into the rolling, twisting smoke that was carried by the wind. Later it would rain down over the desert. The more arduous task was going to be securing the well head and shutting in the escaping crude. That process could take days or weeks depending on the wellhead damage caused when Saddam Hussein's demolition teams blew it up.

It was astounding to see the hundreds of wrecked cars and trucks of all sizes as we drove around Ahmadi. Almost all of them had been stripped of their wheels. Even fifty and seventy-five ton cranes were sitting in vacant lots without wheels! Canham had commandeered a large Japanese-manufactured car dealership facility in Ahmadi to be utilized as a light vehicle center in support of the Al-Awda Project. The building had been totally vandalized. Company records had been strewn all over the floors. Plate glass windows had been shattered. Office furnishings were wrecked and the showroom had been emptied of its contents.

The superintendent in charge of the light vehicle operations was our old pal from South Carolina, Roger Riddle. The Riddle had only recently flown in from the Sumatra project. He said hello to us and then told us to follow him into the rear connecting warehouse of the facility where forty-two brand new imported cars were parked, the Iraqi military had removed every single wheel including the steering wheels. Furthermore they had stripped vehicles of their radios, some dash board gadgets, gas tank caps, most of the front seats, and then smashed every windshield, rear and side windows, and the front and rear lights. It was impossible to comprehend the mentality of the dickheads who had done that shit. I was stunned.

The Riddle looked at me and sighed. "Can you believe this shit, Bubba? Where the fuck were their minds at? There is no logic to this destruction."

Later, driving past a pick-up truck that had been blown apart, I noticed an oil-spattered sandy-colored Iraqi combat army helmet laying several yards from the road edge, a potential souvenir of Desert Storm. I asked Don to stop the pick-up so I could retrieve it. He parked the truck, and as I began to walk towards where the helmet was sitting on top of a mound, I realized the pile of sand looked somewhat like a makeshift grave. Suddenly, I recalled the previous night's lecture regarding booby-traps. If I move the helmet will it trigger a detonation? I felt my heart rate jump a-notch. Fuck-it, I thought. I turned and went back to the pick-up. My souvenir aspirations vanished.

The wind had changed direction and a nice afternoon breeze was blowing in from the coast, pushing the smoke away from Ahmadi into the western desert. Since we were still in a holding pattern due to the lack of equipment and personnel. Don and I decided to head the pick-up south on a divided highway that led into the highly productive Burgan Oil Field, which consisted of several hundred oil wells in close proximity to each other.

**

A mile or so south of Ahmadi, we encountered a wall of smoke that intersected the highway and a screaming inferno. The asphalt road surface was drenched in oil making it difficult to maintain traction. Don figured it was too dangerous to continue and parked the truck on the shoulder of the road. The smoke coming from the eastern side of the highway was the result of several wellhead fires and a ground fire feeding on black sticky crude that covered a huge area of the desert surface. The crude was several inches thick. The abyss opposite the ground fire was a blown-up wellhead that spewed its red-orange flames several hundred yards in opposing directions parallel to the desert.

We were looking at the infamous Long Horn or Moustache. The escaping product, a mixture of crude oil and natural gas, roared with a noise so loud that we should have been wearing ear protection. It was the same well I had heard during my stroll around the shop facilities earlier that day. We stood looking at, listening to, and smelling what nature had unleashed. It was truly a superlative scene. Although destructive and wasteful, the fires, the smoke, and the different colors and patterns held a mystique that was uniquely exhilarating.

The mess hall at Fintas Towers functioned cafeteria style, the same as I had experienced in Alaska, offering an excellent variety of meat, fish, and poultry dishes. It also had a salad bar and an array of desserts. When the Al-Awda Project peaked, and under the project management company's direction, a total of six full-service mess halls would provide some twenty-seven thousand meals a day for the total oil well fires project personnel.

I loaded my plate and sat with a couple of compatriots from the Indonesian project. Some of the guys were talking about an accident that had occurred at approximately five that afternoon near the wellhead fire that had been baptized as the Longhorn. Two British reporters from the London Financial Times had been driving their small Japanese-manufactured car and had either stalled or were succumbed with panic when they became engulfed in the wall of smoke that Don and I had encountered several hours before the disastrous event.

Suddenly an articulated water-tanker that serviced the Canadian fire fighting team, Safety Boss, struck their vehicle from behind. A second semi-trailer loaded with pumping equipment that been travelling behind the tanker was also involved in the accident. The car containing the reporters was catapulted into the exceedingly high temperature ground fire on impact and instantly exploded in flames. Both semi-trailers skidded on the oil-slick surface upon impact and those drivers experienced an identical fate. All five occupants of the three vehicles were incinerated.

Utilizing a segment of fire fighting equipment, the burned-out hull of the reporter's car was recovered within an hour from the holocaust. It contained the skeletal remains of the driver still with his arms out-stretched and hands fused to the steering wheel. His companion was a crumpled pile of chalk-white bones in the passenger seat. The two semi-trailers had traveled too far into the inferno to enable salvage. The only remains of those drivers, all of whom were Egyptian, con-sisted of bones that were found weeks later.

In mid-March the first oil well was controlled. One fire fighter from the Red Adair team and a United States Army Corps of Engineers captain simply walked up to the wellhead and shut off the valve, closing off the escaping crude. A total of eleven wells were controlled that month. Additionally, the Philippine labor force was beginning to enter Kuwait. They flew from Manila to Dubai, where the Kuwaitis had set up a pre-clearance facility at the Dubai International Airport. Evergreen Airlines was flying twice daily into Kuwait with its human cargo.

Don and I were in business manufacturing an assortment of items required by the fire fighting teams because of the ongoing equipment shortage. The Canadian fire fighting team, Safety Boss, had comman-deered and refurbished several Russian made Iraqi military trucks that had been abandoned in the desert.

A small amount of equipment began arriving into Kuwait. It resulted in controlling sixty-eight more of the smaller fires, but prog-ress slowed due to the decision to attack mountainous wells that were producing huge amounts of smoke and obstructing some flight operations in and out of the airport and polluting the skies above Kuwait City, which was slowly resurrecting itself from the ravages of the war.

As Kuwaiti citizens began to return, additional check-points along the highways and streets, manned by the Kuwait militia, began to pop up. They were well armed with automatic AK-47s M-16s, and Kalashnikov assault rifles. They displayed an attitude of heroics, which was somewhat confusing considering the majority had run with their tails between their legs when Saddam Hussein had shown up at their front door.

I was associated with a dozen or so Kuwaitis in the fabrication shop who had remained in Kuwait during the entire occupation and Desert Storm. Some had been members of the Kuwaiti resistance. These individuals had a serenity that only they understood, and they displayed nothing but congeniality at all times. As we became better acquainted, they revealed situations that had occurred during the invasion. I learned that in the course of the first several weeks after the Iraqis' arrival, many Kuwaitis were given identification papers and passports by the Iranian Embassy stating they were citizens of Iran, which allowed them to exit by the invaders. However, the Iraqis discovered what was going on and the practice ceased.

I was also told that for several years leading up to the invasion there was an individual who pushed a cart around the streets of Kuwait City selling peanuts. Several days after the Iraqi military arrived, the peanut seller was seen wearing the uniform of an Iraqi Army colonel. Additionally, six weeks before the invasion, the Iraq government sent a delegation to Kuwait to investigate the possibilities of building similar oil facilities in Iraq that already existed in Kuwait. The Iraqi delegation was given an escorted tour of the refineries and other oil installations by unsuspecting Kuwaitis. It was exposed after the invasion that the delegation was comprised mostly of high-ranking intelligence officers in the Iraq Armed Forces.

It has been said that in love and war the ordinary rules of life do not apply. One of the Kuwaitis in the shop relayed to me how he had gone into Kuwait City early one morning during the occupation and came across the most barbaric scene he had every witnessed. Three deceased naked Kuwaiti women in their early twenties were hanging by their necks from ropes that were tied to overhead traffic lights. It was evident the victims had been raped and their breasts had been violently severed from their bodies. The Iraqi soldiers, it seems, broke many of life's rules.

I had been in Kuwait for four weeks and I could feel how polluted my lungs were. They were in worse shape than if I had smoked a pound of weed with Willie, the red-headed stranger. I had been breathing in a lot of polluted air, which resulted in lung congestion with all the symptoms of a heavy bout of the flu: continuous coughing, sneezing, and pounding headaches. To make matters worse, once the violent coughing started, the strain often resulted in the old quick step to the toilet. I knew it was time to visit the doctor and I hoped he had kept the plug in the jug since his arrival in Kuwait.

Doc informed me that a dozen or so other folk had shown up at his facility with the same symptoms I had. Luckily after several days of rest and medication, they were all back on their feet and doing well in no time. He gave me a bunch of pills and offered to drive me back to Fintas Towers where he had other business to attend to. I thanked him for his generosity and we both walked to his vehicle.

During the half-hour trip, the Doc turned to me and said,

"Bubba, you probably don't know this, but we are seeing some terrible things at the field hospital."

"Every other day a young woman of either Kuwaiti, Philippine, Indian, or Sri Lankan origin is dropped off at our doorstep, presumably by a relative or friend, we don't know. Her anus is ripped and usually bleeding profusely. Then we have to perform immediate surgery to try and reconstruct the rectum to its former state."

"What the hell is going on Doc?" I asked him.

He sighed. "All the women have the same story. The returning Kuwaiti men join the local militia and are issued United States Army fatigues along with M-16 rifles and live ammunition," he said.

"They roam around Kuwait like conquering heroes, brutally sodomizing these women at loaded gun point. To make it clear that they mean business, they often fire off a couple of rounds, threatening the poor women into submission. These sub-human ragheads are a law unto themselves and answer to no one!" he said.

Of course at that time there was no infrastructure in Kuwait and that meant no police. Shit, I thought. There are no good guys or bad guys when it comes to these Arabs. There's no difference between these chicken shit Kuwaitis that ran like mongrel dogs or the fuckin Iraqi military when it comes to humanity. Apparently they were all tarred with the same cowardly brush!

I had a Philippino guy working for me in the fabrication shop who had been in Kuwait a couple of weeks. He had told me one of the reasons he had taken the job and come to Kuwait was to try to find his missing female cousin who had been working as domestic help before the war. Unfortunately he found out through other Philippine folks who had survived the occupation that she, and about twenty other female domestic helpers whom the fleeing Kuwaitis had deserted, had been rounded up by the Iraqi Army and taken to the

Mina Abdula oil refinery, which was several miles from Ahmadi City. During their incarceration of a week to ten days, about fifty or sixty Iraqi soldiers had raped and tortured the women. When the soldiers had tired of their insanity, the women were forced to line up along the edge of the refinery pier, some so badly damaged that they could not physically stand, and all were mercilessly shot. Their lifeless bodies fell into the oily waters that floated their remains out into the Persian Gulf.

***

Outside of the United States, the largest General Motors dealership, with respect to volume of business prior to Desert Storm, was located in Kuwait City. Don and I, still in need of equipment, traveled with Canham's chief procurement officer, who had come out of retirement just for the Al-Awda Project, into Kuwait City to visit the dealership.

The dealership was owned and operated by three Kuwaiti brothers who were of Iranian and Kuwaiti parentage. All of them stood over six feet in height, and they each weighed at least 250 pounds; huge men for Arabs. The largest and oldest of the brothers had been held captive and tortured by the Iraqis for 21 days. He told us that it had seemed like a lifetime. He also told us that on the morning of the invasion, he and his brothers had hastily lined up side by side across one end of their warehouse 45 brand new GMC Blazer vehicles and built a false wall concealing them. The Iraqi military, bivouacked one-hundred yards from the warehouse, continually entered and exited the premises, stealing whatever they could find during their occupation. With the occupation over, the brothers could now joke about the dumbness of the Iraqis, never realizing how much smaller the warehouse was on the inside compared to the exterior.

After going to the dealership, we made a few more calls around the city. Unfortunately we weren't able to find any equipment. With that we returned to Ahmadi and the black rolling, overhanging cover. The smoke never diminished, ferrying its cargo of black rain across the desert and out to sea.

One television channel was being piped into Fintas Towers. It was a cable show out of Saudi Arabia. Each evening it was the same thing: a Saudi mullah preaching and explaining the Koran. It sounded similar to some of the Bible stories I'd heard as a kid. Gerry and I often sat in the sparsely furnished living room in front of the television set with the sound turned off. We often reminisced about Sumatra. One evening I got to telling him about the Black Hawk turkey shoot I had seen on television the night before I left London.

"Was that the Highway of Death shit?" he asked.

"It was," I nodded.

Gerry was silent for a moment. Then he spoke.

"You know, we should take a drive out to the highway and check it out ourselves. What do you think?" he asked. We decided to leave work an hour or so earlier the following day.

At 4:30 P.M. the next day we were on our way, taking the third ring-road out of Kuwait City and then onto Highway 80, which ran through the desert to the border towns of Abdali, Kuwait, and Safwan, and ended in Basra, Iraq. After a couple of miles heading west on Highway 80 we encountered the beginning of the massacre.

We parked and began to walk through the destruction of hundreds of abandoned, damaged, and completely destroyed vehicles. The carnage stretched, uninterrupted, for at least a mile.

As we wandered through the twisted hulks of cars, buses, trucks and military vehicles, I turned and looked in Gerry's direction and said,

"Hey Gerry, can you smell what I smell?"

"Sure can," he answered.

It was the strong odor of decaying flesh. The US Air Force had bombed both the front and rear ends of the mile-long convoy of retreating Iraqi military and civilians, Kuwaiti hostages, and Palestinians. It had been rumored that a shallow mass grave containing several thousand bodies had been dug alongside the highway by United States burial teams. Needless to say, smelling that potent stench proved it wasn't a rumor.

We noticed a huge bomb crater with a Nissian pick-up truck nose-first in it on the west end of the highway, its tailgate level with the surrounding desert. Many of the vehicles had peeled off the highway into the desert, obviously trying to escape. Even a couple of army tanks were several hundred yards into the desert. None of them had made it. Munitions of all kinds lay between the wrecks. The Explosive Ordnance Disposal teams had stacked hundreds of rocket propelled grenades, rockets, hand grenades, and AK-47 rifles in the center of the divided highway for later retrieval.

I managed to expose two rolls of film in the first thirty minutes we were there. It really was incredible destruction; I had never seen anything like it before. I looked at Gerry and slowly shook my head in disbelief.

"This is the aftermath of that helicopter shoot-em-up show I told you about Gerry," I said.

"Man," he answered. "Can you imagine the terror on the ground during this shit?"

I couldn't, and part of me was relieved that I couldn't. With that we got back into the truck, and as the sun was about to disappear below the desert rim, we drove away from the Highway of Death and headed back to Fintas Towers and supper.

***

As the battle to control the fires continued there was a perpetual need for water. Canham's earthworks department planned ahead and dug approximately four hundred water lagoons over the ensuing months. The lagoons were lined with heavy plastic sheeting to stop seepage, and each one was capable of containing one million gallons of sea-water. Prior to the conflict the Kuwait Oil Company had built pipelines from the desert to the coastal oil refineries for crude transportation. By reversing the pumping and piping systems, sea-water was then able to be transported through the pipelines to the lagoons in the desert. This strategy allowed sufficient water for fire fighting and well blow-out control.

There was no operational telephone system in Kuwait. Instead we were all issued hand-held Motorola two-way radios. This was our only means of communication between our respective departments and project personnel. Canham had also installed several satellite dishes that were utilized for project overseas business calls. In an emergency, project personnel could use the satellite system. However, under the local war zone conditions, this was strictly only for emergency situations.

A project-wide memorandum had been issued to all employees. It read:

We want to reassure you that your families can get urgent messages to you in Kuwait through the Canham system. Emergency messages directed to the offices listed below will be relayed to you through the Project's emergency contact telephone and or fax system and return calls will be authorized. As a reminder, please ensure that your family members are aware of these emergency contact numbers. The telephone numbers for the Project's Canham offshore support offices are as follows...

There were telephone numbers for Canham's offices in San Francisco, California, London, England, and Melbourne, Australia.

Until the Kuwait telephone system was destroyed during Desert Storm, the Kuwaitis who remained in the country were sending facsimiles to the allied forces headquartered in Saudi Arabia. These facsimiles described locations and military equipment the Iraqis had distributed throughout their country. One of the Kuwaitis I was working with explained how one morning during the occupation an Iraqi Army lieutenant came to his house and demanded to use the telephone. The Kuwaiti handed him his cordless telephone. The lieutenant had obviously never seen equipment without connecting cables before. Believing he was being hoodwinked, he uttered threats of personal violence, threw the telephone at his host, and stormed out of the house.

The Al-Awda work force was increasing daily. Sixty skilled and semi-skilled Philippinos and a dozen Pakistanis on loan from the Italian company, Saipen, worked in the fabrication shop producing a variety of items for the fire fighters. Kuwait Oil Company also had personnel from India, Egypt, Syria, and Bangladesh working as welders in the shop.

Field services manager Bill Bass came by the facilities and informed me that both the fabrication shop and Don's machine shop would have to extend their work hours within the next couple of weeks, increasing from ten hours to twenty hours a day. We were already operational seven days a week. The added hours were required to accommodate an increase from four fire fighting crews to eight. Extra Philippinos, Thais, and Indonesians would be imported into Kuwait for both the field and shop expansions.

Hundreds of unemployed Palestinians and Somalis who had been employed in the oil fields before the arrival of the Iraq army were now wandering around Kuwait. The Kuwaitis had treated them as low life slaves so they hooked up with the invaders hoping for a better deal in life. I had been given strict instructions that neither nationality was to be given a job. Within six months of the war ending, each and every Palestinian and Somali had been deported. I knew that I would need supervision assistance though, so an old pal I had worked with in Sumatra, that Seminole Indian from Florida, Charlie Blackcloud, was offered the position. A couple of weeks later Charlie was working with me in Kuwait.

Cleaning up Kuwait was a monumental task. The Iraqi military had built hundreds of bunkers and slit trenches throughout Ahmadi. These had to be searched and cleared by Explosive Ordnance Disposal teams before the cleaning crews could go to work. Prior to the invasion the Kuwait Oil Company had stockpiled large quantities of oil field drilling pipe and structural steel items used in the oil industry, some of which the Iraqis had not removed.

The yards in which the material was stored were strewn with garbage, broken household and office furniture, clothes, footwear, children's toys, bullet-belts from army tanks, and those countless dirty Iraqi military-issue green and cream striped blankets. Everything was covered in a layer of black crude oil that had been raining down on most of Kuwait for several months. As the crews moved through the storage yards removing the debris, a young Philippino laborer gathered up a pair of old worn-out oil-soaked steel-toed work boots.

Instantly the concealed explosive device detonated, destroying both the boy's hands and a section of his forearms. He was rushed to Ahmadi Hospital, which was staffed by both Canham and local medical teams, and his life was ultimately saved. However, the remnants of his forearms had to be removed several inches below the elbows. Either the booby-trapped boots had not been considered a threat by the Explosive Ordnance Disposal teams, or the layer of oil and the blowing sand had not exposed them when the team conducted its search.

I received a work order from Evergreen airlines to have a crew come out to the airport and remove some structural steel columns from inside a warehouse to make it accessible for helicopters to be wheeled in for undercover maintenance. I showed up with a crew as requested, but as we wandered around the building I noticed a huge bomb crater with a freezer someone had dumped into it. One of the crewmembers carefully climbed into the crater and opened the freezer lid and almost immediately threw up. The freezer contained rotting human body parts. Several days later I was told the freezer had been loaded onto a truck and carried out into the desert and buried. No one had bothered to find out where the human remains had come from, but it was assumed they were Iraqi army personnel.

In support of the Kuwait hospital and the Al-Awda Project, Canham had built a forty-bed field hospital on the outskirts of Ahmadi. It was specifically designed to support fire fighting efforts with dedicated burn facilities, operating rooms, and complete support services. It was staffed with one hundred professional medical personnel, paramedics, and other staff who were on duty at seven smaller medical stations throughout the oilfield. This was the facility where Doc was stitching sphincters. Two medically equipped helicopters, identical to the type used by United States military during the Vietnam conflict and flown by Evergreen personnel (also veterans of that Asian conflict), were on twenty-four-hour call for medivac situations. They were on stand-by on the helipad in Ahmadi.

A couple of weeks after Charlie Blackcloud arrived in Kuwait he wanted to call home. The local telephone system had been destroyed by the Iraqis and as the Canham satellite system was for emergency use only, we decided to visit the United States military base that had been christened Blackhorse. We had been informed that we could use the telephones installed for the troops, all we needed was our passports for entrance onto the base. We headed out after work, and as soon as we reached the military base Blackcloud and I headed to the Quonset building that housed the telephones.

When the little blonde lady in Odessa answered her telephone, she told me she got quite a scare when the operator who connected us identified himself as being from the United States military communication center in Saudi Arabia. I quickly told her I was fine and that I was sorry about the scare. I had no idea of the routing or that it was going through Saudi Arabia or the military.

After Blackcloud and I finished our telephone calls, we headed over to a KFC outlet on the base and sat down with a box of fried chicken and two cold Cokes (almost all of the major fast-food chains were on base). I told Charlie about the telephone scare and he told me that the same shit happened with his wife. She said she almost had a heart attack when she answered the phone after the operator had identified himself. Of course we felt bad for half-scaring the women, but it had been great to have been able to hear their voices for a little while.

Historical geographical, geological, and engineering records concerning the majority of oil wells in Kuwait were mostly destroyed during the occupation. Consequently, fire fighters and Canham personnel responsible for the recovery had to physically examine the burning wells. This was almost impossible for several months after liberation owing to the constant heavy smoke overhead that resulted from the fires.

An accurate count and evaluation of the burning and damaged wells was impossible to come up with due to the lack of surface access on bomb-damaged and oil-flooded roads, as well as unexploded ordinance. Satellite photography and helicopters had to be utilized to understand the exceedingly difficult task of determining the scope and nature of the problem. Coming to terms with the millions of barrels of oil, roaring fires, and densely concentrated smoke that was abundantly discharging from 749 oilwells, twenty-four hours a day, was a serious condition without a blueprint; it had never before been confronted.

In Kuwait a fire fighting team generally consisted of four thoroughly trained specialists and approximately eight other personnel, including equipment operators for the cranes, backhoes, and bulldozers. The remaining members tended to be semi-skilled labourers who attached and manned fire hoses and pumps and performed other associated duties.

Surrounding the majority of burning well heads in Kuwait were huge piles of unburned petroleum product known as coke. Some of these mounds grew in excess of twenty feet and had the consistency of concrete. They also had a habit of discharging a continuous barrage of small explosions, spewing small red-hot missiles in all directions. Most of the well heads had been protected from wandering Bedouin tribesmen and their animals by being encircled with chain-link fences. However, most of them had become a twisted mangled obstacle owing to the intense heat that was in excess of 2,000 degrees Fahrenheit.

Water would be pumped onto the wellheads to extinguish the fires and they would still have boiling bubbles on the surface sand twenty-four hours later, which was transforming into glass. The twisted, melted metal was removed by using the hooked end of an Athey Wagon that was attached to a bulldozer. An Athey Wagon resembles a crane boom in a horizontal position and is approximately sixty-feet in length. It has a hook on one end with the other end mounted on wheels. Explosives would then be used to try to remove the coke piles before attempts at taming the raging infernos could commence.

***

Several weeks after my arrival in Kuwait, Butch came by the fabrication shop and asked me if I would be interested in joining him and a friend of his for dinner at the Holiday Inn, the only establishment open for business in downtown Kuwait City. His friend had just arrived from the United States.

The interior of the Holiday Inn had been refurbished after the Iraqi vandalism, however scars of the war remained visible on its façade. The trip into Kuwait City from Fintas Towers should have only taken half an hour if we actually knew the way. We didn't.

During the drive, Butch turned to me and said something I would recall at a future date.

"Bubba, there are some opportunities here to pick up a little extra cash," he began. "I called a Caterpillar dealer friend of mine in Atlanta, Georgia, a week ago. I gave him Canham's purchasing agent's name and number and he sold two brand new D9 bulldozers, fully loaded, to this project. He dropped six thousand dollars into my bank account as a finder's fee."

"No shit," I said. "No shit."

Fifty minutes later, we finally pulled into the parking lot of the Holiday Inn. I learned that Butch's friend was a professor from a university in one of the southern states. During dinner he explained that he was in Kuwait trying to sell his idea of killing the oil well fires by enshrouding them in solidified carbon dioxide, also known as dry ice. In retrospect, I guess his idea was not accepted; it never was used.

After leaving the Holiday Inn we headed back to Fintas Towers. Butch started talking again.

"Ya know, Bubba, some bad-ass shit happened to the poor bastards who were left hanging in the wind when the Kuwaitis fled. We just hired an old Philippine man as a cleaner for the office. I mean the old guy is around seventy if he's a day and speaks good English. Anyhow, the other day he was telling me and Bill Bass about how one afternoon during the occupation he was walking along a street in Ahmadi when a half-dozen Iraqi soldiers grabbed him and threw his ass into the back of a pick-up truck."

"What?" I asked incredulously.

Butch nodded. "Yup, they drove out of Ahmadi into the desert. The old man said the Iraqis had crates of booze in their pick-up and they were all swallowing it like pigs at a trough. Half an hour later they stopped where a huge bunker had been dug into the desert and he was dragged out of the truck and tossed onto the desert sand. That was when he saw at least a dozen naked brown women. Most of them were crying while others were screaming. Drunken Iraqi soldiers were molesting them. Some of the women were being raped. Some were being forced to perform oral sex while others were being sodomized.

"Man, that's fuckin' bad shit!" I muttered, shaking my melon.

Butch continued. "Then the old man said that a couple of Iraqi soldiers suddenly grabbed him and ripped his clothes off. He figured he was going to be raped. Instead they dragged a young Philippine girl over to him and forced her to perform oral sex on him. He said it took forever to obtain an erection, and when he did they made her get on her hands and knees and poke her ass up in the air. Then, with a pistol barrel in his ear, they forced him to sodomize her. The entire time that was happening, the Iraqis were drinking, laughing, and hollering, just having one hell of a party."

"Are you fuckin' kidding me?" I said.

Butch shrugged as we drove along. "Bubba, the old fella said that shit went on for hours and hours and it got worse. Just before the sun came up, one drunken Iraqi soldier stuck the barrel of his loaded AK-47 into the vagina of one of the women and pulled the trigger, killing her instantly. Apparently this turned into the highlight of the party, and other soldiers began doing the same thing to the other women. The old guy said that all of the women had been murdered that way. Once they were all dead, he thought he was going to be next."

"So what happened?" I asked quietly.

"Well, the drunken Iraqis stacked the bodies in a pile like cord wood, one on top of the other, in several layers. When they were done, they poured gasoline over the bodies and one of them tossed a match onto the corpses. They continued drinking, laughing, and smoking their Camel shit as they stood around and watched the cremation," Butch said.

"That's really bad shit, Butch," I said.

"Eventually the drunken murderers became bored watching their victims burn. A couple of them then approached the old man and picked him up by his hands and feet. He thought for sure he was going into the fire, but they tossed him into the bed of a pick-up truck and drove him back into Ahmadi. They dumped him, naked, on a street and drove off hollering, drinking, laughing, and firing live rounds into the air as they headed back to the desert," Butch said.

It was incredibly difficult to believe the horrendous story, but I knew that it was true. Butch added that the old guy had tears rolling down his cheeks and his hands were shaking by the time he got through telling his tale. I could understand the tears, and I couldn't help but think about those poor women. I was almost in tears myself.

***

It goes without saying that conventionally fighting oil well fires is extremely dangerous anywhere. A huge problem in the Kuwait desert was the sudden wind changes that occurred almost instantly without any warning. Firefighters would be upwind and as close as fifteen feet from the 2,000 degree Fahrenheit infernos. Another reason for trying to stay upwind is the deadly hydrogen sulphide (H2S) gas contained in many oil wells. It is both colourless and odourless and, if inhaled, it attacks the nervous system and renders death in minutes. The firefighters' action would be directed from behind a metal heat shield fabricated out of corrugated iron for protection. All firefighting crew members wore heat-reflecting suits with a continuous spray from water hoses manned by other team members. Death was literally only a sudden wind change or a broken water pump away.

The Chinese firefighting team found out the hard way just how suddenly the wind could change. Crewmembers were operating a brand new D9 Caterpillar bulldozer, clearing the area around a well-head fire, when one of the notorious wind changes suddenly made the fire turn toward them and engulf the bulldozer. Within minutes the bulldozer and operator were totally consumed in fire.

Many of the desert fires were extinguished by using a compound of dynamite, C4 plastic explosives, and a dry chemical called Purple K. This mixture, when exploded, would rob the atmosphere of oxygen, snuffing out the fire. However, sudden wind changes could easily reignite the well heads, and they often did. Depending on the size of coke piles and the pressure of the well-head, varying amounts of each explosive were packed with desert sand into an empty 55-gallon barrel. The barrel was then hung from the end of an Athey Wagon, which was connected to a bulldozer. Then with the barrel swinging from the opposite end it was manipulated out into the searing fire, exploding it in less than a minute. The United States Army also participated in the fire fighting efforts by utilizing its armored military vehicles, standing off at 250 yards and firing 165 millimetre rounds. Direct hits with exploding shells destroyed the coke piles, ultimately snuffing out the flames. However, the practice was soon considered a risk in the event of an overshot and was halted.

As time rolled by, more of the Kuwaiti families whom had high-tailed it out of their country when they realized invasion was inevitable started to return. Some had their homes in Ahmadi. I heard that one family of four had opened the front door of their war-damaged home and were met with a huge explosion, instantly killing them all. The hinges of the door of the house had been booby-trapped by the invaders, setting off what the Explosive Ordnance Disposal experts said was a wired stash of C4 plastic explosives.

CHAPTER 8

Don and I were able to get our fabrication and machine shops up and running productively within the first five weeks of being in Kuwait. To get to and from work each day we traveled in the pick-up I had been issued. Don was supposed to be getting a new Chevy as soon as the next barge load arrived from Jebel Ali in a week or so. By the time we left our shops for the day, it would be around 7:00 p.m. as we made our way back to Fintas Towers, headlights blazing. It was always on the dark side of twilight at that time, even when the wind was blowing the smoke due south, almost missing us in Ahmadi.

The returned Kuwaiti militia, in all its infinite wisdom, had set up a check point along the main road in and out of Ahmadi about two miles from the edge of the town. Depending on the wind direction, this meant that most of the time they were under clear skies. Don and I had been stopped every time. The only exception was when we travelled in the early morning to our shops when the Kuwaitis were still sleeping. The routine shit the militia would do was to walk up to your vehicle while cradling an M-16, glance to see who was in the vehicle, and ask if everyone aboard was American. Then, with the barrel of the M-16, motion you to drive on.

On one particular evening, I slowed the pick-up to a standstill at the check point, which was basically just a tent adjacent to the edge of the black top. The Kuwaiti militia turkey got up off a chair he had been sitting on inside the tent and headed our way. As he was exiting the tent, I noticed a big old hubble bubble hash pipe in the light inside the tent. It was standing upright with half a dozen smoke tubes that ran from its base where the smoke was supposed to be drawn through the water pool. The tubes were set on a hook on the top where the smoker mouth-piece was located. This should be interesting, I thought, a stoned assbag with a loaded weapon!

He walked across the road to my opened window and glanced inside.

"You American?" he asked.

"Yes," Don and I both answered in unison.

"Go." He replied, motioning with his M-16. I took my foot off the brake and pushed the accelerator without hesitation. We slowly moved on, but as we did we both began to hear extremely loud rifle fire. Don whipped around and looked out the rear window.

"It's that crazy fucking Kuwaiti shooting his rifle," he exclaimed.

The loud shooting wouldn't stop. The M-16 was on full auto and a stream of hot lead was blasting all around us. I wasn't sure if I should duck for cover or just keep driving.

"What is that crazy bastard doing?" Don hollered over the gunshots.

Suddenly there was a loud whack. It sounded if a stone had been thrown from a passing vehicle into our vehicle. Immediately after, the truck's rear window exploded in a thunderous blast. Simultaneously I felt something wet slam against the right side of my face, arm, and my hand on the steering wheel. I turned my head to see if Don was okay and instantly threw up all over myself, the steering wheel, and dash-board. Instinctively my right foot pushed the pedal to the metal, not believing what I had just seen. I looked over at Don again and threw up more bile.

The gun fire finally ceased but I could hear someone hollering in the distance. "Oh Fuck! Oh Fuck!" Then my ears popped back into reality, and I realized the person hollering was me. I shut my mouth and concentrated on keeping the truck between the white lines on the road. I knew I was travelling fast, but I couldn't see how fast because the speedometer was covered in my vomit. However, I could see the left turn north to Fintas Towers was coming into sight. I slowed a little bit to make it; the last thing I wanted was a wreck. For all I knew, that crazy fucking hash smoker might have still been on my trail. I took a chance and looked at Don again.

"Motherfucker!" I hollered. Half his melon was missing. The left side was all over the inside of the cab, on the dash-board, and on the windshield. It was at that moment that I realized what the wet shit had been that had hit me.

I tried to wipe the steering wheel clean to stop my hands from slipping in the puke I had spilled on it; I needed to get a grip for the upcoming turn. Puke was everywhere. The stench of it was thick. There was also the distinct smell of shit; I guessed Don's sphincter had relaxed. I made the turn and gunned the pick-up, knowing we'd be back at Fintas Towers in five miles. I made the turn and Don's body hit the passenger door and window. Blood was pumping out in little squirts from where his chin used to be.

Finally I pulled into the front of Fintas Towers, jumped the curb and drove up over the sidewalk on to a wide flat paved area between the sidewalk and the front steps leading up into the Fintas Tower lobby. I slammed on the brakes and came to a stop several feet from the steps. I switched off the engine and blared the horn. I continued to blare the horn as I opened the door and tried to step out.

"Help!, Help!" I screamed.

Moments later, men came running down the stairs wondering what had happened. I recognized some of them, others I had never seen before. Once they took a look at me and Don, they began hollering orders.

"Get an ambulance," someone demanded

"We need the medics!" someone else shouted.

It was then that my knees gave out and I hit the deck. The next thing I knew, a medic was passing some powerful shit under my nose that seemed to burn inside. I came to, shaking my head.

"We-we were shot! We were shot! Don's been shot!" I stammered.

"We know," the medic said calmly. "Have you been shot?"

"No, I am okay, I think," I replied.

"Don is being cared for," the medic continued. "We are going to put you in the ambulance and take you to the Canham field hospital to check you out."

"Don's fucked, isn't he?" I asked quietly.

The medic hesitated a moment before responding. "Yes, he's fucked," he said softly.

At the hospital they sat my ass in a wheel-chair and a nurse wheeled me into an examination room where Doc was waiting for me.

"How you doing Bubba?" he asked with a smile. "I heard you had a little excitement tonight."

"I am so god damned thirsty," I muttered.
"I need a drink of water."

The Doc nodded. "Shock will do that to you," he said.

"Shock will do what?" I asked, confused.

"It will make you thirsty," he clarified. Then he gave me a plastic bottle of room temperature water and proceeded with a cursory physical.

"Do you know if you have any injuries?" he asked.

"No," I replied, shaking my melon. Suddenly a lump of gray matter and some other shit fell from my hair onto the floor. The Doc and I both looked at each other.

"I need a shower," I blurted.

"No problem. We will get you to the shower and cleaned up, and then you may need a sedative to sleep," he said.

"We will keep you here over night just to be sure you're okay. You have had one hell of a nasty experience."

As the Doc was speaking, California Ken, Bill Bass, and a few Kuwaiti officials entered the examination room. They began asking me if I was okay. When I shrugged, they said that we all needed to talk. First they wanted to know where had the shooting occurred and if I could describe the assassin. They wanted to find him as soon as possible. I explained the location of the checkpoint and recalled that the murdering hash-smoking assbag had been wearing a new GI desert camouflage uniform. I added that he stood about five-foot-four and had a slim build. With that they thanked me for my time and said they would stop by tomorrow morning. They told me to rest up while they went to apprehend the culprit before anyone else got blown away.

Once I was alone with the Doc again, he led me down the hospital corridor to the shower room and opened the door.

"Put these on after you shower," he said, handing me a set of green hospital scrubs. Then he said he would be back in thirty minutes to see how I was doing.

"Thanks," I replied.

I stepped into the shower room and closed the door. Then I turned the shower on as hot as I could handle the water and stepped under the shower head, clothes, boots, the lot.

I stood there for I don't even know how long, just letting the water wash away all the shit. Sometime later I saw that the shower-head was connected to a flexible hose. I carefully unhooked it and bent down to spray the puke and gray matter off my boots. Once they were clean, I kicked them off and out of the shower, and then stepped back under the cascading water. I took my time cleaning each item and tossing them out of the shower stall and stripped down slowly until I felt as clean as I could possibly feel.

Twenty minutes later, dressed in my green scrubs, I picked up my wet clothes, rung them out, and dumped them into the empty garbage bin. Then I pulled out the garbage bag, tossed in my boots, and headed for the shower room door.

Doc was waiting in the hall with two pill containers in his hand. He smiled and handed me the containers.

"I have given you 21 sleeping pills and 42 anxiety capsules. Take one sleeping pill a night if you are having problems sleeping. Do not take more than two anxiety capsules a day," he explained. Then he added, "And this is important, Bubba: Do not mix narcotics or booze with these, okay? And only take one when your melon is twisting bad about the events of tonight."

I nodded. "Okay."

As we headed down the corridor, the doc looked at me.

"We have a bed for you down at the end of the hall. I suggest you take a sleeping pill and rest. We will have some fresh clothes brought over from your room at Fintas Towers if that's okay with you."

"That's fine," I replied. "Will you please tell whomever goes to my room to bring back my Tony Lama cowboy boots, too?"

The doc smiled. "Okay Bubba. Have a good night. I will have someone wake you at 8:00 a.m. for breakfast. At 9:00 a.m. there will be a meeting with California Ken and his group. Rest well Bubba," he said. "You know, I am really sorry for what you had to go through today."

"Yea, me too," I said quietly.

I entered the small room and noticed a single bed and a side table. Half a dozen plastic bottles of water were on the side table. I took the lid off the sleeping pill container Doc had given me and popped a pill. Then unscrewed the cap off one of the bottles of water and swallowed half of its contents. I pulled back the bed covers, turned out the light, hit the fart sack, and passed out in a matter of minutes.

"Wake up, Mr. Bubba," a gentle voice said quietly into my ear. "Wake up Mr. Bubba. It's 8:00 a.m."

I felt a light hand on my shoulder and slowly opened my eyes. There stood a smiling Philippine female. She looked like an angel dressed in a nurse's white uniform. Once she saw that I was awake, she smiled again and headed for the door. As she was closing the bedroom door on her way out she added.

"You must shower and hurry, Mr. Bubba!"

I stretched and noticed my clothes and my Tony Lama cowboy boots had been delivered sometime during the night and were placed neatly on a little chair in the room. I hadn't been disturbed once until the little brown-faced angel gently shook me awake. Those sleeping pills sure worked well, I thought. With that I showered quickly and then headed for the hospital mess hall.

Bill and Butch sat and drank coffee with me while I attempted to eat a little breakfast. I never got past a few bites of dry toast. I felt a bit awkward as Bill and Butch just stared at me, but I figured they just wanted to make sure I was okay.

Butch spoke up first. "How you doing this morning Bubba?" he asked.

Bill piped in too. "Yea, how's it going now that you've had a little time to rest? We are really sorry this shit happened."

I shrugged, "Well, right now I'm okay, but who knows down the road," I replied. "I mean that was some nasty shit last night. You don't even know the half of it. I just hope they hang and quarter that hash-smoking fucker who blew Don away."

Bill and Butch just nodded solemnly. We were all pretty quiet while we finished our coffee.

At 9:30 a.m. I was taken to the field hospital board-room, which was a typical worksite trailer. It contained comfortable padded chairs and a long table with a polished wood surface. Seated at the table were California Ken, Bill, Butch, a United States Embassy official, an FBI agent from the Embassy, two official-looking Kuwaiti's dressed in their full Arabic regalia, and an interpreter. There were also several other Canham representatives there, but I had no idea what their position was nor did I care.

California Ken and several others had set up tape recorders that were clearly visible on the table and several microphones were placed around the table, too. One was placed directly in front of me. When everyone who needed to be there was present, California Ken opened the meeting.

"Good morning," he said. Next he stated everyone in the room was present to witness a verbal statement from Bubba Cottonmill regarding the events of the previous evening that led to the death of Don Johnson.

He noted that the statement would be in English and also translated into Arabic. A hard copy of the statement would be distributed for signatures an hour after the meeting concluded.

With that I began recapping exactly what had happened from the time Don and I left our work shops. I explained how we had come to a standstill at the check point. I noted that I had seen the hubble-bubble hash pipe in the tent. I finished by explaining my arrival at the hospital.

"Bubba, are you positive you came to a standstill, a full stop, and not a rolling stop at the check point?" California Ken questioned me.

"A dead stop," I said matter-of-factly.

California Ken nodded and sighed quietly. "The check-point militia stated that you drove through the check-point without stopping," he said. "They claim that the accused militia chased you down the road, firing his rifle in the air in an effort to make you stop. When you didn't, he fired into the vehicle thinking you and Don Johnson may have been terrorists."

I couldn't believe my ears. "That's absolute bullshit," I answered.

Suddenly the FBI agent reached for the microphone in front of him.

"Bubba, we believe what you are saying," he said, looking directly at me. "We examined the area of highway where the shooting took place. Through an interpreter, we asked the militiaman, Mohammad is his name. We asked Mohammad how far he ran down the highway, shooting at you. He said, 'Maybe a hundred yards or so.' We then asked him if had altered the scene in any way. For example, had he picked up any items and moved them? He said, 'No.' We then asked if he had moved any of the shell casings. Again, he said, 'No.'

The FBI agent paused a moment to let that information sink in. Then he continued. "We found no shell casings along the highway and our United States Army expert gathered up all of the empty shells at the check point location. After further investigation, he stated the number of empty shells found at the check-point location was equivalent to a loaded M-16 magazine," he said. "Our conclusion is, and the Kuwaitis have also agreed, that Mohammad did not pursue your vehicle. We believe that he did stand at his post and empty his magazine into and around your vehicle, striking it twice. One shot hit the rear right-hand tail light arrangement, totally destroying it. The second hit was through the rear cabin window, passing through Don Johnson's head and burying itself in the doorpost metal that separates the windshield and door."

I was relieved to know that they believed my side of the story, but I wondered what would become of Mohammad. I wanted him to pay for what he had done.

The FBI agent continued. "As a result of these findings, and in agreement with the Kuwaitis, Mohammad has been removed from his post in the militia. He is not to own a weapon for the remainder of his life, and there will be no further charges against him. Also no hubble-bubble hash pipe was found in the check point tent. There will be no action taken against Bubba Cottonmill, either. That concludes my report." He set the microphone down.

I was in complete shock. I took hold of the microphone in front of me and pulled it closer, looking directly at the FBI agent "No further action will be taken against Bubba Cottonmill?" I asked sarcastically. "You must be joking, right? This is total fucking bullshit! You have the balls to sit there and tell me every piece of trace evidence that your investigators uncovered confirms what I have told you is correct, and the murderer of an American citizen gets to walk free? I can promise you all one fucking thing: This may be over today in Kuwait, but it's definitely not over in the land of the free!"

California Ken looked at me and spoke up. "Bubba, I respect how you feel, but this is a foreign land; it is a war zone. I am afraid our hands are basically tied. The company is prepared to have you go to London for counselling, though. In fact the London office will handle all arrangements for you. It's your choice if you want to go." Then he added, "But so you know, Mr. Johnson's death certificate will read: Cause of Death, accidental."

Ultimately, Don's family would receive his employer's compensation package for accidental death in the work-place and his body would be flown back to the United States that afternoon. Don's family had already been notified.

Ken continued. "Bubba, you are only three or four days from your two weeks leave. We have arranged for you to fly out of Kuwait this afternoon to Dubai, where you will be met by a travel agent. You can arrange your travel plans with the agent. There is a room that is already booked for you tonight at the Hilton Airport Hotel, if you need it. You can stay the night and leave for home tomorrow, or wherever you want," he said. Then he smiled sympathetically. "And when you are due to return to the project at the regular date, we sincerely hope you will. We would like for you to keep up the good work and assist us with the controlling of these oil well fires."

I thought to myself, man this guy is one cold-hearted son-of-a-bitch. All business. To hell with the lives it may cost! Suddenly I recalled what that old tobacco-chewing oil-well driller had told me many moons ago.

"Ain't no sympathy in the oil patch, Bubba."

I took one look at California Ken and told him I'd pass on the counselling. However, I had no reason not to return and I would see them all in a couple of weeks. With that we all stood up and I immediately left the room without saying another word or shaking anybody's hand. I just couldn't bring myself to do it.

Butch and Bill caught up with me in the hospital mess hall a little while later. Bill sighed and looked at me. "They will need you to sign a copy of your statement after it's written up," he said quietly. "After that, Butch will take you back to Fintas Towers and out to the airport."

"Fine," I answered. "But I will not sign unless California Ken, the Embassy official, the FBI agent, and at least one Kuwaiti have signed and dated it first, and I will need a copy of the statement for my records."

"Of course," Bill said. "No problem."

Forty-five minutes later, with my garbage bag of still-wet clothes and boots, and a manila envelope with a signed copy of my statement in my hand, I climbed into Butch's Cherokee. I couldn't wait to get out of there. Butch was behind the wheel and asked if I needed to go anywhere before we went back to Fintas Towers. I thought for a moment and then requested that he drive me to the fabrication shop. I needed to speak with my old elephant-riding pal, Charlie Blackcloud, before I left.

Don and I had each received a forty-foot trailer to set up as our office. We had arranged them along-side of each other in the open yard at the rear of our shops. When Butch stopped at the fabrication shop, I got out of the vehicle and headed toward my office trailer.

As soon as I stepped through the door, Blackcloud, who had been working at his desk, immediately stood up and shook my hand and asked,

"How ya doing Bubba?" Butch followed behind me and the two of them shook hands, too.

I took a deep breath. "Admittedly I have been better, Charlie," I replied. "Even falling off that jungle elephant was better than this." Without saying anything else, I handed him the manila envelope and said,

"Charlie, inside is a copy of my official statement. Why don't you take a photocopy and read it later. It explains exactly what happened last night," I said, shaking my melon. I looked at him again. "Charlie they have gone and buried this fucking shit just like they are going to do with Don in several days. In fact, they are flying his body out as we speak."

Blackcloud was speechless. He simply nodded and made a photocopy and placed it on his desk. Then he handed the manila envelope back to me. After that, the three of us grabbed a cold Coke from the mini refrigerator in the office and discussed the previous evening's events. The consensus was mutual: we were angry and loathed the assbags responsible for the tragedy. Furthermore, we felt disgusted by the reaction of the authorities. Don had been a good man; he had always been polite to everyone. It just wasn't right.

"So what are you going to do now?" Blackcloud asked, finishing his Coke and setting it aside on the office table.

"I am going to take my two weeks' leave and will be back on my regular return date so that you can take your leave, too," I said simply. "See? Nothing's changing. It's like nothing ever happened!" I tried to calm myself down before continuing. "So if you wouldn't mind keeping an eye on the fabrication shop during my absence, it would be greatly appreciated."

"Of course, Bubba," Blackcloud replied quietly. "You go do what you have to do."

***

I arrived into the Dubai International Airport at 6:00 p.m. The travel agent was there to meet me and we sat down in the airport lounge to talk. I ordered a beer as soon as a server approached us. Dubai was loaded with bars and freely sold alcohol. I spoke with the travel agent for a little while and then I bought an airline ticket for Singapore. I'd be flying with Emirates Airlines and leaving at 11:30 p.m. that night with a stop-over in Colombo, Sri Lanka. I would arrive in Singapore at 8:30 a.m. the following day.

That evening as I found my assigned seat on the aircraft, I saw that I was going to be seated beside a plump brown girl who I guessed was in her mid twenties. I sat down in my seat and introduced myself to her. She smiled and said in broken English that she was from Colombo, Sri Lanka. She added that she was returning home after two years in Kuwait.

"So that means you were in Kuwait during the war?" I asked curiously.

"Yes," she answered. Then she told me how she and two other girls from Sri Lanka and one girl from India had hidden in an abandoned Christian Church in Ahmadi for eight months. She explained how she and the other girls, two at a time, would take turns going out and knocking on doors of houses in Ahamadi. They would beg for food. Sometimes the houses had no people living in them, so the girls would break a window to get inside and help themselves to whatever food they could find, which was usually canned and wouldn't perish.

"How about the Iraqi soldiers?" I asked. "Did they give you problems?"

She told me the soldiers spotted them several times, but they never had any problems. In fact, she told me that one Iraqi military officer, who spoke some English, had asked if he could help them.

Well, I thought to myself. Perhaps some of those Arab pricks do have a conscience.

There were a lot of empty seats on the aircraft when we began heading toward the runway. Half the passengers had disembarked in Colombo. After take-off, I moved to where four center row seats were vacant and stretched out, making myself comfortable. Then I popped one of Doc's sleeping pills.

I awoke to a Lebanese stewardess dressed in the Emirates Airlines uniform gently shaking my shoulder.

"Sir, we have started our descent into Singapore. Please return to your seat and fasten your seat belt," she instructed.

Back on the ground, I left the airport and hailed a cab. As the taxi carried me to the old Negara Hotel, the streets and highways of Singapore were alive with morning traffic. It felt good to see lush green vegetation and thousands of people going about their business in a regular fashion. It was refreshing to see the world was still alive after that shit in the desert. I checked into the Negara Hotel, freshened up a bit, and then headed next door to the Denny's restaurant for a cup of coffee and an American-style breakfast after having declined the airline crap.

I strolled along Orchard Road, just taking in the sights and sounds of the locals and the thousands of tourists that always seemed to be in Singapore. It was not hard to understand, although now much more expensive than it was in my Rig Pig days, it was still an exhilarating location with a vivid culture of Chinese, Indian, and Malaysian people all mixed in a huge salad-bowel. Soon after, however, jet lag began to take its toll on me I headed back to the Negara Hotel to sleep.

Around 5:00 p.m. I hit the Hard Rock Café for dinner. Later, as I walked along Orchard Road, a short ass Chinese Singaporean fell in step beside me. He looked at me and smiled.

"Hello!" he said cheerfully.

I looked sideways at him. "What do you want?" I asked.

"You want beautiful young lady?" he asked.

"Sure," I answered.

"What hotel you stay?" he asked in broken English.

"Negara," I replied.

"You tell me room number. I bring beautiful lady for you make sex," the man said.

"How much?" I asked skeptically.

"Three hundred dollars Singapore," he answered.

"For all night?" I asked.

"All night," he answered with a nod. "I bring your room in half-hour, okay."

I grinned. "Sure," I said. With that, he peeled off.

Half an hour later I was back in my room, waiting for the woman the little shit had promised me. I had no way of knowing if the assbag would show, but nothing ventured, nothing gained, right?

Sure enough, moments later there was a knock on my door. I opened it and there stood the pint-sized pimp with a beautiful young brown-skinned lady standing beside him. The man stepped forward and smiled.

"She come from Mauritius," he said. Then he promptly held out his hand, waiting for the three hundred dollars.

"I will pay her," I said.

"No, you pay me," the pimp replied matter-of-factly. "Up to you if you pay her, too."

I glanced at the girl, who was smiling at me, and then back at the little shit. Finally, I gave him his cash and he immediately turned and walked away. Then I invited the Mauritius beauty in.

The first week or so of my leave was a buzz. Ms. Mauritius would moonlight most afternoons with me. By 6:00 p.m. she'd be gone to her regular job with the pint-sized pimp. She had told me she came to Singapore every six months on a three-month tourist visa. Ten days after our first encounter, though, her visa expired. She returned to that little island nation in the Indian Ocean.

During my remaining leave, I spent my time searching for bars that stood out from all the others. I needed ideas for the bar I would hopefully one day own. I knew that I wanted my bar to be very distinct. I wanted an interior with a difference. Still, the bar and the little blonde lady in Odessa were just dreams for the time being. I visited shanty bars out in the local Kampongs and bars in the tallest hotel in

Singapore. I took notes, but each day I always ended my research at the same location where the famous cocktail, the "Singapore Sling", had originated. It was a colonial-style hotel dating back to the late 1800s that carried the name of the founder of Singapore, the Raffles Hotel. Occasionally in the evenings I would experiment and pop one or two of Doc's anxiety pills, chase the medicine with a few shooters, and ride the roller coaster into the fires.

CHAPTER 9

Charlie Blackcloud met me at the Kuwait International Airport that was now being managed by local Kuwaitis. We drove to Fintas Towers so that I could check in. By then it was lunchtime and we decided to grab a bite to eat and catch up on what had been going on. While we were eating, Charlie began giving me an update on everything. Apparently the shit was happening in Kuwait. The shop was humming along but it was barely keeping up with the work load. A Canham pick-up truck had been driven over a small bomblet out in the desert, leaving six men injured. One of them received serious wounds to his chest from the shrapnel. Another had one of his feet badly blown apart. The remaining four guys who were cut and bruised are now working on light duties in our shop. Additionally, Canham had a bulldozer operator get burned up. He had been operating his machine near one of the lakes of oil and the fumes given off by the lake somehow got sucked into his dozer, catching it on fire.

Then Charlie dropped a bombshell.

"Bubba," he said slowly. "I got some sad bad news to tell ya."

Noticing his voice had changed, I looked up from my lunch plate and I swear to god Charlie had tears in his eyes.

"Gerry got blown up," he said.

I quit chewing my sandwich and swallowed hard.

"Gerry got blown up?" I repeated, letting the words sink in. I couldn't believe it; I didn't want to believe it.

"Charlie, what the fuck are you saying?"

Charlie took his glasses off his face and wiped his eyes before continuing.

"Our old pal from Sumatra got blown up by a booby-trap in a crane he was trying to start up," he said quietly.

I suddenly felt like I had been punched in the guts. My melon began to spin and I thought I was about to faint. I flashed back to the evening Don had been murdered, and in the process I dropped my glass of water onto the tiled floor of the mess hall. It seemed to fall in slow motion and shatter in a hundred pieces as it hit the floor, but I didn't hear a sound. I just stared at the floor and the scatted broken glass shards in the spilled water.

A hand touched my shoulder and reality came rushing back into my melon, bringing me back to the present moment with all its noise.

"Are you okay Bubba?" Charlie asked.

I took a couple of deep breaths and looked around the room. I noticed one of the mess hall attendants was already sweeping up the broken glass. I turned to face Charlie.

"Is he dead Charlie?" were the only words that came to me.

After lunch Charlie quietly drove me to The Riddle's light transport department where I was issued a new red Chevy pick-up truck. Once inside the truck I decided to go visit with Gerry's assistant, Roy, and find out what exactly had happened to my old pal. Roy was in the crane compound, speaking with some of his Philippino helpers. As soon as he saw me, he smiled and excused himself from the helpers. We shook hands and he suggested that we go into his office trailer to talk.

"What the hell happened Roy?" I asked as soon as the trailer door shut.

Roy shook his head sadly, remembering the day.

"Well, Bubba. Gerry and I were out scouting for equipment. We located a 150-ton crane with all its moving parts down near the Mina Abdula oil refinery. We figured the Iraqis must have missed it since it looked to be in good shape. Anyhow, the field services manager told Gerry, 'If you can make it move, it's yours,'" Roy explained.

"So that's what you guys tried to do?" I asked.

Roy nodded. "Gerry climbed up into the operator's cab and turned the key, but the battery was dead. So that's when we hooked up some jumper cables from our pick-up truck to give it a boost. I stayed in the truck to make sure the engine didn't fade and Gerry twisted the key again. This time there was power. What we didn't know was that the booby-trap was wired up to the ignition. The charge was hidden below the seat and rigged to blow out horizontally, not vertically," he said. He stopped for a moment before continuing. "The blast severed Gerry's left leg at the knee and his right leg half-way up the calf. The shock-wave blew apart the cabin of the crane, and a piece of flying metal hit the pick-up truck's windshield. When it exploded, I almost soiled my Carhartts, but I am okay," he said.

"I am glad you are okay Roy, but what about Gerry?" I asked quickly.

Roy continued. "A couple of Brits working close by heard the blast and called for medical support. Then they rushed over to us and pulled Gerry out of the twisted crane cab. They applied a makeshift tourniquet around his thighs while they waited for help to arrive. Gerry was unconscious at that point. Man, I thought he was dead!" he said, shaking his head. "There was not a lot of heavy bleeding because the heat of the blast had cauterized his shredded wounds. He was rushed up to the Canham field hospital and they tell me Doc did one hell of a job saving his life. Anyway, Gerry has since been medevaced to London."

"So he's gonna make it, right?" I asked.

Roy smiled and nodded. "Yes Bubba, he's gonna make it, just without his legs." By then, Roy's eyes were overflowing with tears. I knew these guys were tight. He continued. "Gerry is a lucky man Bubba. The bomb disposal guys said if it had been a vertical blast, Gerry would be up with the angels."

As I drove back to the fabrication shop. I started thinking about how shook up Roy was and how Gerry had been through the Vietnam War without a physical wound and had to come to this shit-hole to get blown up. Gerry was a noble guy who never spoke evil of anyone.
He was respected by everyone who had the pleasure of working with him. Wiping away the water from my own eyes, I made up my mind that I would go to London on my next leave and visit with him.

Work in the fabrication shop continued to pile up. Canham had all supporting facilities switch to working two ten-hour shifts in a row. We hummed for twenty hours non-stop, Blackcloud and I ended up having to work some weird hours, covering both shifts. There was no fucking the dog, so to speak, on this project. We were definitely earning our cash.

I approached Bill and told him I needed help in the fabrication shop; it was just getting to be too much. He asked if I had any one in mind and I told him I knew of a guy who had worked in Duri, Sumatra, for three years. Then I told Bill what his name was and waited for his response. Bill smiled. "Sure, I remember Scar. He was a piping superintendent for PT. Petrochem," he recalled. "Well, its fine with me. Let's try to get him."

Scar Tissue and I had grown up and worked together for years on oil drilling rigs all over West Texas. I had often wondered why Mr. and Mrs. Tissue had named their only son Scar. They either had one hell of a sense of humor, or maybe in their younger hippie days they had messed with that South Texas small thornless cactus, peyote. I had heard that folk could really trip out on its psychoactive ingredient, mescaline. The funny name never seemed to bother Scar, though, in fact he did a lot of crazy shit over the years to help validate it. These activities included wrecking dirt bikes and getting into bar room fights, which both managed to leave their marks. But I guess Scar could've had it worse, his sister was named Pulpy.

Scar and I had started out as "gofers," meaning that we'd go for this and go for that when we first started working together. We were just your run-of-the-mill rig pigs. With our hands aching at night from all the work we finally said 'piss on it' and decided to get some skills. That's when I took up welding and Scar took up pipefitting.

We stayed with the rigs for a couple of years. I focused on welding while Scar earned his paychecks as a maintenance motorman. One night during a wild weekend party in Midland, Texas, Scar and I got to drinking and shooting the shit. We figured there had to be a better way to make a living. We had both done our time in a bunch of shitty-ass countries and saved a little cash. I made the decision to go to university; Scar went to Odessa College for a couple of years and graduated with an associate degree in petroleum engineering technology.

I always recall and chuckle about an adventure Scar and I had in Dallas one Saturday night. We had completed drilling a well outside of Tyler that had come in dry. On Monday morning the rig would be stacked and moved to another location. I looked at Scar and grinned. "In the immortal words of that rock and roller, Little Richard, 'It's Saturday night and we just got paid', what are we waiting for?"

With that we checked in at the Hilton Ranchman in Dallas, deciding that we were going first-class all the way. Four hundred and fifty dollars later, we were in our two-bedroom suite on the seventh floor. We immediately hit the cocktail bar and after an hour of hard sell to a couple of Dallas cowgirls, we were invited to a party room on the top floor. We partied for a couple of hours trying to get laid but there were too many cowboys and not enough cowgirls.

The night was still a pup so we decided to go for a drive. Unfortunately it was thirty floors to the basement parking lot and we both needed to piss like a couple of Texas gushers, what can ya do? When we reached the basement, our bladders were empty and the elevator carpet was soggy.

We headed to the outskirts of Dallas and wound up in a little bar on a lake. After a couple of rounds with the bartender, an attractive Latino woman in her thirties, we began chatting with her a bit. I jokingly told her that Scar was a CIA agent who had just returned from

Iran, which, at that time, was experiencing an Islamic Revolution. Technically, Scar had been in Iran on a refinery project, but he'd been home for eight months. He laid enough Iranian bullshit on her at the appropriate times. I think she may have believed him.

After the bar closed for the night she joined us for a drive around the lake in my 1965 Ford Custom 500. She climbed in the back seat with Scar. I drove around puffing on a joint and held a long neck Lone Star between my legs in the front seat until the folk in the back seat quit playing hide the wienie. Just a couple of natural-born West Texas rig pigs. It would be good to have him around again. He would be in Kuwait within two weeks.

***

Working the night shift brought its own sub-human activities, Kuwaiti style. Hundreds of pieces of heavy-duty earth-moving equipment, cranes, and trucks of all sizes were parked by their day shift operators for refueling by the night shift personnel. Armed Kuwaitis manned check points in and out of the oil fields where the refueling trucks would pass through. One night a young male Philippino driver was stopped and ordered out of his vehicle at gun point. He was forced to kneel and perform oral sex on his captor. Once that was over, he was then bent over the front of his vehicle and brutally sodomized. The young Philippino had to receive medical attention and get stitched up. After he healed, he was flown back to his home country. He was paid several thousand dollars by Kuwaiti officials while his attacker walked free. There were several other incidents of brutality against third-country nationals. No justice ever prevailed.

Some unusual oil well fire fighting equipment began to arrive into Kuwait. A Hungarian oil well fire fighting outfit showed up with a contraption never before seen. The motorized section for land travel was a Russian World War II T-34 Army tank, stripped of its turret and gun assembly. Two World War II Russian MiG aircraft engines were mounted onto it. Built behind and above the engines was an enclosed control room that gave the general overall shape of a railroad caboose.

A remote control operator connected with a hundred feet of umbilical cables to the machine in conjunction with the control room operator directed the tank's land movement. Pressure piping to the engine's air intake had been flanged to the high-pressure hoses and pumps sucking water from the recently dug lagoons. Depending on the size of the wellhead fire, pumps that could deliver anywhere from two thousand to six thousand gallons per minute were used. As the high-pressure water was sucked through the MiG Engines, the exhaust fans spit out a huge atomized cloud of high-pressure moisture, smothering the oxygen and snuffing out the fire. However, that was the easy part. That raging oil fountain was the real beast. The Hungarians had christened their red painted pride and joy "Big Wind."

Another world player in the oil patch that is ranked among the top three drilling companies in the world is Santa Fe International Corporation, which was founded in 1946 and is headquartered in California. In 1981 it was purchased by the Kuwait Petroleum Corporation, an agency of the Kuwait government. Santa Fe is still managed by United States executives who were running the show at the time of the acquisition. When Iraq invaded Kuwait in August 1990, Santa Fe had nine hundred employees of mixed nationalities in the country. The company's European and American employees were taken hostage by the Iraqi military and held captive for five months before being released. Before capture the Santa Fe person- nel had been engaged in the operation of ten land oil drilling rigs. Since changing ownership, Santa Fe had drilled approximately four hundred oil and gas wells in Kuwait. At the war's end, most of Santa Fe's equipment was in Iraq or busted.

Santa Fe began its Kuwait rebuilding efforts by providing personnel to assist the professional firefighters and coordinating with the Kuwait Oil Company on the implementation of new firefighting teams to support the initial four groups and the arrival of new service companies. The Kuwait Petroleum Corporation also manned up a firefighting team of Kuwaiti personnel. The only female to play a role in the field fighting the fires was on the home grown team. A petroleum engineer with the Kuwait Oil Company, she had been responsible for saving some computer data files relating to the Kuwait oil fields before they could be destroyed by the invaders.

When the time finally came, and the last fire was extinguished, it would be Santa Fe's principal responsibility to reclaim the wells and restore production. Planning for this work actually began in October 1990. Within two months of the Iraq invasion, it was well understood from military intelligence reports coming out of Kuwait that the Iraqis had stolen or vandalized most of Santa Fe's equipment. A Santa Fe task-force based in Houston, Texas, began to identify and acquire drilling rigs, along with support equipment and personnel camps suitable for use in Kuwait. In mid January 1991, just hours before the bombs and missiles of Operation Desert Storm lit up Bagdad, a vessel departed Houston with two complete drilling rigs, personnel camps, and spare parts destined for a staging area in Qatar. It arrived in Doha in late February 1991, three days before the Iraqi retreat.

Extinguishing oil well fires in Kuwait was an equipment intensive exercise. Some of the equipment required for a typical crew of firefighters included ten blow-out preventers, six one hundred-ton cranes, four Caterpillar D9 bulldozers, at least four all-wheel drive trucks, ten pick-up trucks, ten thousand sacks of oil well cement, two tons of dynamite, six Athey Wagons with sixty-foot-long booms, and several miles of six-inch diameter pipe, depending on how close the water supply was. Tons of liquid drilling mud material would be required to be forced down the well-head to block the escaping oil. Support equipment such as helicopters, mobile welding shops, medical support teams, living quarters, food, and drinking water supplies were also all part of the show.

There had to be a logical sequence for fighting the Kuwait oil well fires. Each well-head fire had to be surveyed to assess the damage. A well-kill plan had to be devised, which included a fully developed list of required equipment and personnel. Then the equipment had to be located and pulled together. For Kuwait, that meant long distance shipping, especially for unusual types of equipment. The actual killing of the fire sometimes wouldn't begin for several weeks after the initial survey.

By June, equipment was arriving into Kuwait. Enough was coming to allow an additional team of firefighters for each of the four original companies. Furthermore, the infrastructure had grown sufficiently to allow several new American and a number of international firefighting teams to mobilize into Kuwait. These teams were coming from Iran, China, Canada, Hungary, Romania, France, Russia, and Britain.

***

The Shamal wind was blowing and visibility was no more than ten feet in any direction. Driving conditions were especially dangerous due to the mixture of heavy smoke, wind, and sand. However, the project wheels kept turning, although at a much slower pace. I took a walk around the shop floor, checking how much outside sand and smoke was blowing in through the holes in the old worn-out walls with the odd bullet hole. Some outside shit was definitely finding its way in. As I began passing out dust masks to the shop workers, a man wearing red coveralls and carrying a wide-brimmed red hard hat walked into the shop. He was about five-feet-ten inches tall with a full head of white hair.

I looked at his face and immediately recognized it belonged to that famous oil well firefighter, Red Adair. He smiled at me and extended his hand in my direction.

"Just thought I'd get in out of the sand for a bit," he said. "How's everything going here?"

I shook his hand and smiled back. "Fine," I told him, not wanting to come across as a star-struck fan.

He wandered around the shop for ten minutes or so before coming up to me again.

"Well, thanks for letting me take a breather in here. Good luck." With that he was gone.

I couldn't believe Red had entered my shop! I was in awe of the guy. He was a living legend. Red Adair had gained international fame in 1962 when he and his team of oil well firefighters tackled and extinguished the eight-hundred-foot high gas well blow-out in the Algerian Sahara Desert. The well had been burning out of control for six months and had been nicknamed The Devil's Cigarette Lighter.

In 1991 Red Adair had turned 75 in Kuwait. Canham arranged a birthday celebration in his honor, but no one below the rank of manager was invited. Unfortunately my rank was superintendent, which left me uninvited. If nothing else I could at least now say that I had shaken his hand.

In the early months of the Al-Awda Project, nothing of any significance was happening. The firefighters were raising hell with Canham. The Kuwaiti officials were so fucked up, waiting for a pay-off, and no one was signing project purchasing documentation to get the ball rolling. Basically everyone and everything was in a deadlock.

Canham was exerting political pressure wherever it could. Red Adair even went to Washington, D.C., to kick ass and rattle the cages of politicians. He managed to embarrass them into bringing pressure down on the Emir and Crown Prince, the rulers of Kuwait.

About the same time Red was raising hell in Washington, D.C., Bill had taken Butch aside and given him a small manila envelope.

"Butch, around noon today a C5-A will be landing at the Kuwait International Airport. Part of its cargo is a black Cadillac Limo. This envelope contains the ignition key. Drive the Cadillac to the burned-out Kuwait government buildings in downtown Kuwait City," he instructed. Then he handed Butch the street address.

"Park the Cadillac, toss the key onto the passenger side floor, get out, lock it up, and climb into my car. I'll be waiting for you."

Butch followed Bill's instructions. Later he told me that the Cadillac's tail bumper was almost touching the black top surface as he drove. What-ever was in the trunk was packing a whole bunch of weight. Everybody's thought was that it was gold.

A month after the Cadillac, which was never seen again, had been delivered, shit started to happen. We guessed the squeaky wheel was being greased. Between Red Adair raising hell in Washington, D.C., and the contents of the Caddy's trunk, convoys consisting of heavy-duty earth moving equipment, twenty-wheel trucks by the dozen, and a multitude of light transport vehicles began arriving. It was all rolling in like a carnival parade coming to town, almost bumper to bumper, along the three or four miles that delivered everything into Ahmadi City from the Mina Abdula dock. The necessary supplies and equipment remained continuous for the next couple of weeks. Eventually it began to thin out, but a steady flow continued for months.

***

July arrived and Canham International had transported nearly ten thousand people and six thousand vehicles in less than six months into Kuwait. It was the most massive mobilization in the company's history. The fastest "fast track project" on record. An entire city of equipment operations, management staff, communications, transportation, and purchasing for the effort sprang up in the desert. Canham also laid more than ninety miles of pipeline across the desert. This piping system was capable of delivering twenty million gallons of seawater per day to the wellhead fire sites.

I was returning to Ahmadi City one afternoon, along the same stretch of road where Don had met his Waterloo, when suddenly the horizon filled up with rocket after rocket, bursting in the air. I quickly pulled the pick-up over onto the shoulder of the road to stop and watch. Fire-ball after fire-ball exploded and brilliant flares with red and green tracer bullets lit up the afternoon sky. I wondered what had happened.

We had received several memorandums signed by California Ken warning us about the dangers of messing with live munitions that had been discarded and left in buildings and warehouses, or even in the desert by the Iraqi military. However, the memorandum didn't mean shit to one desert worker. A retired Indian Army sergeant had picked up a hand grenade, pulled the pin, and tossed it into the open desert. The million dollar toss, so to speak. The grenade landed on a pile of sand that concealed a buried Iraqi Army ammunition dump. As the grenade exploded, shooting its shrapnel down into the ammo, all hell broke loose. It reminded me of a scene out of that Vietnam movie epic, *Apocalypse Now*.

It was the middle of July and the temperature was dangerously high. The Sumatra jungle had been hot and humid, but it was never much above 100 degrees Fahrenheit. The middle of summer in the Kuwaiti desert had unbelievably stifling temperatures that averaged

140 degrees Fahrenheit. Needless to say, water intake was essential. Around noon one day, a Philippino welder collapsed on the shop floor. The little brown guy had turned white and was delirious. I quickly loaded him into my pick-up truck and carried him to Canham's field hospital. He was admitted for dehydration and immediately put on intravenous fluids.

Later that day Blackcloud decided to conduct a little heat experiment with an uncooked egg he had snatched from the mess hall. We laid a shovel out in the sun to let it suck up a little heat, and then Charlie cracked the egg on top of it. When it hit the shovel it immediately started sizzling! A couple minutes later, we were looking at desert fried-egg.

It seemed that the hotter the sun burned down on the travelling smoke across the desert, the more it melted the oil droplets the smoke was carrying. They'd come down like black rain, spilling on everyone and everything. Another problem being encountered by the extreme heat was a huge headache for the bomb disposal teams. Within a two-week period, two Iraqi Army tanks that had been sitting out in the desert mid day heat just simply blew to pieces! When their operators deserted their post, the abandoned tanks remained with full loads of ammunition. The intense heat inside the steel tanks was close to 190 degrees Fahrenheit. The bomb disposal experts said the internal heat of the tanks was setting off the smaller rounds of ammunition which in turn lit up everything else.

One afternoon the shop was humming along without any problems. I turned to Blackcloud and said, "Piss on it Charlie. Let's head to the desert and do a little sightseeing and take some photographs."

The roaring oil well fires in the desert were incredible. The whole scene before us was horrific historical aftermath that we would never see again in our lifetime. Several fires roared in erratic directions from fractured wellheads. We saw massive swirling, multi-colored smoke. Black oil inches thick covered the desert. Huge lakes of oil, some of them had oil well fire reflections on their shimmering surface. Abandoned cars and pickup trucks were strewn across the desert, bogged down and relinquished by the fleeing Kuwaitis heading for Saudi Arabia.

We watched as firefighting teams pumped thousands of gallons of water in multiple arcs that glistened against the dark smoky environment while the brilliantly mixed red, yellow, and orange oilwell fires screamed a hundred feet into the air. We saw deserted anti-aircraft gun emplacements and loose hand grenades scattered between crates of munitions with Jordanian Army Forces markings. Mile after mile of mine fields lay in front of us. Twisted Iraqi military personnel carriers and blown-up army-trucks with the remnants of live and dead mortar shells were all there, too. We even saw the odd dead camel and army tanks buried in the sand, leaving only the turret exposed.

The Iraqis used a technique of digging their tanks into the desert for camouflage purposes, which turned out to be a primary cause of why they lost so many when the United States tanks roared into action. The buried tanks were unable to dig out and move quickly. Some even had flat batteries and the United Sates weapons simply blew the tops off the tanks. It was amazing to see tank after tank buried in the sand with their turrets alongside of them blown to rat shit. Then there were the bunkers; they were scattered throughout the desert.

Charlie parked the truck next to a mound of sand where bricks and sand bags formed a doorway with steps leading down into an underground bunker at least twenty-five to thirty feet below the desert surface. The steps leading down into the bunker were slabs of white marble. The bunker had a living room with a table and a couple of chairs, a portable toilet, and one bedroom with a bed. All the floor surfaces consisted of white marble. At one end of the living room was an escape tunnel leading up and out from the bunker. It was large enough for a medium-sized man to crawl through. We noticed that there were remnants of a smashed communications system on the table. Charlie and I guessed the bunker may have been some kind of officer command center during the occupation. The furniture and white marble had been looted from shops, warehouses, and deserted homes in Ahmadi and Kuwait City. These bunkers had been built the same way as the ammo dumps. A backhoe would be used to dig a large hole, and then rafters were laid across the top, followed by sheets of plywood placed over the rafters, then desert sand would be used to conceal the bunker.

After a couple of hours of breathing the smoke, concentrated fumes, and low oxygen because of the fires, Blackcloud and I were beginning to experience a petroleum high. We both agreed that it was time to head back to Ahmadi. As we drove the winding desert track between the oil well fires, I hit the play button of the cassette deck in the truck. The group Damn Yankees fired up with their hit "High Enough" with the lyrics, "Can you take me higher." I grinned. Appropriate, I thought.

***

I found another memorandum on my bed. This time it was from the doc. It was addressed to all staff, and was titled, "Survey of Pollution Impact on Staff Health." It read:

> The preliminary report from the Environmental Protection Agency does not show any concern on health hazards due to the air pollution in Kuwait.
> The analysis however is not conclusive but the recorded levels of carbon monoxide, sulphur dioxide, hydrogen sulphide, and aromatic hydrocarbons are not significant.

The only problem facing the employees is the large amount of particulate in the atmosphere. Those particulate are made essentially of carbon and their size prevent them from penetrating the pulmonary alveoli. The natural cleaning system of the bronchi should eliminate them.

Well right on Doc, I thought. I just hope it's the truth because I would hate to die a slow painful death from this shit we are breathing. I had heard about the Gulf War syndrome and that returning coalition solders were complaining of illnesses following their participation in the war. There had been some speculation about the causes of their illnesses and some of the factors considered included exposure to the depleted uranium from the tank busting bombs and other chemical weapon exposures after the bombing of the chemical weapons factories in Iraq. Then there were the prevailing Shamal winds, blowing that shit down over Kuwait and Saudi Arabia, blanketing the troops along with the burning product of the oil wells.

That night I remembered the brief phone conversation I had had with the blonde lady in Odessa from the United States military base, Blackhorse. She had asked me why I was in Kuwait, considering the danger. Shit, I thought at the time. I don't exactly know why I am in Kuwait. I had actually considered quitting every day. But whenever I felt like quitting I would always remember the cash stacking-up in my ass national. My answer to her was simple.

"I guess it's the same reason most folks give when they are going off to war: 'Someone has to do it,'" I said.

***

Butch came by the fabrication shop around 8:00 one morning.

"Come on Bubba! Me and The Riddle are taking a helicopter ride up to North Kuwait and there's an empty seat," he exclaimed. "We'll be back by lunch. Let's go!"

He didn't need to ask me twice. I hollered to Blackcloud that I would be back in a couple of hours and he gave me the thumbs up sign. With that I climbed into Butch's Jeep Cherokee.

The Riddle was already standing by the four-seater helicopter waiting for us when we arrived. We said hello to each other and then all boarded. Butch sat up front beside the pilot. The Riddle and I sat behind them. Then we put on our headphones that came equipped with microphones and sat back for the ride. Soon we were up and away, listening to the pilot speaking with the military air controllers. We flew parallel with a rocky ridge that protruded very distinctly out of the desert, perhaps ten, maybe twenty feet above the desert floor. It ran from somewhere below Kuwait City all the way to North Kuwait and further and followed in general parallel with the winding Persian Gulf Coast, approximately twenty to twenty-five miles inland.

The oil field facility in North Kuwait consisted of the largest pipeline gathering system in the country. It brought the crude from two local producing oil fields into a central gathering center, where separating the oil from natural gas and dirty water occurred. The gas was wastefully burned off and the dirty water was spread over the desert. The crude was then pumped down the pipeline to the refinery's near Ahmadi.

It was these oil fields that the wacky Iraqi, Saddam Hussein, accused the Kuwaitis of directional drilling from and sucking oil out from under the Iraqi desert. I never heard an official denial of the directional drilling. North Kuwait also consisted of living accommodations for several hundred oil field workers but the facilities had been heavily damaged during Desert Storm.

For years another thorn in the side of Iraq had been the establishment of the country of Kuwait. Iraq claimed Kuwait had been part of its Ottoman Empire's province of Basra. Its ruling dynasty, the al-Sabah family, had concluded a Protectorate Treaty in 1899 that assigned responsibility for its foreign affairs to Britain. Britain drew a line in the sand, making it the border between the two countries, and deliberately tried to limit Iraq's access to the ocean so that any future Iraqi government would be in no position to threaten Britain's domination of the Persian Gulf. Iraq refused to accept the border and did not recognize the Kuwaiti government until 1963. The wacky Iraqi was still claiming Kuwait as the nineteenth province of Iraq. In 1990 he decided he wanted it back.

Fifteen minutes into the flight we could see the oil pipeline Saddam's boys had been building on top of the desert floor. The pipeline had begun at a refinery somewhere near the Bagdad oil fields. Its destination was the Persian Gulf and was intended to flow with petroleum product for export. They had made it as far as the rocky ridge when the United States Air Force started shaking Bagdad.

The pilot advised us the flight time to North Kuwait was thirty minutes without a Shamal wind blowing. He dominated most of the conversation telling us what we were flying above and pointing out areas of war damage. Butch asked a few questions, but then the headphones went quiet for several minutes. When they crackled alive, the pilot asked, "Hey, Riddle, when you gonna come visit your old pals at Evergreen? You can take us for a ride in one of the Slicks, just like the old times! What do you say?"

The Bell UH-1 helicopter was often referred to in Vietnam War slang as Slick or Huey. It transported troops and cargo in and out of the combat zones.

The Riddle's voice entered my earphones. "I'll do that one day," he crackled.

I flashed back to that steamy afternoon when Roy, the New Orleans crane man, had visited my fabrication shop in Sumatra for a Coke break and a cool down. He had mentioned that The Riddle used to fly Cobra gunship helicopters during the Vietnam War. On his leaves from Sumatra he would fly black ops down in Central America. Maybe The Riddle wasn't such a riddle after all.

During the first week in September, Canham began distributing a daily Al–Awda Project update report regarding the wellhead fire locations of each firefighting outfit. On September 7 the first report I received stated:

Total oilwells damaged, 749. Total oilwells controlled, 362. Number of firefighting teams, 16.

I figured that the way the project was going, it would be all over by Christmas time. I had been sure, as most others were too, that it would never be less than a good three year paying project. The image of my Gulf Coast bar was beginning to fade.

A guy came by the fabrication shop to submit an order along with a roll of blue-print drawings to fabricate a piping system for the restoration of a Gathering Center Station, or GCS as they were called. He was working on a heavily damaged GCS out in the Bergan Field, twenty miles from Ahmadi. The Bergan Field has more oil wells per square mile than any oil field on the planet. Because the oil wells are spread all over the desert, the product is pumped to a common GCS.

Miles of flow lines lay on supports across the desert surface to a multitude of GCSs. When the product from the oil well passes through the equipment in the GCS, it is stripped of the dirty water and gas that comes with it. The final product, crude, was then pumped into the main line, carrying it to either one of the three oil refineries on the Kuwaiti coast before the Iraqi Army blew the shit out of the GCSs and the refineries.

I looked at the guy's face as we introduced ourselves.

"Have we met before?" I asked him. He seemed familiar for some reason.

"Yes," he answered. "My name's Bob. We met on the Alaska pipeline project. You were with Alyeska on Pump Station No. 3. I was the piping supervisor for the contractor, Veco."

"Sure, now I remember!" I said with a grin. "It's a small world, huh?" Admittedly, I was still having a hard time actually recalling him on the job.

"So how did you wind up here?" I asked.

"Well," he began. "I don't live in the United States any more. I've been living in Thailand for the past twenty years. If the job market gets tight in Southeast Asia, or I get bored with the bar, I occasionally pick up a fill-in job in the United States if the money's right, sometimes for three or four months." Bob explained. "About a hundred years ago I used to work out of the Pipefitters union, Local 496, in San Francisco. I still have a few good union buddies there who steer me to the odd good money project. Alaska was one of those jobs for me," he added. "But most times I am at my bar in Bangkok."

He told me the Canham Bangkok office was only a couple of blocks away from his bar and a bunch of Canham head honchos often drank there. After he talked with a few of them one evening, he ended up hiring on for the Kuwait rebuild.

"Shit, man! That's cool," I told him. "And it's great to see you again. Where is your bar in Bangkok?" I was envious; owning a bar was my goal!

"You ever been to Bangkok?" he asked.

"Sure," I said, recalling my time in the Nana Hotel with my little Thai lady friend, Noi.

"It's located in the Nana Plaza, on Sukhumvit, Soi Nana," Bob explained.

"Yeah I know where that is," I answered.

Bob grinned. "Really? Well, next time you are in Bangkok, come visit. I am on the second floor of the plaza. My bar is called the Hog's Breath. Many folks know me as Bangkok Bob," he said. With that he turned and started walking back to his pick-up truck.

"I will. You can bet on it!" I hollered after him.

Later that evening, I was thinking about the name, the Hog's Breath. Suddenly I had a flash back. I remembered seeing the Dude from Dallas wearing a black t-shirt in the base bar one evening back in Sumatra. On both the front and back of the t-shirt it had a red and white picture of a furious wild boar with blood and shit dripping from its tusks. Written underneath the hog logo it said, "Hog's Breath, Better Than No Breath." Under the slogan was some shit about a bar and location. I was sure it had said Bangkok. I also knew the Dude from Dallas had spent some time in Thailand. At that moment I decided that after I visited Gerry in London, I would go get wasted in Bangkok.

CHAPTER 10

Dillard Dillpot was a thirty-year Canham hand. He had come into Kuwait a week or so after me and was well-connected with Canham's upper echelon. Basically he was one of the "good old boys". His position was area manager somewhere out in the desert. When he drove up to the fabrication shop one day, I was a little puzzled to see him. I wasn't sure why he would visit. I knew it couldn't be work-related; our departments didn't mesh that way.

After ten minutes or so of general bullshit he asked a question that came out of left field.

"Have you known Bill Bass for long?" he asked casually.

"Couple of years," I replied, wondering what he was getting at.

Bill had worked for PT. Petrochem in several Indonesian locations for close to ten years. The PT. Petrochem project in Central Sumatra covered three separate oil fields. Each field covered thousands of jungle-covered acres. All three were under exploitation by Caltex Pacific Indonesia. Bill was a long time friend of the PT. Petrochem project manager, California Ken. They had worked together for the military contractor, Brown & Root, during the Vietnam shit. When that show was over, they hitched their horses in Jakarta, Indonesia. Several weeks before my arrival in Sumatra, Bill had been assigned a recently vacated area manager's position in Duri.

Dan the Special Forces man had told me how Bill was nothing but a chicken shit womanizer. I knew Bill had left behind a string of Asian wives, both in Vietnam and in Indonesia, and I understood his current Indonesian wife was his third in ten years. Dan told me he continually sexually harassed the Indonesian office girls and he had been reprimanded many times for it. However, Bill was Bill, a fucked-up womanizer, and he never quit. Dan also said that his own wife of six months had worked as a secretary for Bill in the PT. Petrochem Duri office before he had met her. He added that if he ever found out that Bill had harassed her, he would rip his fucking head off and piss down his throat. When I saw the look on Dan's face as he spoke, I definitely believed that Special Forces man was capable of doing just that. Dan's love for his new wife was so strong that he had become involved with the Muslim faith and had been circumcised to be eligible for the marriage.

Dillpot continued, "Well, I hear he's fucking up."

"No shit!" I answered. "What's he gone and done now?"

"He has that young piece of tail in his office and the door is always closed," Dillpot said. "It seems he spends more time fucking around with her than he does his job."

I sighed. "He does have a reputation with the ladies," I replied.

Then Dillpot dropped a bomb shell. "Well, he's about to get his ass run off," he said matter-of-factly.

I didn't say anything and only nodded. He made his bed, I guess he'll have to sleep in it, I thought to myself. A couple of minutes later Dillpot was gone.

Later that day I was speaking with The Riddle and he told me that Dillpot had visited him, too. Dillpot basically said the same thing about Bill; he was on very thin ice. Bill had hired almost every superintendent and there were ten of us for the field services department, including myself. I guessed Dillpot was front man for the Canham hit squad out for some Bill Bass blood. I started realizing that Dillpot was gathering a consensus. Canham did not want a superintendent rebellion on its hands.

The consensus must have been favourable. Ten days later Bill was fired for incompetence. He had dicked himself out of a high-paying project. I heard that California Ken had fought tooth and nail to block the termination, but the entrenched Canham good old boy establishment outnumbered him. Ken and Bill were long-time buddies and Ken had hired Bill for the Kuwait Fires Project.

Ten days later I said good-bye and good luck to Bill. He told me he was going back to his area manager position in Duri. If nothing else Bill had all the right connections.

When the Al-Awda Kuwait Fires Project first kicked off, the Field Services Department was one of the first departments to be manned, owing to the nature of the project. It was a war zone, and Kuwait had to be rebuilt from the ground up. The first priority was to establish civil work; support civil works with earthworks equipment, including cranes; support the earthworks with mechanics; and support the mechanics with the machine shop, welding/fabrication shop, and mechanical repair shops for cranes, heavy and light duty equipment. All of this work came under the Field Services Department.

California Ken had come out of Sumatra, and in turn he hired Bill off the Sumatra project. Bill had to set up his department and hired those he believed could handle the work. He turned to his most recent project to select personnel, which was Sumatra, and that's how most of the field superintendents, including myself, wound up in Kuwait. Like a lot of opportunities, it's not what you know, but who you know.

Naturally, all of us field superintendents were acquainted with each other and so we had a tendency to sit together in the mess hall simply because it's easier to eat and bullshit with people you know versus with strangers. However, because we came across as a bit cliquey, the Field Services Department had been labelled as the "Indonesian Mafia" by the other folks on the project, mostly the Brits. Some even went so far as to call us "Bass's Bastards".

Early one morning I heard Butch talking on his two-way radio. He was cussing up a storm and sounded really pissed with someone or about something. When he signed off, I called him and asked him to stop by when he got the chance.

He came back, "I am just pulling up to your office now."

Moments later he stormed in and sat down across from me. Before I could even ask what was going on, he started talking.

"Bubba, the people running this project are nothing but a pile of chicken dick motherfuckers – the whole fucking bunch, California Ken included!" he muttered. "I have had about all I want of this shit. As a matter of fact, I am on my way to go and pull the pin. That son-of-a-bitch general manager can stick the whole fucking deal up his hairy ass!"

He shook his head in disgust and stood up. Then he held out his hand to shake mine before leaving. He headed for the door, stopped, and turned to face me. "Hey man, in case I don't see you again, Bubba, hang loose, mother goose. Stay low and take the dough."

I nodded. What else could I say? "See ya, Butch," I said quietly. I had a feeling that would be the last time I saw him.

Several days after Butch's departure, rumors were all over the mess hall that Butch had been given two options: resign or be fired. Rumor had it that Butch had been bootlegging whisky. Supposedly he was having crates of whisky flown in on the United States Air Force C5-A and C-130 aircraft, as well as the Russian Antnov. The whisky-laden crates were mixed in with the bulldozers, buses, earth moving equipment, and oil well head assemblies. Apparently the crates of whisky had been labelled with the code words, "Spare Parts". Butch's major task was to organize and supervise all unloading of the giant aircraft.

A few months before Butch left, guys started hinting that whisky was available. However, it was illegal: the Muslims of Kuwait did not allow alcohol into their country. If Butch had been caught smuggling booze into Kuwait, he would have found himself doing some heavy-duty hard time in a Kuwaiti prison for many years. For how long, only God knows.

After listening to the rumors, I flashed back to the evening I had joined Butch and his professor friend for dinner at the Holiday Inn. During the trip into downtown Kuwait City I recalled how Butch had told me there were opportunities to pick up a little extra cash. Then it crossed my mind that the nasty shit he had hollered over the two-way radio the morning he quit was for show or some kind of a cover up. Either way, it was out of character for that Georgia man. I wondered who had ratted him out. The so-called Indonesian Mafia had now lost two of its top Capos.

By the end of September, 426 oil well fires had been killed and one extra firefighting team had been engaged, giving a total of seventeen teams participating in the Al-Awda Project. Sixty-four wells had been controlled within a three-week period and more than half of the original fires were now extinguished. Shit, I thought to myself. The show is half over. In a way, we were working our way out of a job.

There was another memorandum on my bed. This one was from the United States Embassy in Kuwait.

It was addressed to all employees and the subject line was titled, Terrorist Activity. The memorandum read:

Please note the following message from the head of the Consular Section at the U.S. Embassy.

As mentioned at a recent Warden's meeting, the potential for terrorist action is always high in the Middle East. Because certain groups may use terrorism in an attempt to disrupt the Middle East Peace Conference scheduled to begin in Madrid on October 30, all personnel should heighten their awareness.

Remember that most terrorist action involves surveillance of the target or targets before any attack. As you move around the city, be alert to your surroundings. If you notice anything suspicious, please contact the local authorities and notify the Embassy or the Consular Section. If you wish to call after hours or on weekends, please ask for the Duty Officer.

A list of telephone numbers was below the memo in case someone was moved to call.

The following morning Canham broadcast a project-wide radio message, stating:

With regard to last night's memo from the United States Embassy, all employees in charge of a vehicle must refuel when the fuel gage of their vehicles displays half empty. You must only drive on the top half of your fuel tank. If there is a terrorist alert, all drivers are to head in a southerly direction to the Saudi Arabian boarder for muster. Again, ensure your fuel tank is never below half full, over and out.

***

There is an area a couple of miles outside of the city of Dubai known as Jebel Ali. It is a section of the United Arab Emirates that is utilized as a duty-free port, and it is surrounded by a security fence and armed security guards with United Arab Emirates military manned gun emplacement. The Al-Awda Kuwait Fires Project was leasing numerous warehouses in Jebel Ali for material and equipment storage that was arriving from worldwide locations.

An unconfirmed report had been circulated around the Al-Awda Project that Canham had placed an order and received three pallets, each weighing twelve hundred pounds of C4 explosives for fire fighting purposes. When the request was made to ship the three pallets from Jebel Ali to the Al-Awda Project, one pallet was missing. Apparently, everyone in Jebel Ali was innocent and the pallet was never located. Months later an Israeli Embassy somewhere in South America was reportedly blown up with C4 explosives. I didn't require any convincing to stay alert; I knew first-hand what those assbags were capable of.

Work was piling up big time in the fabrication shop and shit was happening fast in the desert. Scar and Blackcloud were switching to a week on nights and a week on days. Man, they both had the red ass and were turning nasty! Some days I couldn't look sideways at either of them in fear that they would bite my fucking head off. I sent a memorandum to Bill's replacement, requesting an ex-pat for the night shift, and marked it For Your Urgent Attention. That afternoon, Human Resources brought me a half-dozen resumes of possible candidates that were currently in the field assisting the firefighting efforts.

I chose the resume of a guy I had known in Sumatra. John was from Houston, Texas, and was a damn good piping supervisor. He would be ideal for the night shift. John had one downfall, though: he was a bad drunk. But Kuwait was alcohol-free, so I assumed that John would be okay. Blackcloud and Scar both grinned and said, "Thank God!" in unison when I told them they didn't have to work any more nights. They wanted to know who was going to mind the night shift and I told them about John. Blackcloud had known John in Sumatra and didn't hold him in very high esteem. He had seen him drunk too many times in the base bar and down in the Bali Rajah District. Scar was yet to meet John.

"Bubba, are you aware that Canham is considering running John and a couple of his buddies off?" Blackcloud asked curiously.

"No," I replied. "I hadn't heard that. Why would they want to run him off?

"Well, John and two of his pals went sightseeing in the desert in one of the project's brand new Chevy four-by-four pick-up truck," Blackcloud said. "They pulled off a recently graded strip in the desert being used as a road and sat eyeballing a heavy-duty oil well fire. Of course, the wind changed. They had parked in the recently heaped sand left at the road's edges by the road grader and the pick-up sunk. When the driver fired up the truck to get the hell out of harm's way the truck just dug itself further into the soft sand. Basically, it was bogged, balls deep, and they couldn't move."

"Oh man," I said, rolling my eyes. "Then what?"

"The driver's door window exploded from the intense heat. They quickly escaped out the passenger door and ran for their lives over the oil-soaked desert," Blackcloud continued. "The driver had the left side of his face and arm burned; John and the other guy escaped without a scratch. Canham got pissed off when it was learned they were sightseeing and a new pick up was totalled, burned to a steel skeleton."

I shrugged. "Maybe this night shift will save his bacon," I said.

John fired up on the night shift two days later and his bacon was saved. A couple of days later I was drinking a Coke in the office trailer and shooting the shit with Blackcloud when I turned and asked, "Charlie, do you remember the time our night shift guy had his melon busted down in the Bali Rajah District back in Sumatra?"

He shook his head. "No, I was on leave when that happened," he replied." Tell me about it."

I continued. "John had hooked up with a skinny, gnarly-toothed young lady from the Indonesian island of Java. She was tall for a female Indonesian; she stood three or four inches above the average woman. Also, she was a Muslim-turned-bad and loved the booze. In fact, I'd seen her falling down drunk several times," I said. "Anyhow, one evening after John and Gnarly Tooth had poured a bunch of booze into themselves and were staggering around like a couple of drunken sailors in the parking lot outside the little one room-bar, screaming abuse at each other. Gnarly Tooth threw a haymaker punch at John and missed. But then John counter-punched and connected with her gnarly tooth. She landed hard on her ass, screaming obscenities. John just left her there in the dirt and drunkenly waddled off to his little worn-out yellow PT. Petrochem pick-up truck."

"Seriously," Charlie asked incredulously.

I nodded. "As he was bent over trying to fit the key in the door lock, Gnarly Tooth came up behind him and swung a two-by-four chunk of wood, catching John on the left side of his melon and knocking him to the ground, out cold," I replied. "Blood was gushing out of his head."

"Then what?" Charlie asked.

"Well, a couple of the ex-pats in the bar rushed to his assistance and carried him to the Caltex hospital on the base and roused the doctor. John had a concussion and required ten stitches in his melon. He was kept in the hospital until the following morning and reassessed. The doctor needed to report how the injuries occurred, so he asked."

"Did the guys cover for John?" Charlie asked.

I nodded. "The ex-pats told the doctor that John was drunk and had fallen down the stairs at the single-man quarters where he lives. Apparently the doctor figured it was a lie. He mentioned that it must have been one hell of a heavy, uncontrolled fall to sustain those injuries and then he winked," I said. "Nothing was ever said to PT. Petrochem's upper echelon. It was accepted that John had flipped down the stairs and busted his melon. John healed and carried on."

Charlie shook his head. "Sounds like he's one lucky son-of a-bitch to be alive," he said

I completely agreed.

***

The first week of October ended with a total of 544 oil well fires tamed and 151 still burning. At that rate, I guessed I would be back in Texas for Christmas. However, all hell broke loose around 2:00 one afternoon. Helicopters filled the skies, ambulance sirens screamed around the roads of Ahmadi City heading out to the desert, and radio calls for paramedics went out to all of the firefighting teams. Canham issued a radio call for all personnel to switch to the emergency channel and continue to monitor the situation until further notice.

The wacky Iraqis had a habit of digging deep holes in the desert and burying their ammunition. Basically it was same method of construction they utilized to build their bunkers. Dig a hole, dump in the ammunition, and cover it with plywood and desert sand. It had happened before in the 140 degree heat. Ultimately, the shit blew up. Just like some of the army tanks. Well, one particular stash of underground ammunition was the so-called mother of all stashes. The explosions were huge.

The Kuwaiti Army and the British Royal Navy had helicopters in the air, trying to assess the situation. The fire power coming from the ammunition dump was so intense that the helicopters could not fly closer than a mile-and-a-half from ground zero. The first reports over the Canham emergency channel reported that forty people were already injured; the shit was hitting the fan. An hour later however, Canham emergency channel stated that no injuries occurred and one Iraqi military ammunition dump was totally destroyed. We were allowed to switch our radios back to our working channel. Luckily, Saddamn Hussein's shit killed no-one in Kuwait that noisy afternoon.

***

I noticed another inter-office memorandum on my bed that evening. It was addressed to all employees and its subject line was titled, Your Safety. The memorandum read:

I want you to keep reminding yourself and those around you of the dangers of mines, munitions, and other unexploded ordinance.

There is no work out there worth risking your mobility or your responsibilities to your family for.

California Ken had signed the memorandum. Right on, I thought. You're right on top of this shit Ken, but a few horses have already bolted.

By the middle of October, the project peaked as far as personnel and equipment went. Twenty-seven teams were fighting and killing the oil well fires. They had successfully extinguished 622 blown-up and busted well heads; only seventy-five were still burning. It was nice to see that the sky was turning bluer each day, and what was left of the smoke in the wind was heading due south. In fact it was now a rare day to be engulfed in smoke. The project adrenalin flow was ebbing; the vision of my Gulf Coast bar was growing dimmer.

One evening I was sitting at the end of the rectangular dining table, eating my dinner when The Riddle came up to the table with his tray of food.

"Hey Bubba. Mind if I join you?" he asked casually.

"Not a problem," I answered. "Have a seat."

The Riddle sat down next to me and began to eat his food. We chatted between bites, munching on the food and moaning about the end of the project coming into sight and wondering where we might end up after the Al-Awda Project was over. The Riddle then began telling me that Ricky Skaggs, the bluegrass singer, was going to be performing at the Blackhorse military base in a couple of days. We were totally immersed in our conversation when, out of the blue, an oversized hand clamped down on The Riddle's left shoulder. I looked up to see an overweight sack-of-shit with no neck, a large beer belly, and a bald head. He was an ugly, loud-mouthed, nasty-looking piece of shit.

"Hey, Riddle, you fucking little prick!" the man snarled. His eyes were dark and angry.

No Neck had no time to say anything else. Riddle was under attack. He grabbed his steak knife off the dining table in his right hand. Then with incredible speed, The Riddle stood, twisted to his left and plunged the knife into No Neck's left arm. He kept moving. He hooked his left foot behind No Neck's right ankle and punched him in the chest with his left elbow at the same time. Then he pulled his own left foot forward, bringing No Neck's right foot out from under him. No Neck hit the mess room floor like an overweight sack of shit. Security personnel were on the scene in a matter of seconds. A medic arrived hurriedly and patched up No Neck's arm. It was only a superficial wound. However, I fully believe that if The Riddle had wanted to fatally puncture that bald-headed chicken fucker, he definitely would have.

An investigation was convened the next day. Being a witness, I told the investigators exactly what I had seen. I figured The Riddle went into self-preservation mode; there was just no telling what No Neck's next move would be. From my perspective, it was entirely self-defense. Being the aggressor, No Neck was dismissed instantly and was on a plane out of Kuwait the following day. The Riddle was asked to submit his resignation, giving a two-week notice. He would be paid all monies owed to him including his bonus. No bonus for No Neck.

The Riddle was paid off, including his two weeks' notice, three days later. Last I knew, he was headed back to South Carolina. I now had no doubt that The Riddle had been a government-trained

Cong killer. There were lots of stories around the mess hall after The Riddle's departure, and a lot of guys speculated about the bad blood between No Neck and The Riddle. Apparently, they had come close to violence on several occasions during the Al-Awda Project. One thing was certain and unanimously agreed: No Neck was a low life, red neck, piece of shit, but Roger Riddle would always be The Riddle.

As of October 31, 686 oil well fires had been killed, and eighteen firefighting teams had been demobilised. That left nine teams to complete the shit.

As the fires were being killed, more and more Kuwaitis had been returning to their country and ordering in domestic help from their usual sources of exploitation: the Philippines, Sri Lanka, and India. A steady flow of brown females began arriving.

Kuwait plays host to numerous nomadic Bedouin tribes as they roam through different Middle Eastern countries. I had seen several of their tent cities in different areas of the desert in my travels to the fires. Most of them were located in the desolate area, fifty or sixty miles south of Ahmadi City. This area of Kuwait has virtually no oil wells and is mostly open desert to the Saudi Arabian border.

One of the rumors going around was that Kuwaiti Ali Babas were running a scam and bringing in young women who believed they were entering Kuwait as domestic help. They would be met at the Kuwait International Airport by a Kiuwaiti dressed in the full flowing Arabic Hijab, and he would assist in getting them through Immigration with a fistful of dollars under the table to the appropriate official. The women would leave with the Ali Baba in his Mercedes Benz. He would drive them into the desert and meet up with several Bedouin tribe elders, bargain, and sell the women to the highest bidder. The bought chattel would join the Bedouin elder's other concubines, and sometimes they would be sold at a later date to human slave traders.

The Philippine Embassy had issued a bulletin reporting two Philippine women missing. They had last been seen passing through Immigration at the Kuwait International Airport.

The women's families had called the Philippine Embassy in Kuwait after there had been no contact with their relatives for three weeks. I never heard if they were ever located.

Another incident occurred at a check-point along the thirty-mile-long divided highway that led from Ahmadi City west into the Magwa and Burgan oil fields. The Kuwaiti militia had set up check points at either end of the highway. The militia manning these check points were mostly in their mid-twenties to mid-thirties with a fucked up attitude of hatred toward those who had liberated their country. Perhaps they were listening to the broadcasts by that tall streak of pelican shit down in Saudi Arabia, Osama Bin Laden, who was on a continuous broadcast rant regarding the demon infidel.

They all dressed in desert camouflage military uniforms and packed fully loaded M-16 rifles. Nothing was new there, but these guys would point the barrels of their weapons in each driver's face, stick the barrel through the door window, and motion for the glove box to be opened. On other occasions, they would order the drivers out at gun-point and have them tilt the seats of their vehicles forward. No one understood what they were looking for. Ultimately they'd grunt and motion for the drivers to get back into their vehicles and fuck off. Canham received numerous complaints from its employees regarding this treatment, but all of them received the same response: it's their country; we were just guests. It was a hell of a way to treat guests. However, Canham did promise to raise the issue with the ruling Kuwaitis. Soon after that things went a little hay wire.

A five-foot-six-inch Australian Vietnam veteran pulled up to a stop at one of the check-points. The armed militia guard ordered the Aussie out of his pick-up truck. As he was exiting the vehicle, the guard prodded the Aussie in the chest with the barrel of his M16. At that moment the little guy's military training kicked in. He immediately snatched the carbine from the Kuwaiti's hands and smacked him alongside of his head with the rifle butt, knocking him out cold. The Aussie then rendered the firearm useless and tossed it into the desert. With that he stepped over the unconscious Arab, climbed into his pick-up truck, and drove off. That same afternoon, the Australian Vietnam Veteran was on the Evergreen Airlines 4:00 flight from Kuwait to Dubai. My only regret was I had not got to shake his hand.

One day Blackcloud received a radio call to go to Canham's office and call home immediately. He hurried to his truck and was gone to the telephone quicker than a New York minute. Half an hour later, he walked back into the shop. I looked up at him from my desk.

"Everything okay, Charlie?" I asked.

He sighed."I have something to tell you," he said slowly.

I motioned for him to sit down across from me and waited for him to continue.

"You remember back in August when I took my two-week break in Egypt, met my wife in Cairo, and we climbed the pyramids?"

"Yeah, I remember," I replied

Charlie continued. "Well Bubba, on my return, I was wandering through the duty free side of the Dubai International Airport waiting for my flight back to Kuwait, when I stumbled upon a big black Mercedes-Benz, five hundred-series that the airport was raffling off to the travelling public. The raffle rules claimed that the company raffling it off would ship the vehicle to the winners home address, no matter what country the winner was from," he said.

I remembered that luxurious limousine. In fact, I had purchased a ticket the last two times I had returned to Kuwait, dropping two hundred bucks total.

"I know exactly which vehicle you're talking about," I said.

Charlie nodded. "Well, after the Egypt trip, I checked my vacation budget. I was way under what I had planned to spend. The price of a ticket for that Mercedes black beauty was one unused boarding pass, which I had, and one hundred United States dollars, which I also had."

The suspense was killing me. "So what are you getting at Charlie?" I asked, trying to hurry him along.

"Bubba," Charlie said, grinning from ear to ear. "I bought a ticket and I won that sucker! That was why I had to call home immediately. Some Dubai airport official called the old lady with the good news and she called Canham to have me call her. Man she was pissing herself with excitement!"

I burst out laughing. "Congratulations, you lucky bastard!" I cried. "Now that's the kind of call home we all need!" At the same time I started thinking that another of my hard earned two hundred dollars had gone for a shit.

***

By November 2, only four fires remained. On November 5, we were down to three fires with four remaining teams. The final three wells were capped and the remaining fire-fighting teams were demo-bilized, except the Canadian team, Safety Boss. They would perform the ceremonial kill of the last Kuwait fire in the desert of the burned-out Burgan Field.

In mid November a gathering of dignitaries, including the Emir and Crown Prince, firefighters, and a bunch of reporters, gathered to view Safety Boss control the last oil well that had been sabotaged by the Iraqi Army. The event brought the most destructive and point-less act of Saddam Hussein's aggression against his small neighbour to an end.

Later, the United States Embassy in Kuwait issued a bulletin stating:

The extinguishing of the last oil well fire will see the end of a defeated Saddam as completely as did last winter's military campaign. This second coalition, composed of Kuwaitis, American, British, Canadians, French, Iranians, Chinese, Hungarians, Romanians, and Russians, threw aside national differences and cooperated with one end in mind. The results have been the extinguishing and capping of a total of 727 oil wells. Never before in the history of the oil well control industry, has such a project been undertaken. That it was completed so rapidly, only eight months, has come as a surprise not only to many would be experts, but also to the firefighters themselves. This total may well exceed the total number of oil wells capped in history before this event.

Son-of-a-bitch, I thought. I had a role in an historic happen-ing, and it only lasted eight fucking months. When I first arrived in Kuwait, I had no doubt it would last three years. My thoughts then turned to something else that had always been in the back of my mind: will I ever get that bar somewhere along the Texas Gulf Coast?

A few days later, Canham issued a report project-wide listing the number of oil well fires killed by each fire-fighting company.

Leading the pack was Canadian Safety Boss with 176,
50 ahead of their closest rival American Boots & Coots: 126,
American Wild Well control: 120,
The legendary Red Adair Co., Inc.: 111.
Kuwait Oil Company: 41,
American Abel Engineering-KOC; 39,
American Cudd Pressure Control: 23,
Iran Nioc: 20,
Canadian Alert Disaster: 11,
China; 10,
Hungary, France and Kuwait production maintenance: 9 a piece,
Canadian Red Flame: 7,
Rumania and the British: 6 a piece
The Russians: 4,
Final total: 727.

November ended and Canham circulated an inter-office memorandum advising all employees that the Al-Awda Project would officially end on December 31, 1991. All monies and bonuses would be paid up to year's end. Effective January 1, 1992, a new Kuwait project would begin. It would be referred to as Al-Tameer, which, translated into English, meant, "The Rebuild." At the bottom of the memorandum was a tear-off section that needed to be returned to all employees' supervisors. It asked if employees wanted to terminate with Al-Awda once the project was officially complete or remain and sign on with Al Tameer.

A simple "yes" or "no" was required by all.

During the Al-Awda Project we were paid for seven days a week for six weeks at ten hours a day, even though we worked many more hours than ten a day. We'd have fourteen days off and free flights in and out of Dubai to Kuwait. We were also given cash that equalled the price of a return economy class airfare to our home-towns or closest airports. There wasn't an American on the project who received less than three thousand dollars per two-week break. That money became known as our "fistful of dollars".

Conditions would change with the Al-Tameer Project, though. An employee would be expected to work six ten-hour days, having Friday off, the Muslim holy day. Three months would be spent working in Kuwait, entitling the employee for a two week break and an economy class return ticket to London. Any further travel would be at the expense of the employee. After reviewing the new terms of the contract, Charlie Blackcloud and I both marked "no". Scar and John marked, "yes". I recalled a lyric from a the Bob Dylan song: "For the times they are a-changing".

Before Charlie left Kuwait we stopped by the Canham main project office to collect a couple of project souvenirs the Kuwaitis had decided to give each of us. A blue-baseball-type cap with the slogan, "Kuwait Fires Project," and a brass belt-buckle with a well-head on fire embossed on it.

Blackcloud left Kuwait on December 15. A few weeks before he left, he had told me he had sent a letter to one of the Indonesian ex-army general's working for Caltex on the PT. Petrochem project we had been on. Charlie and the general had become good friends, owing to the fact that Charlie was supervising the general's section of the Sumatran oil field operations. There had been no construction delays and this made the general look very competent in the eyes of upper management in Caltex. Charlie told me that he had asked the general for his old job back and the general had responded very positively in writing saying: "Mr. Charlie, you come back whenever you are ready, just you telephone call to me and I make the papers for you".

"So, Bubba, I am going home to Florida for Christmas and then I'm headed back to Duri after the New Year," he said to me. Way to go Charlie, I thought.

When Blackcloud won the Mercedes Benz he was told he had a choice: the car or the cash equivalent of the car. I was curious as to what Charlie would choose. Before we parted ways I asked him what his plans were.

"What are you going to do about the Mercedes-Benz?" I asked

Charlie grinned. "I am taking the cash!" he said without hesitation.

That afternoon as we were getting ready to leave the office and head to the airport, Charlie approached me. "Hey, Bubba, give me a copy of your resume and if you want to return to Sumatra, give me a call. I will give your resume to Bill Bass and twist his arm if I have to."

"Shit Charlie," I said, feeling touched that he would try to get me a job. "That's great! Thanks man."

With that I drove Charlie to the airport and sincerely hoped that we would get to work together someday again. He was a good man. I pulled up alongside the curb in front of the Kuwait International Airport departures. Charlie and I shook hands one last time. We both wished each other well and then Blackcloud disappeared into the Kuwait airport.

Several days after Charlie's departure, I was woken up in the early morning by loud, thunderous explosions. Brilliant white flashes were darting across my bedroom walls. My first half-awake thoughts were that the wacky Iraqi was back in town. Confused, I looked out the window to see the rain was pissing down. It was a thunder and lightning storm; a wild electrical Kuwaiti winter storm was watering the desert.

On December 21 it was my turn to leave the Al-Awda Kuwait Fires Project. Scar was remaining and would manage the steel fabrication shop. John would work with him on the day shift. The night shift had been abolished a few weeks earlier. Roy from the crane department had completed his contract and went home to New Orleans, Louisiana. He had no interest in remaining in Kuwait, especially since he never really got over his pal and mentor, Gerry, getting blown up.

As planned, I had visited Gerry in his London hospital on my one of my two-week breaks. He had lost a lot of weight since I had last seen him, but then he had been through hell. He seemed to be on top of his shit, though. However, that may have been because of the happy pills the hospital was feeding him. Several months later, he was repatriated to his home in California where he would face a bunch of physiotherapy. I promised him I would visit him there.

Kuwait was a completely different country now, with its blue skies and black lakes of oil. Migrating birds would be fooled by the reflecting sun and swoop down into what was not water. They died by the hundreds. The Al-Awda Project had been a career pinnacle for me. In the beginning, no one knew what to expect. Sadly, some good men had died and others had been seriously injured. Some of us had made lifelong friends. There is no doubt that the Kuwait fires burned a scar on the souls of those who experienced it.

THAILAND

CHAPTER 11

I arrived in Odessa in time for Christmas by way of airports in London, New York, and Midland, Texas. After several weeks rolled by, I had to contemplate my next move. I had been on a couple of outings with the blonde lady and our discussions about my ideas of owning a bar on the Gulf Coast did not scare her away. In fact she was very encouraging. However, I still did not have the cash I needed to initiate my plans, and I knew that there was just no way I could hang around Odessa. My melon was still spinning with the experiences of the previous several years. I needed more of that foreign adrenaline and cash flow. Finally, I made the decision to head back overseas. I told the little blonde lady farewell and promised to call her when I arrived at my destination. Then I bought a one-way ticket with Cathay Pacific Airlines to Singapore. Hell, once I'm in Singapore I can always give Charlie Blackcloud a holler, I thought.

Before I left Texas I had called Scar, who was still in Kuwait. I asked him how things were going there. Surprisingly he told me that California Ken had left the Al-Tameer Project. I was interested to learn why.

"Did he quit?" I asked curiously.

"No, I heard he was run off," Scar said. "Rumor has it that he had refurbished his Penthouse suite at Fintas Towers with white carpeting and white leather living room furniture, which he back-charged to the project. That, coupled with the four or five young males that were sharing his Penthouse suite, was not appreciated by the head honchos of the Kuwait Oil Company. They had him removed from the project."

"Wow!" I exclaimed. "Seriously?"

Scar chuckled. "Yes. Last I heard, he opened up an employment agency in Bangkok and formed a partnership with an associate of his, the CEO of an engineering, procurement, and contracting firm in Thailand," he said. "Other than that, Kuwait was just another shitty job in the Middle East."

What a bunch of chicken shit hypocrites the Kuwaitis are, after all the social atrocities they committed, I thought to myself.

A couple of days after my arrival in Singapore, I decided to fly up to Bangkok and contact California Ken. I would keep Charlie Blackcloud as a back-up. Bangkok's Don Maung Airport terminal looks like a cluster-fuck at first glance, with its thousands of people going every which way, but as you follow the multilingual signs, you quickly realize there is a method to the Thai madness. It helped that I had seen this chaos before.

I checked in at the Nana Hotel around 5:00 p.m. It had taken ninety minutes for the trip from the airport, even though it usually took around thirty minutes. During the mid-1990s, rush hour traffic in Bangkok was horrendous. I showered and headed across Soi Nana and up to the second floor of the Nana Plaza. I grinned when I finally found the bar, Hog's Breath. I eagerly stepped inside the establishment and sat my ass on an empty bar stool. I waited for my eyes to adjust to the dimly lit interior. The place was small, about fifty feet wide and a hundred feet long, and the bar ran the full room length along the left wall as one would walk in. Half way down the right side was a small raised stage with two floor-to-ceiling stainless steel poles. The eight or ten girls renting their bodies each evening would rub up against the poles as they tried to rouse the interest of the male patrons. I waited for the bartender to approach me, and when he did, I leaned in and asked.

"Hey, is Bangkok Bob around?"

The bartender nodded. "He in the back," he said in broken English. "I tell him."

"Thank you," I replied.

Moments later, Bob emerged from the darkness. We both grinned and shook hands when we saw each other. We hadn't seen each other since Kuwait.

"Welcome!" Bob exclaimed. "So glad you were able to find the place, Bubba. How long are you in town for?"

I shrugged."Honestly, I'm not sure Bob," I said. "I'm going to contact California Ken tomorrow. He may know of some job opportunities for me."

"Bubba, you just may have arrived at the perfect time!"Bob said.

He then explained how Ken had been in the Hog's Breath several nights back and he had mentioned that he was looking for ex-pat staff for his Thai affiliate company, Siam Engineering.

Apparently Siam Engineering had recently won several contracts for fabrication works on both the Shell and Caltex refineries that were under construction in Rayong province. Both oil companies demanded ex-pat supervision of all Thai contracting companies. Construction had only recently commenced, and both projects were two years away from completion.

Bob went on to tell me he had recently picked up a construction manager position in Thailand with a company that was based in Baltimore, Maryland. This company had recently signed a fifty million dollar-contract with the Thai Government to build three Cutter Suction Dredgers for Thai harbour maintenance. When Bob was done speaking, I nodded.

"Well, I sure hope you're right about everything, Bob," I told him. "And congratulations on the construction manager gig!"

It's legal for an ex-pat to own a beer bar in Thailand, but it's illegal to work in it. Because of this owners, such as Bangkok Bob, would hire a local as a bar manager and then hang around to watch their cash registers and hope for the best when they were not around. The Thai government will not issue a work permit for a position that a Thai person can fill. For the next few hours, Bob and I sat drinking Singha beer and swapping stories about the Kuwait Fires Project. We also discussed California Ken being run out of Kuwait and spoke a few words of disgust about the result of Don's murder. It ended up being a fun evening and I was glad I had gotten in touch with Bangkok Bob again.

At 10:00 the next morning I called California Ken and we set up an appointment to meet and possibly discuss my future working on a project with him. Two hours later I was sitting in his office in Bangna, an outer Bangkok suburb. California Ken told me that he had been in touch with Bill Bass down in Sumatra, asking him if he knew of any good fabrication shop managers. "Bill mentioned your name, Bubba, and told me he would try to track you down," he said. "Right now I am looking for a fabrication shop manager for a facility down near Pattaya City."

"It's a twelve month contract, with the possibility of extending," California Ken said. "Would you be interested in the position, Bubba?"

I didn't have to think twice about his offer. I assured him I would be and asked him to thank Bill for thinking of me. But as we continued to chat briefly about what the position would entail the recollections of Don's murder suddenly flooded my melon. This was the second time in as many days that Don's memory had surfaced. I realized my head was twisted on that matter, and I wasn't sure what I needed to do to get over it.

I spent the remainder of the day completing the paper-work for a Thai work permit, and soon I had a twelve-month signed contract in my hand. As I was riding in a cab back to the Nana Hotel I recalled a couple of lyrics from a John Denver song, "Some days are diamonds; some days are coal." Today was a diamond.

The following morning I was on my way to view the fabrication shop with the Siam Engineering Manager. He was a short fat Thai with a PhD in mechanical engineering from some university in the state of Virginia. His English was near perfect and he drove a late model black Mercedes Benz sedan; a rich man's car in Thailand. I guess it was considered a rich man's car in West Texas as well. He estimated the journey to the fabrication shop would take approximately an hour-and-a half.

We traveled a highway heading south east out of Bangkok down into the province of Chonburi, where both Pattaya City and the fabrication shop were located. As we drove along the heavily congested road, I was amazed at the number of dead dogs there were. It seemed like we came across a puffed-up stinky dead dog on the shoulder of the roadway every few miles. Confused, I asked my travelling companion why there were so many dead dogs. He casually told me they were orphans and it was their karma. Most Thais are devout Buddhists so I guessed it was a Buddhist answer.

Later I would learn that dogs of all types and sizes roam and fornicate with abundance and die daily by the hundreds in Thailand. Some would die of starvation and being badly flea-bitten, others would simply die of old age. But most of them got hit by cars and were scatted along the streets and highways, victims of unexpected road kill. However, woven into the social fabric of Thai Buddhism and Thai culture is a belief of reincarnation. Those who believe say that dogs are particularly effective in repulsing evil sprits. Because of this belief, dogs are rarely voluntarily killed.

Around noon we were half-way to our destination when PhD suggested we stop for lunch. He pulled the Mercedes Benz into a small parking lot just off the highway in front of an open-deck restaurant. After we were seated he insisted on ordering.

"No problem," I said with a shrug. "Go ahead." Shit, I couldn't read the menu anyhow. The whole fucking thing was in the Thai language.

A little while later several dishes of fish and vegetables were set on the table, and two over sized soup bowels of milky-colored liquid with floating chunks in them were placed in front of us. I picked up a spoon and sipped the liquid from my bowl. It was sour and nasty. Then I glanced over at the Siam Engineering Manager, who was already slurping away at his bowl. I dared to ask him what it was.

He stopped slurping for a moment. "Fish guts soup," he said matter-of-factly with a grin.

Immediately I dry-heaved, realized I was coming across as rude and unappreciative, and tried to cover it up with a phoney cough. There was just no way I could stomach that Thai delicacy.

After our almost choke and puke lunch, we drove another thirty miles and then we turned west off the highway. Soon we were in jungle country, following a twisting, winding, narrow road for ten miles or so. Finally, PhD turned through an open gate in a six-foot-high brick wall that ran for several hundred yards on both sides of the opening. We entered an open yard in front of what looked like an old worn-out factory building.

"This is it!" he announced.

The yard contained stacks of steel plates and pipes and a couple of small mobile cranes.

I learned several days later that a resident of Taiwan owned the facility, and when he was in business in Thailand, the fabrication shop had actually been a condom factory. Siam Engineering, in its Thai wisdom, figured it could convert an old worn-out fuck rubber factory into a steel fabrication shop over night. Guess I was stuck with it. As the saying goes, don't worry about the things you have no control over.

I was issued a company Isuzu pick-up truck. Unfortunately it wasn't much better than those shitty pick-up trucks we had used in Sumatra, but what the heck? It was free, including gas.

That night I rented a hotel room in the heart of Pattaya City on Beach Avenue. My room window on the tenth floor looked out over the sparkling waters of the Gulf of Thailand. At night I could see hundreds of bobbing, flickering lights of small boats as they fished the local waters. It was definitely a refreshing change of scenery from the lights I had seen in Kuwait.

***

Pattaya City is home to approximately seventy thousand permanent residents. On any given day, or night, several thousand tourists roam the streets looking for pleasure. I guess the most surprising sight for me was the amount of very old twisted white men, many incapable of straightening their permanently bent backs, waddling down the sidewalk with a love grip on a beautiful young Thai lady. Some of these guys were in their eighties and nineties; their girlfriends didn't look much older than eighteen.

Seeing them look so happy, I had to smile as I recalled a lyric from a song sung by Jennifer Warnes, "Could it be love, I wonder!" The Thai people have a name for old-men who prey on young women. They call them snake head! Pattaya City was bursting at the seams with snake heads and beer bars, all stocked with a dozen or so ladies renting their bodies. In the midst of the beer bars was an area called "Boys Town," a special place for the male gay folk. A variety of food, both Thai and western, was in abundance, restaurants and street food stalls competed for your pocket full of the local currency, the Thai Baht.

Although Thailand has an emerging middle class society, poverty is still abundant. It is not as severe as Indonesia, but it is sad enough to force thousands of females into selling the only commodity they have. However, there is a confusing contrast. The English language newspaper, the Bangkok Post, in 1992 published in the business section that their research showed that in Thailand, females hold 45 per cent of senior management roles in an assortment of businesses, which is far ahead of the global average of 20 per cent. Seems I am not my sister's keeper in Thailand!

It was a twenty-three-mile drive to get to the fabrication shop, but it was a very picturesque drive through the ever-changing tropical jungle flora. On my trips, I often gazed out at the coconut farms with shops selling the shredded product and pineapple plantations intermingled with palm trees and flowering bougainvillea of multiple colors. However, I couldn't take my eyes off the road for too long. Every couple of miles, off to the left or the right, was a different factory building. Since the area was very rural, no public transport system existed. The hundreds of small motor cycles, being driven by both genders of all ages, travelling to and from the factories, created one hell of a congested highway.

The Thais I was working with told me that none of these motorcyclists were licensed. On a weekly basis I would witness busted-up people and motorcycles; most had accidentally slammed into heavy-duty hauling trucks. The chaos never seemed to end and the highway shit just kept happening. Another problem was the cops. I was regularly stopped for an imagined traffic offence. I would hand the smiling officer a hundred baht bill, about four United States dollars. He'd thank me and tell me to be on my way. This was Thailand. Either way, it beat the hell out of that fucking Middle Eastern desert.

During my second night in Pattaya, I woke myself up with my right hand rubbing the right side of my face. Once I got over being disoriented, I realized I'd just had a bad-ass nightmare about Don getting his melon blown apart. Moments later, my mind would play tricks on me and I would think I smelled vomit, shit, and that indescribable odor of human blood and gray matter. I would have to reach for my Vick's nasal inhaler to clear the stench before trying to sleep again.

The smell brought back memories of a fella I met during my time on an offshore jack-up drilling rig in Nigeria, West Africa. I was working with Homer, an old gray haired crane operator from Kentucky. One night after our shift had finished, Homer and I were sitting on the heli-deck drinking a Coke when he told me about one of his World War II experiences. He told me he had been involved in the invasion of Sicily and then on into Southern Italy. It was during this time that he and a half-dozen other GIs were on night patrol when they encountered a swarm of Germans. He said that suddenly it was every man for himself, and each soldier had to scatter for cover along the farmland terrain. The first building he came across was an out-house. Opening the door, he realized it was a two-holer. He lifted the lid and saw it was full of shit. He had no choice but to lower himself into the human waste up to the middle of his chest, and then lower the lids. He told me he could hear the Germans hollering outside and constant rifle fire. He positioned himself in a corner as far away from the two holes as possible and crouched down to where the shit was up to his chin. Within seconds, the shitter door was flung open and a flashlight was beamed in and down the seat holes. Luckily for Homer, no German soldier did a thorough search of the outhouse. Apparently the stench was too overbearing. Homer told me it had taken all his strength to control the nausea he was experiencing. He said that he had crouched in that crap-loaded hole for eight hours. Finally, when all sounds of war had dissipated he heaved himself out, stumbled out the shitter door, and hit the ground on his knees, throwing up like there was no tomorrow. Homer finished his story by saying, "Bubba, it's been more than forty years since that night, and I still wake up some nights smelling that god-awful shit."

At least once a month I found myself having some kind of a nasty flashback to Kuwait and the shooting. I figured it was most likely post traumatic stress disorder. Sooner or later, I knew I would prob-ably have to do something about it I just wasn't sure what. Still, I desperately hoped I would not suffer the recurring nightmares and accompanying aroma for as many years as old Homer had. After the flashbacks, I often recalled a line from that Crowded House song "Don't Dream It's Over": "You will never see the end of the road while you're travelling with pain".

It took me a couple of months to get the shop up and running. Needless to say, it wasn't easy. Siam Engineering was a poor boy operation. The whole fucking company had way too many chiefs and not enough Indians. Everybody wanted a piece of the pie, and most of the Siam Engineering Bangkok management team seemed to be getting it. Several individuals on the team had put together their own small contractor groups and put them to work on Siam Engineering projects, including the fabrication shop. They just sat back and watched the money roll in. These little contractor groups were milking Siam Engineering, leaving a bare minimum for operational costs. Fortunately, I had two very knowledgeable Thai supervisors. Both of them had overseas working experience in the oil fields of Saudi Arabia, and both had a good handle on the English language.

Terdsak supervised the fabrication work while Sakda assisted me with everything and took care of safety conditions within the shop. Both these guys had known each other since childhood and came from the city of Ubon, province of Ratchathani, which is an area in Thailand often referred to as Isaan. It's located in the north-east of the country, close to the mighty Mekong River, which forms the border between Thailand and the Lao People's Democratic Republic. Without these two men I would have quickly been in deep crap. Slowly they taught me the Thai way of doing things. The steel tanks, pressure vessels, and piping items we fabricated in the jungle shop were transported to the refinery sites in the industrial complex near the city of Maptaput in the south-eastern seaboard province of Rayong, located some forty miles east of Pattaya City.

Some of the fabrication work we were involved with required detailed blueprints for the shop floor fabricators to work from. We had a clever little draftsman in the office. After he had drawn up a bunch of drawings he would roll them up, hop on his motorcycle, and head into Pattaya City, where he would have a half-dozen copies made up. Then he would head back to the shop. One fateful day, as he was crossing a dual-highway in order to get onto the road leading back to the shop, the draftsman only got halfway across when he was smacked by a Mercedes Benz travelling at a very high speed. An elderly Chinese-Thai lady had been driving the Mercedes Benz. Apparently she hadn't seen the draftsman. He was killed instantly and the old lady lived to drive another day. The shock of the death and the reaction of the office crew took a few turns that were all new to me.

A few days after the draftsman's death, several office girls would faint without any warning. Some of the male engineers would piddle in their pants. Confused by their behaviour, I pulled Sakda aside and asked what the hell was going on. He explained to me that in Thai culture, ghosts were a fact of life, and some of the office staff believed the spirit of the little draftsman was floating around the office. We needed to set him free, but only the Buddhist monks could do that.

Nine Buddhist monks arrived at the shop the following day. They all sat in a line joined by clasped hands and a continuous string that went from one monk to the next. Then they chanted for a half-hour in that position. The entire office crew, myself included, all knelt in front of them with clasped hands, too. When the monks finished chanting, we offered them bowls of rice and fruit and also filled their alms bowls with food. After they had eaten a little, the head monk took a bowl of holy water. Then with the other monks, we all followed in a procession through all the offices and the fabrication shop area as he splashed holy water as he walked with a hand-full of straw, sprinkling it everywhere. He was setting the little draftsman's spirit free. After the monks visit, all was well in the shop again and the Thais went back to smiling.

One evening over a few Singha beers, Sakda, a man in his fifties, told me he had grown up on his father's farm. At age nineteen, a Thai-born Chinese land-grabber swindled the family rice-paddy farm away from his father. Early one morning, as the swindler was looking over his latest acquisition, Sakda simply walked up behind him with a loaded 22-caliber revolver and shot him in the back of the head, killing him instantly. The swindler fell to the ground and Sakda just kept walking. As the eldest son, it was his duty to avenge his father and his family to save face from the humiliation of losing their land.

I had been in Pattaya City for several months when I decided to go spend a weekend in the capital city and check in on Bangkok Bob at the Hog's Breath bar. He had told me the dredge construction project was in shambles. Apparently the Baltimore-based company had a signed contract with one shipyard in Bangkok to build the three dredges, but then it went and shopped the project around to other local shipyards, trying for a lower price. The shipyards were in contact with each other, and that's when the Thais went on the warpath.

Bob said that he was used to paying bribes to both the local Bangkok mafia and the police to continue the operation of his bar without any strong-arm problems or police raids using the excuse they were looking for underage girls, but the money going under the table from the Baltimore company to Thai government agents and the shipyards was unbelievable.

"Bubba, these under-the-table payoffs are in the hundreds of thousands of dollars," he said quietly. He also said he didn't know how all the corruption would end up, but he'd sure like to get his hand under the table and grab a fistful of the profits if he could.

During my visit to Bangkok, I visited the Chatuchak Weekend Market. I had never seen anything like it! There were fifty acres and row after row of small stalls selling everything and most anything one could imagine, including wild animals. It was a shopper's paradise and I ended up buying a few souvenirs and clothing items. Back in my hotel room in Pattaya, I decided to empty one of my suitcases of old worn-out shit to make space for my new purchases. I upended the suitcase and a manila envelope landed on top of the pile. I picked it up, realizing it was my statement from Kuwait. I removed it from the envelope and read through it carefully. When I finished reading, something dawned on me and I checked to see if I had a contact address for Don. I was in luck. Not only did I have his Santa Barbara, California, address but also his home telephone number.

I went out for a beer and tried to clear my thoughts. I had never heard a word about Don or his family after his remains were flown out of Kuwait, and I was curious as to what repercussions, if any, had occurred. I certainly had no closure regarding the incident. I wondered how Don's wife was coping with her loss. Three Singha beers later I decided to call Don's home telephone number.

***

After two rings, a woman answered the phone. I asked to speak with Mrs. Johnson. The woman responded that I was speaking with her. I then took a deep breath and explained who I was, and that I had worked with her husband, Don, in Kuwait. I also told her that I had been the driver of the vehicle in which Don was traveling the night he had been shot and killed in Kuwait. When I was done speaking, there was no response from Mrs. Johnson. I waited for what seemed like an eternity for her to speak. When she didn't, I swallowed hard and asked, "Are you still there, Mrs. Johnson?"

Her response rattled me. "Is this a joke?" she demanded. "Or are you just a sicko?"

I was dumbfounded. "Mrs. Johnson, this is no joke," I said slowly. "Don was shot and killed by the Kuwaiti militia as we were leaving a highway check-point one evening on our way home from work. If you want, I can send you a signed copy of my statement which is also signed by a representative of the United States Embassy, Kuwait, an FBI agent, Canham's Kuwait project manager, and a Kuwaiti official."

Don's wife was quiet for a few moments. I assumed she was letting the information sink in. Then she spoke, telling me that she had been informed that her husband had died as a result of a traffic accident one evening while he was returning from work. That was it. There was silence from her again, and then she said, "Yes, please forward a copy of your statement to me. I would very much like to see it."

I told her that I would courier my documentation to her along with my address and contact numbers and for her to hire a good lawyer.

"Mrs. Johnson," I added. "Don was murdered, and you have been lied to. Tell your lawyer I am available for whatever information he may require."

Mrs. Johnson's voice was trembling with emotion as she thanked me for contacting her. There was no doubt in my mind that she was absolutely shattered. I told her to contact me after she had received my documentation if she wished to pursue this injustice. With that I said good bye and hung up the phone.

A god damned traffic accident? I thought. I was pissed off big time. To think Don's wife hadn't been told the truth about her husband's death was immoral. I hoped she would go see a lawyer. Maybe a little payback would help her feel some kind of closure and help me feel a little more at ease with what had happened, too.

***

The more I learned about and tried to understand Thailand, the more I appreciated the uniqueness of Thai culture. During my two years in Sumatra, I had often tried to get inside the heads of the Indonesians I worked with. My conclusion was the most important facet of their being was Islam. I guessed with all the corruption in Indonesia, there wasn't much else. However, in Thailand a man who was most revered: His Majestry King Bhumibol Adulyadej, Rama IX. I had seen the king on television many times before, and he came across the screen as a gentle, intelligent individual. He was a travelling king who regularly visited with citizens across his nation. He even taught them new and productive methods of rice farming and urban development. His affection for his people showed through his actions a rare quality in leadership. The affection in return was bountiful by his followers. He is also the wealthiest monarch on the planet.

The majority of Thais practice the Buddhist faith, except for several southern provinces that border with Malaysia where the majority of the population follow Islam. These folks are raising hell with bullets and bombs in their quest for an independent Islamic state, or to hook up with Islamic Malaysia. But the Thai government is stubborn, and the killing continues. Although gentle by nature, when pushed the Thais can turn nasty, as experienced by an international accounting firm.

Three sugarcane mills owned by one wealthy Thai family were in economic woes. The Thai bankruptcy court appointed an accounting firm to work on a debt-restructuring program for the three mills. The foreign chartered accountant appointed to the restructuring program was apparently getting close to exposing the family of corruption, and he was shot to death while travelling in a minivan to the site of the mills. The shooting occurred as the vehicle slowed at a bend in the road about five hundred meters from one of the mills. An inspection of the murder scene revealed that seven of the eight bullets fired from the nine-millimeter handgun had hit the accountant at fatal points. Four Thais who had also been travelling in the minivan were unhurt in the shooting.

This evidence stunned the police but it also gave them an idea of how skilled the gunman was. At the time of the shooting, he had been riding as a passenger on a motorcycle traveling at an estimated speed of between ten and fifteen miles per hour over an uneven gravel road. The English language Bangkok Post newspaper followed up on the accountant's murder, linking the shooter, who was not apprehended, to either the Thai Military Special Forces or the Thai Police SWAT team. Both are trained to stand on a moving motorcycle and destroy a target. Later, several family members of the mill owners were charged with conspiracy to commit murder.

***

On most Sundays I liked to do a little sightseeing and people-watching around Pattaya, especially at the beaches. It was interesting to see the young Thai women from the affluent families go swimming in their very modest bathing suits. They'd almost be covered from their necks to their knees. It was contrasted notably from the skimpy outfits worn by their bar-girl sisters and the majority of female tourists, most of whom were topless. What was almost repugnantly indecent, however, was seeing the hundreds of middle-aged Russian women, almost every one of them grossly overweight and topless lounging at the beach while their saggy baggy tits bounced on top of their protruding bellies.

One Sunday I noticed that a bunch of marines and sailors were wandering the streets, and several United States navy ships were at anchor in the Gulf of Thailand, which splashes the beaches of Pattaya. During the second quarter of each year, the United States and the Thai military hold war games known as "Cobra Gold". I assumed that's why all the Marines and sailors were present.

On this particular Sunday, I stopped by a McDonald's restaurant for a hamburger lunch. After waiting approximately fifteen minutes to place my order, I was finally served and took my meal to a small table to eat in peace.

As I was eating, I noticed a blonde in her mid-thirties who was standing in line, waiting to order food. Suddenly, a dark-skinned-Arabic looking guy grabbed her ass. She turned and confronted him and he raised his hands as though to apologize or say he hadn't done it. As soon as she turned back around he grabbed her ass again.

Instantly, two solidly built United States Marines had the guy by an arm apiece, and they half-dragged half-carried the assbag to the front doors, which were already being held wide open by two of their fellow Marines. The jerk-off was dressed in t-shirt and knee-length baggy shorts, the two Marines who were holding the ass-grabber literally threw him into the street with such force that he skidded across the concrete sidewalk on exposed knees, finally falling on his face, when he stood up blood was dripping down his knees. Completely embarrassed, and no match for the Marines, he skulked off.

I started to laugh and almost choked. The two marines who had tossed him out went over to the blonde lady and I could hear them tell her, "Don't worry about those low life sub-humans sunshine; as long as we are in town we will protect you." After the shit in Kuwait I felt the incident gratifying.

Early one morning, Sakda came into my office at the fabrication shop and asked me if I knew a Canadian man named Mr. Luke. Luke was working for Siam Engineering on the refinery project in Rayong. I told him I did know him. I had first met Luke in Kuwait. His ass was always seated in Canham's main office in Ahmadi. I was never sure what his position was, but I had heard he was a good buddy of California Ken. They had both worked together on a project in Indonesia.

I had once overheard Luke mouthing off in the mess hall in Kuwait about how he and another buddy of California Ken's had been given the task of going to Jakarta and Bangkok to assist with the hiring of two thousand personnel through PT. Petrochem in Indonesia and two thousand Thais through Siam Engineering in Thailand for the Al-Awda Project. All he and the other guy had really done was party for the two months they were out of Kuwait. I often wondered how much the kickback was from PT. Petrochem and Siam Engineering to California Ken from his old CIA pals for using their respective companies for the lucrative contracts of supplying four thousand bodies for the project, not to mention another two thousand workers from the Philippines.

Once a month, all Siam Engineering managers would attend a meeting at some fancy hotel in Pattaya City. After the meeting, Siam Engineering would wine and dine us. It was at one of these functions where I had bumped into Luke for the first time since Kuwait. He had told me he was an area manager on the Caltex refinery project and was having one fuck of a time getting the Thai workers to do things the right way, – his way.

I was curious to know what Sakda had to say about the guy. "What happened to Luke?" I asked, thinking there may have been an accident of some kind.

"This morning California Ken and Siam Engineering Manager take Mr. Luke from the project," Sakda replied in his style of broken English.

"Why did they do that?" I asked.

Sakda told me Luke continuously pranced around his area screaming, shouting, and waving his hands in the air, cussing out the Thais and calling them bad names. The workers had lost face, a huge cultural insult. Apparently the previous evening the Siam Engineering manager had received an anonymous telephone call, advising him Luke would be killed on the job the next day. He was "a bad man for Thai people." The Siam Engineering manager wisely took the threat seriously and Luke was removed from the project for his own safety.

During the mid 1990s, numerous projects within the petrochemical industry were under construction within the Maptaput Industrial Estate of Rayong province, including the two refinery projects Siam Engineering was involved with. Many of the Japanese, Korean, and American companies that had existing petroleum facilities were expanding. One Korean outfit had imported its own supervisors from Korea for its expansion program.

It is general knowledge within the international oil patch construction industry that Koreans have a terrible reputation for abusing their subordinates. One such supervisor made the mistake of slapping several faces that belonged to a couple of his Thai underlings. The Korean went missing. His pick-up truck was discovered several hundred miles to the east of Maptaput. It had been parked in the grounds of a Buddhist temple near the Cambodian border. The unfortunate, but stupid, Korean was discovered in a roadside ditch not far from his project site. He had been shot at close range right through his head.

Police investigations learned the Thai workers on the Korean project site had pooled their wages and hired a local police officer to whack the Korean. The cop was arrested and is doing time in the monkey house, as Thais refer to a prison. It is said he will most likely receive a royal pardon in the not too distant future.

Many prisoners are released on the King's birthday each year, and the cop had taken revenge for Thai people who were being abused by a foreigner. This murder had occurred several months before Luke had been removed from his post. He was one lucky son-of-a-bitch.

***

At 2:00 a.m., the telephone beside my bed rang like the chimes of Big Ben. This was the third night in a row I had been woken up by the telephone ringing at some ungodly hour. The previous two nights, it had been a drunken assbag calling my room number by mistake. I picked up the receiver and hollered into the mouthpiece.

"Do you know what god damned time it is?" When I heard the response, however, I sat up, wide-awake.

"Excuse me sir," an American-accented female voice began. This is the office of Weinstein and Weinstein, Attorneys at Law, in Santa Barbara, California. We are trying to contact a Mr. Bubba Cottonmill."

"You got him," I answered. "And I apologize for cussing."

"Sorry about the time, Mr. Cottonmill. We weren't sure what time it is there," the woman continued. "Mr. Jacob Weinstein would like to speak with you."

"Put him on," I answered.

"Mr. Cottonmill, I am Jacob Weinstein," he said. "My law firm is representing Mrs. Donna Johnson, the widow of Mr. Donald Johnson. Mrs Johnson has advised me that you had spoken to her and forwarded documentation in reference to the demise of her late husband."

"That is correct," I replied, wondering what the lawyer had to say. I knew it would be something about Don.

Finally, it seems that Don will get the justice he deserves, I thought excitedly. "Not a problem!" I told him.

"Thank you, Mr. Cottonmill." Jacob said. "Also, would it be possible for you to come to Santa Barbara?"

"Yes," I replied. "But I'm not sure how soon with work."

Then he mentioned something that had crossed my mind but I hadn't bothered to pursue.

"Mr. Cottonmill, additionally, my colleges and I would like to discuss possible avenues for you regarding the incident that occurred in Kuwait," Jacob added. "We believe that you have probable cause for punitive damages with regard to mental duress and or delayed stress syndrome."

I responded by telling him I would gladly discuss the matter at a more appropriate time. He asked me to contact his office when I had a schedule; his office would handle all arrangements.

With that, I said thank you, we both hung up the phone, and I tried to fall back asleep. However, with news like that, it was easier said than done.

The fabrication shop was humming along and it was nice to know that we were beating our work schedule. It was Friday. I wanted to go see Bangkok Bob and lay the shit on him about what I'd gotten myself into regarding the whole Kuwait mess. I checked into the Nana Hotel around one p.m. and decided to rest for a couple of hours before walking across Soi Nana to the Hog's Breath. To pass the time I picked up the latest edition of the Bangkok Post newspaper.

One of the headlines brought back memories of Dan, the Special Forces man I had worked with in Sumatra. It read, 'Discovery of Agent Orange Dump Haunts Thailand.' The article went on to read, "It is the infamy of Thailand's involvement in the Vietnam War that is coming back to haunt the country. Workers upgrading a runway at an airport in Hua Hin, 60 miles south of Bangkok, became ill after uncovering a dozen barrels of the chemical identified as the deadly Agent Orange, the herbicide used by the U.S. Air Force against Vietnamese troops. Also, local villagers living near Hua Hin had complained about their water buffalo becoming ill and dropping dead after drinking water from local streams, and many of the village children had higher cancer rates than the rest of the country. Some of the barrels had corroded and the chemical had leached into the water table.

The U.S. Embassy in Bangkok at first denied it was Agent Orange but later admitted that carcinogenic chemicals had been tested on the local flora near a Thai military base not far from Hua Hin and the U.S. military had indeed tested Agent Orange in Thailand in the early 1960s with the full knowledge of Thai authorities. This was according to a United States Embassy spokesman citing declassified CIA reports in Bangkok two months after the discovery was made.

I wondered how Dan would feel if he knew Vietnam wasn't the only country suffering from what he had called chemical warfare.

When I strolled into the Hog's Breath, Bangkok Bob was sitting at his usual personal corner table. That's where he had the controls for the bar music and television. He had his hand wrapped around a can of Singha beer.

"What's new, Bubba?" he asked.

One of the bar-girls approached me as soon as I sat down next Bob. I ordered a beer and then I handed Bob a copy of my Kuwait statement. "Bob, this shit has been twisting my melon ever since it happened," I said. As he began to read it over, I told him in detail about my conversations with Don's wife and her lawyer.

When he finished reading the statement, he took a large swallow from his beer can and looked me directly in the eyes.

"Bubba, I think you may have opened up the proverbial Pandora's box," he sighed. "You do know that this means California Ken will be involved. He's one of the signatories on your statement. "

"I know," I said quietly. "I don't know how this will all shake out, but I do know I owe it to Don to let the truth, the real truth, be told."

"Bubba, I have known Ken for many years, and I know other folk who have known him a lifetime. They all say the same thing," Bob said. "On the surface, he's fine, but cross him, and he can be very nasty." His eyes widened as he spoke.

"Meaning what exactly?" I asked.

Bob sighed, "Just watch your back, Bubba," he said. "And I hope the outcome of this takes those twists out of your melon." With that he handed back my statement to me.

I already knew that Ken was a cold-hearted bastard after the shit that went down in Kuwait. Oh well, I thought. Let the chips fall where they may. I ordered another beer when the bar-girl approached again.

Bob changed the subject. "This dredger project has gone from bad to worse," he said. "The Thais are ready to do a number on this chicken dick from Baltimore, but I think there may be a possibility where you and I can walk away with a wheel-barrow full of cash."

Naturally, I was intrigued. "Oh, really?" I asked

Bob nodded. "Yea. Just try to hang in for as long as you can with Siam Engineering," he said. "What I am trying to organize may take a month or so."

I told him that I still had five months left on my original twelve-month contract and that I was going to take a week or ten days off and fly to Santa Barbara, California, to go talk with Don's wife's lawyers.

After returning to Pattaya City from my weekend in Bangkok, I contacted Weinstein and Weinstein and told them of my arrival and departure dates into the United States. My twelve-month contract with Siam Engineering stated I was due a two-week paid vacation at its completion, and one week could be taken after six months of service. I organized the dates to coincide with the Thai New Year, which falls in mid April. "Happy New Year" as the Thais call it, is actually celebrated on three different dates in Thailand: our Western New Year (January 1), the Chinese New Year (either at the end of January or the beginning of February), and Thailand's official New Year, known as Songkran on April 13, which is the equivalent of Thanksgiving and Christmas rolled up into one. It is the most important holiday of the calendar year in Thailand, and it officially lasts four days. In fact, people working away from home all over Thailand travel hundreds of miles to be with their loved ones for Songkran and they stretch the holiday anywhere from seven to ten days. That gave me heaps of time for my trip. I telephoned the little blonde lady in Odessa, and told her about my plans to go to Santa Barbara, and asked if she could meet me in Los Angeles.

My Cathay Pacific flight arrived into the Los Angeles International Airport at 7:30 on a beautiful sunny morning. After passing through Customs and Immigration, I headed to the car rental booth and chose a dark green ML-350 Mercedes Benz SUV. Weinstein and Weinstein was picking up the tab, so I thought 'to hell with it! I'm going first class.' The little blonde lady was arriving from Texas at 10:30 a.m. I rented one of the self-contained, hourly-rental, airport refreshment rooms. I shaved, showered and put on fresh clothes. At the airport hotel reservation counter I managed to reserve a suite at the West Beach Inn in Santa Barbara. The reservation clerk told me the hotel was located across from the beach on West Cabrillo Boulevard, and only three blocks from downtown State Street. This was the location of the Weinstein and Weinstein law office.

I was waiting in the domestic terminal and my tired jet-lagged eyes lit up like neon lights as the blonde lady walked through the arrival doors and into my arms and put a lip-lock on me I would never forget. During the hour and a half drive to Santa Barbara I explained why I was in California, but leaving out the gruesome details of Don's tragic death.

At 10:00 the next morning I walked into Weinstein and Weinstein's law office as prearranged. The expensively furnished office was located on the twenty-first floor of a steel and glass high-rise with a magnificent view of the Pacific Ocean. It was obvious that this was no "Cheap Charlie" outfit. I approached the receptionist, who politely escorted me into a lavishly furnished office with thick carpeting, a huge mahogany desk, and several oversized brown leather chairs around the room. There was also a brown leather U-shaped couch that faced the desk. The walls were highly polished walnut. To complete the aesthetics, a half-dozen framed degrees hung on the walls. I sat down in one of the chairs and waited for Jacob to enter the room.

Moments later he appeared with a well-dressed woman whom I guessed was in her early fifties. Jacob first introduced himself and then he turned to the woman and introduced her.

"Mrs. Donna Johnson, this is Mr. Bubba Cottonmill," he said with a kind smile.

Instinctively I stood up, took several steps towards Don's wife, and hugged her. "I'm truly sorry about Don," I said quietly.

We sat down after we were all formally introduced. Jacob then opened a file that was already on his large desk. Before he spoke I asked that both of them call me Bubba. Mrs. Johnson then added that she would prefer to be called Donna. Jacob nodded at both of us and then proceeded.

"The reason Donna is here, Bubba, is twofold: first to meet you, and second to confirm to you that it is her wish to pursue, through the avenues of the law, compensation relating to the untimely death of her husband, Don."

"Fine," I said. "What is it you want me to do?"

Jacob continued. "We have set up a hearing with the grand jury next month. Since you will be returning to your residence in Thailand before the hearing, we will require a video-taped statement concerning the events in Kuwait that resulted in the death of Don," he said. "If you are in agreement with this, we will arrange for your statement to be taken here in this office, after lunch today."

I nodded. "That's not a problem," I replied. "That was my reason for coming." I glanced over at Donna, who looked relieved by my willingness to cooperate.

"Thank you," she whispered.

Jacob then went on to explain that since several federal government departments were involved, along with the State of California, the state of registration of the Kuwaiti project management company, he had hired a lawyer in Washington, D.C. to assist with the case. "All applicable documentation had been received, and there is clear evidence of a cover-up regarding the shooting death of Donald Johnson," he said matter-of-factly. He continued to ramble on about the legalities for another twenty minutes or so. When he was done explaining our general game plan, he then stood up and asked if we would join him for lunch in the roof-top revolving restaurant on the thirtieth floor. It sounded intriguing. Donna and I both agreed.

The view of the ocean and the lunch itself complimented each other nicely. Our conversations were mostly relaxed. I talked about Kuwait, my days working with Don, and about our experiences supporting the firefighters. Donna asked several questions about her late husband, about his last days, his last hours, his last minutes. I told her what I could but tried to spare her the goriest of details. I also reiterated to her that Don had been a good, solid, dependable man. When lunch was over and we said our good-byes, I told Donna I'd stay in touch. She thanked me again for all I was doing.

After lunch, Jacob and I returned to his office. Several video cameras and bright lights had already been set up. Efficient, I thought, impressed by how quickly the team moved. I signed an affidavit confirming my statement was true and correct. Then I told Jacob that one of the signatures on my original statement, California Ken, just so happened to be my current boss.

He looked slightly concerned by the news. "Well, that may have some consequences regarding your employment since that individual will be subpoenaed to appear in front of the grand jury," he said. "So please keep me informed of any repercussions."

"Okay, I will," I said with a nod. With that I sat in a chair in front of the cameras and began my story. I told it from the day I met Don in London, and then I spoke about our days in Dubai, and how we arrived in Kuwait. I walked through the horrors of the fires, the unexploded ordinance, the booby-traps, and I spoke about the efforts and frustrations both Don and I had in setting up our support facilities. I finished with that fateful evening and the investigation the following day. By the time I got through speaking about the details of what ultimately had happened to Don a couple of tears had left their tracks down my cheeks. I couldn't control my emotions, I still had a lot of anger and sadness pent up inside.

Jacob thanked me for the videotaped statement and then asked his assistants to leave, except for one stenographer. She would keep a record of our conversation. Then he turned to me. "Bubba, you have grounds for punitive damages. Weinstein and Weinstein would like to represent you and file on your behalf," he said. He added that both my case and the Johnson case would be filed simultaneously if I wished to proceed. Donna had already agreed to this arrangement.

"That works for me," I nodded.

An agreement between Weinstein and Weinstein and Bubba Cottonmill was already written up and required only a signature. It was a one-page document that basically stated Weinstein and Weinstein would be the sole representative of Bubba Cottonmill.

Whatever monies that may be court-awarded would be shared equally between the said parties. I signed, and then asked Jacob what kind of a dollar figure he had in mind. He told me the actual amount had not been calculated, but if an award was granted, he expected four to six million dollars. As for Donna and her two children, he expected that they would receive an award in the double-digit millions. After that we said our farewells and Jacob reminded me to courier my expenses along with a bank account number and location so that I could be reimbursed for all my expenses, and to have a safe journey back to Thailand.

I stayed one more night in Santa Barbara with the little blonde lady from Odessa. I was more than happy that she was there to take care of me. That night I had gotten falling down drunk and blubbered on about the whole Kuwait shit. She was a good listener. The following day we drove the ninety-odd miles down to Los Angeles. We did the tourist gig, Disneyland, Rodeo Drive, a few movie studios, and then it was time to say adios.

I had a six-hour wait before my flight back to Bangkok and decided to visit with an old friend I knew was being cared for at a prosthetics facility in Long Beach. An hour later I was sitting with Gerry, drinking coffee and shooting the shit like old times. It was good to see that he had gained a little weight since I last visited with him in the London hospital. He also had more color in his face. He looked good, considering his unfortunate circumstances, and was even slowly learning to walk on his new legs. I told him what I was up to and he wished me well with what was about to happen. However, he also reiterated what Bangkok Bob had said about California Ken; in his mind, he was an unsavory character. He added that California Ken never called him once since the shit in Kuwait. We reminisced a bit about Sumatra and Kuwait. We were both carrying scars. The difference was that his were physical; mine were emotional. Finally it was time to leave. I hugged my friend and promised to stay in touch, and then I headed back to Los Angeles International Airport.

On the boring twenty-hour flight back to Bangkok by way of Osaka, Japan, I started thinking about how important that little blonde lady from Odessa was in my life. I was going to have to do something about that before it was too late. It also crossed my mind that there could be a little cash headed my way or maybe a lot of cash. Perhaps that Gulf Coast bar would become a reality, after all. The trouble was that I was well aware that court cases can sometimes go on for years. It may never amount to a hill of beans.

CHAPTER 12

I still had a couple of vacation days left so I checked into the Nana Hotel and visited with Bangkok Bob at the Hog's Breath again. I wanted to bring him up to speed regarding the pending court case. Bob wished me well, and then said that his dredger project was almost in enough shit to where he could, and would, within another couple of weeks, make his boss an offer to take the pipelines and pontoons, which were part of each dredger, under his control and have them fabricated in Thailand. Doing so would save the project several millions of dollars.

"It's all a matter of timing now," he shrugged.

Back at the fabrication shop, it was nice to see that no Thais were missing. They had all made it back safely from Songkran. We were in the hottest and driest season of the Thai year. In another six to eight weeks the rain would start pouring down. The wet season brings with it some of the wildest electrical storms imaginable. In fact, many golfers wound up as crispy critters after having ignored the dangers of the deadly lightning to stay on the golf course just a little bit longer, chasing that eighteenth hole.

One afternoon, a couple of months after my return from Santa Barbara, I was sitting in the fabrication shop office with the door closed going through a stack of invoices. I was ten months into my contract. Suddenly the office door was flung open with such force that it crashed against the wall. The crashing sound startled me so badly I almost shit my britches.

California Ken stormed in, carrying a plastic bottle of water. He sat his ass down in a chair in front of my desk and glared at me.

"Who the fuck do you think you are Bubba Cottonmill?" he demanded. "You're a fucking nobody! You're just a fucking peon. You have kicked a hornet's nest, and I will see to it that you get stung!"

Based on the lawsuit, part of me knew that this encounter was going to happen one day. I just wasn't sure when.

"And a good afternoon to you, too," I replied. "Just calm down. What the hell are you talking about, anyway?" I had a pretty good idea but I wasn't letting on.

"Don't play dumb with me, Bubba!" California Ken hissed. "You are involved in a court case regarding Don Johnson's death in Kuwait and I have just been subpoenaed!"

I shrugged. "Why don't you call it what it was Ken?" I asked. Then I leaned forward in my chair. "It was fucking murder."

To my surprise, he didn't respond about Don or what happened in Kuwait. Instead he stood up and took a deep breath.

"Cottonmill, Siam Engineering management has informed me your services are no longer required. The company feels the Thais can handle most of the shop work, and we have another long-time ex-pat employee who will stop by from time to time to check on everything," he said dryly. "Your contract will be paid out for the next two months, along with other monies owing. You are required to turn your pick-up truck into the Siam Bangkok office tomorrow, and at 1:00 p.m. you will be taken to the Immigration Department with your passport where your work visa will be cancelled. If you fail to show up, the matter will be turned over to the Thai police and Immigration."

Clearly California Ken was pissed big time. He unscrewed the top from his water bottle and lifted the bottle his mouth. He was shaking so much he almost missed his mouth altogether. He immediately wiped the backwash from his chin and headed for the door.

I stood up. I wasn't going to let him have the last word, not this time. "Hey Ken!" I hollered. California Ken stopped at the doorway and looked in my direction, waiting. I continued. "There's something I've been meaning to tell you for a long time: go fuck yourself!"

His face turned crimson. He looked at me for a moment, opened his mouth to speak, and then closed it without saying another word. With that, he was gone.

I sat back down and tried to get control of my nerves. Bangkok Bob had been correct, I thought. California Ken certainly can be a nasty little shit when he wants to be. I had no doubts he had run me off because of the lawsuit. I remembered a saying those old West Texas oil-drilling wildcatters used to have, "The greatest risk is not taking one." Well, apparently I had taken one.

Once I was officially through with Siam Engineering, I would forward a copy of the termination documentation to Weinstein and Weinstein. I didn't expect much to happen; United States laws had no authority in Thailand. Although, I figured what had just gone down was considered wrongful dismissal.

I rounded up Sakda and Terdsak and explained the situation to them. I told them the reason why I had been fired and the shop was now in their hands. They both told me they were sorry I was leaving. I went on to explain to them that I may have a deal with another fabrication project in the near future, and I wondered if they'd be interested in hooking up with me again. If Bangkok Bob came through with a deal, these two guys would be tremendous assets.

They both agreed they would come and work with me again any time. With that I wrote down Sakda's Bangkok address and telephone number.

"Sakda, you stay in touch with Terdsak," I said. "If I need you guys, I will contact Sakda and he will contact you, Terdsak." They both agreed with the plan and we said our farewells.

The following day, I checked out of my room in Pattaya City and drove the hour-and-a-half to the Nana Hotel in Bangkok. After I checked in, I headed to the Siam Engineering headquarters. It was all over by 3:30 p.m. Monies owed were to be paid into my account within several days and my work permit was cancelled. I was issued a three-week tourist visa. I climbed into one of those three-wheeled Tuk-Tuks that Bangkok is famous for and headed back to the Nana Hotel. Overall, the termination had been relatively painless.

I wondered how Bangkok Bob's deal was developing. That evening I visited the Hog's Breath and laid out the events to Bob as they had occurred. "It is what is," I said, taking a sip of my beer. "I knew the shit would hit the fan when I told Weinstein and Weinstein I wanted to move forward with the court case."

"Sorry you got fucked over, Bubba, but I am not surprised," Bob replied. "But fuck 'em. Hang around Bangkok for the next week or so because the dredger project is coming our way. The Thais have twisted the nuts of that little assbag from Baltimore, and he is almost ready to see things my way."

***

I called the little blonde lady in Odessa and told her I would probably be on my way home soon. However, there was just one more lead I had to follow up on. After that I spent the best part of a week just relaxing and enjoying myself. One afternoon Bangkok Bob called my hotel room and asked me to meet him at Tony Roma's rib restaurant on Sukhumvit Road for dinner that evening. I told him I would be there at 7:00 sharp. The restaurant was only a couple of minutes walk from the Hog's Breath and the Nana Hotel.

We sat down and each ordered a full rack of baby back ribs. It seemed like Bob wanted to get right down to business.

"Bubba, the dredger pipelines and pontoon fabrication project is ours, providing we can come up with facilities to build them in. The contract includes the supply of sixty pontoons per dredge for a total of 180 pontoons," he said, leaning in. I could tell he was excited about the project. "Just regular type pontoons to support the floating quarter mile long, thirty inch diameter discharge pipeline that is flanged to the tail end of each dredge. That's a total of three quarters of a mile of pipeline required."

Okay..." I said, trying to follow him.

"Anyhow Bubba," Bob continued. "Because of the bullshit the chicken dick in Baltimore pulled, the Thais have ganged up with each other. No one will build the pontoons and pipelines for less than twelve million dollars," he said. "Anyway, I crunched some numbers and spoke with some contacts around town regarding material costs, and I believe these items can be purchased and manufactured here in Thailand for around five million dollars for material, plus the cost of the fabrication facilities and cash under the table for greasing the cogs, if you know what I mean."

"So what's the deal, Bob?" I asked.

Bob took a deep breath. "Well, you know the operation of fabrication facilities. If we could lease a joint, you man it and run it, I will secure the material and welding consumables, and we can both walk away with a shit-load of cash," he said. Then he added. "Enough for that Texas Gulf coast bar you keep talking about."

He finished by saying that he believed he could swing a deal for eight-and-half-million dollars. "It's a savings of three-and-a-half million dollars for chicken dick in Baltimore."

"Bubba, if we work this right, we should be able to split at least one-and-a-half plus million. What do you say?"

Suddenly, something dawned on me. When I had been living in Pattaya City, I had a few beers one evening with a little Australian guy who told me about a fully equipped fabrication shop that was owned by a wealthy Thai pal of his. It had been sitting idle for one hell of long time. He said if I ever heard of any work for that facility to let him know. I told Bob that I liked his idea so far, and that I potentially knew of a place we could use, too. I just had to make a call.

Later that evening I hunted through my business card binder and found the Australian guy's card. I quickly called him up to ask if the facility was still available.

"Too bloody right mate," he said. "It is sitting vacant, just waiting for work."

I arranged for the Aussie to introduce me to the owner of the facility with the intention of requesting a four-to-six month lease.

I had another meeting with Bangkok Bob the following day and explained that there was no problem obtaining the fabrication facility that was located sixty miles south of Bangkok just off the Bangkok to Pattaya Highway near the village of Bang Saray. We could lease it for as long as necessary, three months, six months, or nine months, whatever we wanted. Bob figured we would need twenty thousand dollars to grease the cogs and get the ball rolling.

The next day, we put ten thousand dollars apiece into an operating account under both of our signatures. Bob asked me for a shopping list of equipment and welding consumables, and through his Thai contacts he would organize the purchase and delivery as soon as I had a signed lease. He also told me his boss and other engineering personnel from the Baltimore office, along with the Thai government agents, would want to inspect the facilities to ensure we were competent and capable of fabricating for their project. We signed a lease with three-month increments, that way our asses were covered if time became a problem.

I decided to contact Charlie Blackcloud in Sumatra to find out if he was interested in our little adventure. After discussions with Bob, who knew Charlie from the Al-Awda project, I would offer Charlie five hundred thousand dollars for a six-month deal. If we needed him for a longer period of time, we would negotiate. During one of our conversations, Bob and I discussed the possibility of operating the facilities twenty-four hours for maybe six days per week. Basically we would try for a quick killing. If we could orchestrate that I would need Charlie's assistance to cover the hours. I also contacted Sakda and Terdsak, guaranteeing them a six month contract and doubling their Siam Engineering salaries irrespective of completion date and an extension if we went past the six months. I was happy when they accepted their offers immediately.

Leases were signed for the facility, one five-ton crane, one ten-ton crane, and two Toyota pick-up trucks, one for me and one for Blackcloud. Additionally, a small amount of welding equipment and welding consumables were delivered. The steel for building the pontoons and the forty-foot lengths of pipe, along with the connecting ends that would have to be welded onto each end of the pipe, would be delivered once we had permission to proceed. Charlie was locked and loaded and on his way to Thailand; Sakda and Terdsak were already on site. Terdsak said that he would bring in his crew of workers when we were ready to fire up.

I had arranged with the fabrication facility owner to sponsor both Blackcloud and I for twelve-month work visas. The wealthy in Thailand, as with the wealthy in most countries, are very well-connected with government officials. Work permits in Thailand were a simple formality whenever a handful of cash was offered under the table. It was time for the official visit.

Bangkok Bob, along with his three-man Baltimore entourage and four Thai government agents, arrived in their tailor-made suits and ties around 3:00 in the afternoon. Bob's group travelled in a hotel-provided Volvo, while the government men arrived in a BMW 3231A sedan, which was owned by their second in command. I had seen the same model on a showroom floor in Bangkok with a price tag of two million baht, a pile of loot for a government employee. I guessed that tax-free cash under the table was being put to use.

After formal introductions, the Thai government agents informed me they were officially known as the "Dredger Committee." The committee had total responsibility for acceptance or rejection of equipment, and it would approve all payments once the fabricated items were delivered and accepted. I couldn't help but notice the Thai committee guys were all wearing real Rolex watches, not the cheap copies that were abundant in the streets of Bangkok. Not only were they wearing genuine Rolexes, each man was also sporting a large sparkling diamond ring; these guys were living the high life.

Bob took me aside and told me he had to return to Bangkok with his Baltimore bunch to tie up a few loose ends. He also told me that I would have to invite the committee to an evening of wine, women, and karaoke. It was part of their custom, and I wasn't allowed to do it cheap. I understood what Bob was saying; we had a lot riding on their approval. Although the committee members all spoke fluent English, I decided to ask Sakda and Terdsak to join us for an evening of profit and pleasure.

After initial inspection and a walk around the shop, coupled with a half-hour sit-down meeting, the committee agreed that there were no problems with our facilities. I knew they wouldn't have any problems even before they arrived. On a scale of one to ten our shop was a high eight. The Siam Engineering fuck rubber shop where I had last worked was a low two. With that I invited the committee members to wine and dine. They didn't require any persuasion; they actually told me of the ideal location in Bangkok where they wanted to go. That was completely fine with me. We arranged to meet at 7:00 that evening and Sakda said he knew the location of the establishment the committee had named.

***

The Plaza turned out to be a high-rise building of twenty floors. The first three floors were used for parking the BMWs, Mercedes

Benzes, and the odd Volvo. The fourth floor was a combination of several bars and restaurants that occupied two-thirds of the floor. The remaining floor space was a brightly illuminated glass-enclosed room that was filled with young Thai females in their late teens and early twenties. Each one wore an evening gown. The Dredger Committee members appeared as if they felt right at home the moment we entered the building.

The ladies were seated in a semi-circle on a carpet-covered terraced arrangement. Attached to their gowns, in the vicinity of their left breast, was a round white plastic badge with a black number. Several Thai men dressed in ill-fitting cheap suits were wandering among the patrons, which were all male, asking excitedly.

"Which number you like?"

If a customer desired a particular female, all he had to do was tell the waiter the number that was pinned to the young woman. The waiter, in turn, would advise one of the ill-fitting suits who would fulfill the customer's order and then have that woman join the customer at his table shortly after.

The committee members had arranged for a private room on the sixteenth floor. In reality, it was a large condominium that contained five bedrooms, a dining room that could seat a dozen guests, and a television set for karaoke. It was also hooked up to a closed circuit television that was on a continuous pan of the ladies who were seated in the glass-enclosed room. Adjacent to the dining area was a large bubbling hot tub. Several minutes after we were seated in the dining room the alcohol, Thai food, and Thai ladies arrived

This appeared to be developing into an orgy. These turkeys have obviously done this before, I thought to myself, taking in my surroundings. And this is going to cost big bucks.

Sakda was seated beside me at the table, and within seconds, his arm was around a young beauty, as was Terdsak's. These guys were not wasting time! I glanced over at the chairman of the committee, who was clearly enjoying himself just as much. When he saw me look at him, he leaned in and asked,

"Mr. Bubba, what is your spec?"

"My spec?" I asked, a little confused.

"Yes," he said, nodding. "Big tits, little tits, black skin, brown skin, white skin, fat, skinny, tall, short it's all here. Whatever is your specification, it's here."

I thanked him and told him I would have to think about it a little more.

Across the table from me, two other committee members were loudly discussing the ladies by number. Judging by their conversation, this was not their first visit to The Plaza either. I overheard one of them say, "Number eleven gives good service, but she smokes ganja. Number-twenty two is no good; she no suckie dickie." It was a matter-of-fact-style conversation, the Thai way. Sexist as it sounded, this was an establishment of business, and sexual performance by the seller, in an over-populated industry as it is in Thailand, is important to the buyer.

The party lasted until midnight. The bedrooms had been used and so had the girls; the food had been eaten; the booze had been drunk and was all gone; more karaoke songs than I ever wanted to hear had been sung. There wasn't much left to do but pay the bill and retire for the rest of the night. The total cost for the evening was twenty-five hundred dollars. Admittedly, I thought it would be more.

That crazy party was worth it in the end, though. The following week, Bangkok Bob had a signed and approved contract for eight-and-a-half million dollars. The contract payment schedule included one kick-off payment of two-and-a-half million dollars, two progress payments of two-and-a-half million dollars each, and one final payment of one million dollars to be paid after full acceptance and sign-off by the Dredger Committee. We were officially in business.

The kick-off payment was fulfilled and the material for the pontoons arrived along with Terdsak's crew. Charlie Blackcloud was on-board, the sun was shining, and we were making hay. We decided to work a month on the pontoons, and then have the lengths of pipe delivered. After that we would commence welding on the end connectors.

As the project progressed, both Charlie and I would drive to Bangkok each Saturday evening, check-in at the Nana Hotel, walk across to the Hog's Breath and deliver a package of invoices to Bangkok Bob, who in turn would submit them to the Dredger Committee the following week for sign-off and reimbursement. For once, everything was going exactly as planned.

CHAPTER 13

I received correspondence from Weinstein and Weinstein. The grand jury was to convene within a month, and the State of California was contemplating criminal negligence charges against California Ken. As the representative of his employer, he had approved the distribution of false information regarding the incorrect cause of Don's death. Even though the Kuwaiti authorities had issued a death certificate stating the cause of death as a traffic accident, this was being considered as a collusion of deceit.

After the information sunk in, I figured I had better start looking over my shoulder. I was in Thailand, after all, where assassinations are a common occurrence, be they political or personal. I knew that California Ken was well connected. In fact, I had heard his current gay lover was from the seedier side of the Bangkok sex trade industry. I had a meeting with Blackcloud, Terdsak, and Sakda to explain the information I had received and to get their take on it. Sakda insisted he would obtain a handgun for me to carry, just in case the shit hit the fan. Blackcloud figured California Ken wouldn't be stupid enough to pull any shit. Then he added,

"But you never know about those dickie-licking bastards."

A couple of days later, Sakda handed me a loaded nine-millimeter Glock-17 pistol. I know it's wiser to have a gun and not need a gun than it is to need a gun and not have a gun, but I just felt uncomfortable accepting it. Plus, it was illegal to be packing a pistol. I thanked Sakda for obtaining the weapon for me, but I asked if he would hold onto it for the time being.

"Up to you Mr. Bubba," he replied, taking the gun back.

Two months into the project, we found ourselves working two ten hour-shifts. I would open the shop at 5:30 a.m. and we'd be smoking by 6:00 a.m. Charlie would roll up around 3:00 p.m. We would then have a crew change at 4:00 p.m. and Charlie would shut everything down at 2:00 a.m.

We were on schedule with 120 pontoons completed, leaving sixty to fabricate in the next month. We hired extra welders through Terdsak's connections for the pipeline and quickly had one quarter of that work completed. We knew that the Dredger Committee would be making an inspection visit to our facilities in the near future, and if the members were satisfied, Bangkok Bob would slip one hundred thousand dollars into the hand under the table to the committee chairman, an acceptance fee, or the cost of doing business in Thailand. The committee would then process the documentation, and the progress payment would be made. The committee would also expect to be wined and dined again.

One afternoon I was sitting around, shooting the shit with Sakda, when I asked him what he had done after he had avenged his family over the loss of the rice-paddy farm.

"The United States Air Force was looking for Thais who could speak the Lao and English language, which I could, so I hired on," he replied.

"Doing what?" I asked curiously.

Sakda explained the United States Air Force put him through several indoctrination courses and then sent him into the Lao People's Democratic Republic where he was located on a hilltop in the Plain of Jars with United States supplied communications equipment. It was his duty to assist the B-52 bomber aircraft crews with radio navigation as they came and went from their Thailand bases on bombing missions over North Vietnam.

In the mid 1970s, after the conflict was over, Sakda said he hired on with people he knew to be local Bangkok mafia involved in the sex-slave trade. His assignment was to fly to Japan acting as an escort for six to eight Thai girls in their late teens. On arrival into Japan, Sakda would turn the girls over to the Japanese Yakooza, and they would be put to work as bar girls. His cover was a salesman for children's toys. During the trip to Japan, by way of Taiwan or the Philippines, it was his duty to take care of visa documentation as most of the girl's were illiterate.

He told me he had been paid twenty-five thousand dollars per trip. When he returned from his third trip however, the Thai police and Immigration officials were waiting for him. He was held in custody and questioned for several hours. Sakda managed to produce his briefcase of kids' toys and phony invoice orders he had received from the Yakooza, repudiating any knowledge of the running of prostitutes into Japan. After the interrogation, he decided to quit what he was doing, believing he was now under observation by the authorities. Saudi Arabia, at that time, was hiring thousands of Thais to go work in its desert oil fields. He, along with Terdrsak, immediately hired on, spending the next three years in the sweltering Saudi desert heat.

It was a very interesting story. "Will you ever go back to work in Saudi Arabia?" I asked him.

Sakda shook his head. "Thai people are banned from working in Saudi Arabia now, Mr. Bubba," he answered. "A couple of years ago, one Thai man was working in Saudi Arabia as a janitor in the palace of King Faisal. He stole around twenty million dollars worth of jewels from the palace. It took him several years, but piece-by-piece he would hide them in electrical appliances and smuggle them back into Thailand. Sometimes he would bring them in himself, and other-times he would have his friends bring the appliances back on their holidays. However, his friends never knew he had hidden jewels inside the appliances. When he finally returned to Thailand, he pawned the precious stones to three jewelers in Bangkok. When one highly-prized blue pendant was discovered missing from the palace, the Saudis started an investigation. When they learned about the theft, they immediately contacted the Bangkok police."

"Really?" I asked incredulously. "Then what happened?"

"The Thai police general, who was in charge of the investigation and seven members of his task-force became greedy. During their search and recovery of part of the haul, they murdered the wife and teenage son of one of the jewelers using torture tactics to try and extract information," Sakda said. "Also, some of the recovered jewels they returned to the Saudi's were fake."

"Was the pendant ever located?" I asked.

Sakda shook his head. "No, the precious pendant was never found. However, the police general and the seven task force members were eventually charged with malfeasance, conspiracy to embezzle, and abuse of authority by conspiring to commit murder and were imprisoned. The Saudi Charge d'Affaires pressed the case for his government to our prime minister and issued a statement that no more Thai people would be allowed to work in Saudi Arabia until all the jewels were returned." Sakda explained. "I think the jewels have been sold many times, and some of them have been cut into smaller jewels. No one knows where most of them are now. I think it's safe to say that Thai people will never go back to work in Saudi Arabia ever again.

***

The Dredger Committee visited the shop and inspected the completed pontoons and pipeline sections for size and quality and would approve the items for delivery after Bangkok Bob had submitted the necessary documentation for the first progress payment. We would deliver the items to their storage yard in the suburb of Sumutprakan on the south side of Bangkok.

Once again, the committee also wished to visit The Plaza. Sakda, Terdsak, Blackcloud and I obliged, and that night we all ran up a tab of three thousand dollars. The following afternoon Blackcloud and I visited the Hog's Breath to hand Bob the Dredger Committee's signed-off documentation for our first progress payment of two-and-a-half million dollars. Bob grinned as he looked over the paper work.

"Fellas," he said. "This is our first payment with a profit. After costs. With this payment, we should damn near be a half-a-million bucks in the black!"

Both Charlie and I each had individual Bangkok bank accounts. When Bob received the payment into our joint account that he and I had originally set-up, $150,000 would be transferred into Charlie's account, and the same amount would be transferred into my separate account and Bob's account, leaving the remainder for expenses. The spotlight was beginning to shine on my Gulf Coast bar again.

Then Bob leaned in and looked at me. "Hey, Bubba," he said quietly. "I think I may have fucked up."

I glanced over at him and felt my pulse quicken. "What do you mean, Bob?" I asked.

"Well, a couple of nights ago California Ken was here in the bar, and we got to shooting the shit. He asked what I was up to these days. Well, without thinking, I told him I had a deal going with you and Charlie, and we were doing a bunch of fabrication work for the Thai Dredging Department. As soon as I mentioned your name Bubba, and saw the look on his face, I knew I had said too much."

"What are you saying Bob?" I asked slowly.

"California Ken told me you had created a world of trouble for him, and Thailand just might not be the safest place for you to be," Bob responded. "I am truly sorry, Bubba, I just wasn't thinking!"

I took a deep breath and shook my head. "Don't worry about it Bob, fuck California Ken!" I assured him. "As the saying goes, 'You can't hide from the consequences of the things you do,' right? We have some celebrating to do!" With that we raised our glasses and toasted to our success. Meanwhile, I silently recalled a line from an old Eagles song: "Every form of refuge has its price."

We continued working the two shifts for another month, completing the pontoon side of the contract, and then we eventually went back to straight days. I extended the lease on the fabrication facilities for another three months. Through his Thai contacts, Bangkok Bob had arranged for a trucking company to load out the pontoons and haul them the forty-odd miles to the storage yard where the Dredger Committee would take delivery and process the documentation for payment after they withdrew their fist-full-of-dollars from under the table. Each Saturday evening Blackcloud and I would follow our routine and drive up to Bangkok, check in at the Nana Hotel and meet up with Bob at the Hog's Breath to hand over whatever documentation he required for submittal to the Dredger Committee.

During one Saturday morning load-out of the pontoons, one of the semi-trailer trucks was accidentally reversed right into Terdsak's vehicle. The front end was instantly caved in, which wrecked the radiator and fan assembly. There was no way the vehicle could be driven, and there was nothing we could do to get it to a repair shop until Monday. Terdsak needed a vehicle to visit his family in Bangkok, so I told him not to worry and tossed him the keys to my vehicle. I would just ride up to Bangkok with Blackcloud for our weekly meeting at the Hog's Breath.

***

The recently completed four-lane express highway between Pattaya and Bangkok had shortened the trip by at least forty-five minutes. However, there were tollbooths located where vehicles entered and exited the highway, and they charged what amounted to a couple of bucks for a one-way trip. Vehicles with four or more wheels utilized the toll road; motorcycles were absolutely prohibited from using it. To enforce the law, Thai police officers with their BMW patrol cars were stationed at both toll booths.

The highway ran through rice paddy farms and rubber tree plantations. The busy highway was also fenced-in on both sides to impede the local farmers and their water buffalo from crossing. Terdsak left for Bangkok in my pick-up truck as the sun was almost touching the horizon. I had half an hour of paperwork to complete before Blackcloud and I would follow.

Once I was done finishing up we headed out and passed through the toll booth and entered onto the four lane highway which remained a straight stretch for the next thirty miles. Everything was going fine. Blackcloud was driving and we were shooting the breeze. Suddenly, off in the distance we noticed flashing lights from various emergency vehicles. As we drove along, we realized there was an accident of some kind up ahead. Once we reached the scene, Blackcloud slowed down, and that's when we saw a Toyota pick-up truck in the ditch. We both glanced at each other. My mouth dropped open.

"Goddamn it, Charlie!" I groaned. "That's my fucking truck!"

Charlie pulled onto the shoulder and parked his truck. I quickly got out of the vehicle and looked over at my pick-up truck in the ditch. In the fading light, I also noticed a black motorcycle lying tits up in the ditch approximately fifty or sixty feet from the truck. A thought flashed through my mind. What is a motorcycle doing on a highway where they are clearly prohibited?

A Thai cop began walking briskly towards us, waving his arms and speaking in broken English.

"You must go. Cannot stop here!" he called out.

I stood still and waited until he reached me. Charlie was now standing beside me, too. I spoke slowly in clear words, and pointed at the wrecked truck, explaining that it belonged to me.

"That your truck?" he asked, confused. He shook his melon. "But Thai man drive."

I didn't have time to answer him. Another Thai man in plain clothes approached us and introduced himself in perfect English as Detective Piboon. He was in charge of all highway accidents. I showed him my passport, as did Charlie, and then I explained to him that the pick-up truck was my work truck. I also told him that the driver, Terdsak, worked with me and had borrowed my truck. I wanted to know if Terdsak was injured and what had happened.

Detective Piboon explained that someone had attempted to assassinate Terdsak while on a motorcycle, and there were several bullet holes in the truck's body. Terdsak had been wounded and was currently being transported to the Bangna General Hospital with non-life-threatening wounds. The police had already managed to apprehend the injured motorcycle driver, and it was suspected that a passenger on the motorcycle was no doubt the shooter. Unfortunately, that person had escaped before police arrived on the scene. The motorcycle driver was also taken to the hospital with a suspected broken leg and was under police watch.

Detective Piboon then took down our information and requested we meet with him at noon the following day when he hoped he would have more information. We thanked him and continued on our way to Bangkok, passing through the suburb of Bangna, where Terdsak lay in the emergency care unit. We stopped at the hospital but were told Teredsak could not have visitors that evening as he was still in surgery, so we decided to visit him the next day. Later, when I reached the Nana Hotel, I would contact Sakda and tell him the news about Terdsak. I also made a mental note to call the truck rental company and explain that the Bangkok cops had impounded it until further notice. I would stop by for a replacement in a day or two.

When Charlie and I entered the Hog's Breath, Bangkok Bob could tell something was wrong by the looks on our faces. After I explained what had happened, his eyes grew wide. "Holy fuck, Bubba!" he exclaimed. "I hope it wasn't you they were gunning for. However, I wouldn't be surprised if that shit-ass mother fucking California Ken had a piece of this action."

Charlie looked at Bob. "Do you really think that queer son-of-a-bitch would set up a hit on Bubba, all because of the shit that happened in Kuwait?" he asked.

Bob sighed. "Well, Charlie, I think he's definitely burned up over the pending court case in the United States, especially considering he may be charged with criminal negligence," he muttered.

I glanced over at Charlie, who seemed visibly shaken. I felt bad for him, and I didn't want him to get hurt or caught in the middle of shit that I started. "Charlie, if you want to bow out of this deal, I fully understand," I said. "I know that this shit has turned nasty, and hanging around with me might jeopardize your health."

Charlie gave me a look of disgust as if he was offended I would even say that.

"Fuck you and the big white horse you rode in on, Bubba!" he replied, "This is our war, and I am in it with you 'til the bitter end." With that, he raised his beer.

Bob nodded and held up his beer as well. "And that goes for me too, Bubba," he added.

I grinned and thanked them for their moral support. Then the three of us clinked our beers in unison in a toast to a continued healthy and prosperous project.

We met with Detective Piboon at noon the following day. He told us the motorcycle driver's leg had indeed been shattered and the authorities had already interrogated him using a little gentle persuasion. He confessed his passenger, the shooter, had hired him, but he only knew the guy as Khun Nong.

"So it should be easy to find him then, right?" Charlie asked.

Detective Piboon shook his head. "More than likely, the shooter used a false name," he explained.

Apparently the motorcycle driver and the shooter had been hiding among the rubber trees several miles down the highway from the toll-booth. They had cut the fence to enable quick and easy entrance onto the highway. A third party had been stationed at the toll-booth, waiting for a Toyota pick-up with a certain license plate number to drive through. When it did the third party called the shooter on his mobile telephone to make sure he was ready.

The motorcycle driver told Detective Piboon that the shooter stood up on the back foot-rests of the motorcycle and took aim once they were close enough to the pick-up truck. As he did so, the Toyota swerved, clipping the front wheel of the motorcycle and caused the driver to lose control, which in turn threw off the shooter's aim. The motorcycle driver had told Detective Piboon that the shooter knew that a "farang," or white-skinned foreigner, would be driving the pick-up truck. By then, however, it was after sunset. Distinguishing the driver's actual skin color was difficult. All the motorcycle driver and shooter knew was that the actual driver appeared to have light skin. They had the right license plate number, and money had already been paid for a hit.

Detective Piboon looked at me. "Since the pick-up truck belongs to you, I think it's pretty safe to assume you were the intended target last night, he said solemnly. He glanced at Charlie and then at me again. "Do either of you men have any idea who would want to assassinate you."

"It's a mystery to me," I blurted, lying through my teeth. I looked at Blackcloud.

"I have no idea," he said quietly.

The look on Detective Piboon's face made him seem unconvinced, however, he thanked us for meeting with him and said he would come by our shop to discuss any further developments if they should unfold. We thanked him for looking into the matter and left to visit Terdsak at the hospital.

Terdsak was alert and sitting up in his bed when we walked into his hospital room. His right arm was in a sling and he had a bandage wrapped around his melon. Sakda was sitting in a chair beside the bed. Both men smiled when they saw us.

"How the hell are you, Terdsak?" Charlie and I asked in unison.

"Okay, Boss," Terdsak answered.

Sakda looked relieved that we were there. "Terdsak is very lucky, Mr. Bubba," he said. "If he not drive clever, he dead, for sure."

"Can you tell us what happened, Terdsak?" I asked walking closer to his bed.

Terdsak nodded slowly. "Sure Boss," he said. "I was driving along the highway after the toll booth when I see a motorcycle in my rear-view mirror. I know motorcycle should not be on the highway, so I keep my eye on him. When he get close, I see passenger stand up. I am Thai from the north east of my country; I know of many politicians get shot by man on motorcycle," he explained. "When motorcycle get level to my door, I swing the steering wheel to the right and smack the front wheel of the motorcycle. I feel something hit my shoulder. I over correct truck and crash into ditch. Then motorcycle go wobbly-wobbly and also flip into ditch. Sorry Boss, I broke your truck."

"No problem, Terdsak," I said quickly. "A broken truck can easily be fixed. What about you and your injuries?" I asked. "What did the doctor say?"

"I get one bullet in my shoulder, and I crack my skull when I hit the ditch. Doctor removed bullet. No break bone. Doctor put four stitches in my skull." Terdsak said. Then he added, "Mr. Bubba, I want to know, did crazy shit man from Siam Engineering try to kill you?"

"I don't know Terdsak, but maybe," I answered. What the hell else could I say? It was bad enough that he was hurt because of something I was involved in. I figured that the less he knew about everything involving California Ken and what had happened in Kuwait, the better. But I believed California Ken had caused this shit.

Terdsak then told us he would be out of the hospital the following day.

I smiled. "Well, you go and stay with your family until you are sure you are okay," I said. "And when you feel good enough you can come back to work if you want to. In the meantime, if there is anything you want me to do, just tell me or Sakda, okay?" Terdsak nodded.

"Thank you Boss, and I no tell police nothing about Siam Engineering man," he added.

With that, we said adios and left.

As I walked with Charlie through the hospital corridor toward the exit, Sakda quickly came up behind us and tapped my shoulder. We stopped walking.

"Mr. Bubba, I have many good friends in Bangkok," Sakda said quietly. "I want to have maybe two or three days before I go back to our shop. I go and check-check with my friend about what happen. Then I come and talk with you."

I shook my head. "Sakda, this is not your fight," I said firmly. "You don't have to do nothing man. I don't want you to end up getting hurt, too."

"Mr. Bubba," he persisted. "Terdsak is my family, and you are good friend to me. Bad stupid people make this my fight!"

On the drive back to our work-shop I asked Charlie what his thoughts were on my situation.

"I am not sure I even know what to do right now," I confided.

"Well Bubba, the way I see it, you have several choices," Blackcloud replied. "You could skip the country, or you stay and we fight this son-of-a-bitch together. But remember, we should have this project wrapped up in another six to eight weeks. Focus on that instead of what California Ken may or may not try to do."

I thought about his words for a moment. "Thanks Charlie. You know, that's about the way I see things," I said. "I am going to stay. We've come too far to give up now. Besides, I don't expect any surprises for awhile considering the fuck-up that just occurred.

"Then it's settled," Charlie said.

I hesitated. "I am kind of curious about what Sakda is up to," I added. "I don't think I told you Charlie, but Sakda knows some pretty shady characters with Thai mafia connections." I glanced over at Blackcloud for a reaction. He just rolled his eyes and kept driving forward.

***

The Thai folk working in our shop were ready to kill whomever had hurt their boss. Blackcloud and I had a meeting with their supervisors and assured them that Terdsak was out of the hospital and he would be back with us in a week or so. When Sakda returned, he approached me and had a very serious, yet satisfied look on his face.

"I find out many things, Mr. Bubba," he told me and Charlie. "You no worry about Siam Engineering man. Thai people will take care of this problem."

I looked at Charlie and then at Sakda.

"Listen, Sakda. I don't want you to do anything that will cause you a problem," I said.

Once again Sakda remained persistent. "Mr. Bubba, maybe I will need a bonus of fifty thousand baht to make problem disappear," he said.

I looked at Charlie again. He shrugged and gave a little nod. His silent blessing, I thought. Fuck it. This is war. Fifty thousand baht in local currency amounted to about fifteen hundred green backs.

"I will have it paid into your bank account within the next couple of days," I replied. Shortly after our brief conversation, I called

Bangkok Bob and asked him to transfer the money from our expense account into Sakda's bank account. I added that I would explain everything when we met at the Hog's Breath. Bob told me the money would be transferred as soon as we got off the phone.

Ten days after the highway shooting, Terdsak was back on deck. While he had been on leave, I had his truck's front end and radiator repaired. He told us his shull was healing just fine. However, his arm would be in a sling for another couple of weeks. At least it was healing the right way, and he exercised it a little bit each day.

I received another letter from Weinstein and Weinstein. Jacob indicated an out-of-court settlement was becoming evident for both the Donald Johnson and Bubba Cottonmill cases.

The District of San Francisco and State of California were proceeding with criminal charges against California Ken, owing to the fact that he was the project manager of the Al-Awda, Kuwait Fires Project representing his company. I decided not to inform Weinstein and Weinstein about the highway assassination attempt; there really wasn't a damn thing they could do, anyway. This was a Thai affair.

Our project had progressed to the extent where we had completed two-thirds of the pipeline fabrication. It warranted another inspection visit by the Dredger Committee for our second progress payment. The committee members arrived, as usual, in all their splendour of designer suits, Rolex watches, and diamond rings. As that saying goes, "living well is the best revenge," and these cats were into that. They conducted their tour and congratulated us on the production and quality of the fabrication and readily signed off on the documentation. Of course we then had to provide them with another indulgent evening of wine, women, and karaoke.

***

Detective Piboon arrived at our facilities for an unexpected visit, carrying an iced tea and asking to speak with us. Charlie and I took him into our shared office and we all sat down.

"Mr. Bubba, what happened at your old company, Siam Engineering?" he asked, getting straight to the point. He took a sip of his iced tea before continuing.

"I have a copy of your immigration history, and it seems your Siam Engineering work visa was cancelled-prematurely. Why is that?"

I decided to lay out the whole history for Detective Piboon at that point, commencing with Don's murder in Kuwait, my telephone call to Don's wife, the initiation of the court case, and my premature termination. I reached into my briefcase and retrieved a copy of the latest information from the lawyers regarding the pending charges against California Ken and handed it to him.

He listened to my explanation of everything, silently read the documentation from Weinstein and Weinstein, and then he looked at me.

"Mr. Bubba, our investigations have uncovered some information that point to California Ken's homosexual lover as the possible pro-curer of the assassin. This individual has a criminal record that dates back many years. He was convicted of selling amphetamine, ya-ba, pills to under age boys, and having carnal knowledge of those boys," he said. "At this time we don't have enough evidence to arrest anyone, but rest assured that we will. However, from what you have told me and what you have shown me from your American lawyers, I would suggest this evidence indicates motive for what we know in Thailand as a revenge killing."

"Okay, so now what?" I asked

Detective Piboon continued. "The motorcycle driver has been charged with conspiracy to commit murder. We have no links to the shooter, and maybe never will, but we will be following up on all leads. I am sure one of those leads will take us to the guilty party."

With that, I thanked the detective for visiting and giving us the update. He thanked us for cooperating with him. As he turned to leave, he stopped and said, "Mr. Bubba, all life is based on deception. So you take care."

***

Blackcloud and I made the Bangkok run on Saturday evening without incident. As usual, Bob was waiting at the Hog's Breath at his personal table, and I handed him the Dredger Committee's documentation for our second progress payment. Bob grinned at us. "Well, we are stacking cash now, fellas!" he exclaimed. "So how long before the remaining pipeline work is all wrapped up?"

"I'd say it will be another three weeks and then it will all be over," Blackcloud replied. I nodded; it seemed like a fair estimate.

Bob wanted to know how our injured man was doing. "What's going on, anyway?" he asked.

"He's healing well, Bob," I answered. Then I spilled the beans about Detective Piboon's visit and the information I had received regarding the possibility of charges being laid against California Ken.

Bob rolled his eyes. "Honestly, the dickhead deserves all they can throw at him," he said plainly.

Before leaving Bangkok to head back to our workshop, I called the little blonde lady in Odessa to tell her that I missed her and that cash was really starting to stack up. I added that if everything went as planned, I was hoping to be back in Texas in several months. I didn't bother to mention the Terdsak episode.

A couple of weeks later we were all hard at work trying to complete the project. Most of the fabrication work was over and trucks were regularly hauling several loads out of our shop and delivering them to the Dredger Committee's storage yard. Suddenly a brown BMW police car pulled up in front of my office and Detective Piboon stepped out. This should be interesting, I thought. I greeted him as he stepped from his vehicle. Detective Piboon said hello and asked if Charlie could also join us inside the office. He had some information to speak about that concerned the both of us.

We stepped inside and waited for the detective to speak. "Gentlemen, around 3:00 this morning, I was requested to be present at a crime scene on the four-lane Don Muang International Airport toll-way. Evidently a taxi had made a prearranged pick up for a trip to the airport. The two passengers were picked up from the Bangna condo complex. One passenger was farang, the other Thai," he said. "At that time of night, the toll-way is almost deserted. According to the taxi driver, he noticed two sets of headlights coming up behind his vehicle at very high speed. Thinking they could be part of a street race, he steered his taxi into the far left lane, leaving as much road space as possible for the speeding vehicles to pass. However, as they leveled with his taxi, they slowed to his speed for several seconds. The taxi driver said he could see that both vehicles were black BMWs. Then the one along-side of his taxi inched forward while the other one slowed down. Before he realized what was happening, he was boxed in with one BMW in front and the other on his rear. He said they were so close that both his front and rear bumpers were almost touching the two BMWs. It was impossible for him to make a lane change.

Detective Piboon waited a moment to let the information sink in. Then he continued. "The lead vehicle began to slow so much that it eventually forced the taxi to a standstill. As the taxi driver began to get out of his vehicle to speak with the BMW drivers, he stopped cold in his tracks. He said he saw a Thai man getting out of the vehicle to his rear with a pistol in each hand and moving very quickly toward the taxi. Before the taxi driver had any time to react, the pistol-packing gunman reached the rear passenger door of his vehicle and opened fire." The detective said. "The taxi driver said he heard the door window explode and saw the orange flashes from the muzzles of both pistols as maybe six or eight shots were fired into the backseat of the cab, which proved fatal for the passengers seated in the rear. Following the shooting the gunman glanced at the taxi driver as he turned and ran back to the BMW, with smoking-screaming tires it pulled away from the scene followed by the lead BMW that had been stopped, idling in front of his taxi. Both vehicles were out of sight on the toll-way within seconds."

"So who were the passengers?" Charlie asked.

"The victims were identified by their passports and other documentation on their person. We now know the deceased farang is the individual you both refer to as California Ken, the other deceased person we believe to be his homosexual lover." Detective Piboon replied.

"Holy shit!" I exclaimed. "Are you absolutely positive about that? Man this is wild!"

The detective nodded and continued. "We have evidence that these two persons did procure an individual to cause harm to you,

Mr. Bubba. We also believe that all negotiated monies for the assassination were not paid, owing to the fact that the hit was unsuccessful. This morning's shooting was payback for non-payment."

"What happens now?" I asked. "Where does that leave me?"

"Mr. Bubba, as far as the Bangkok Homicide Department is concerned, we have a few details to complete, but you have nothing to be concerned about. For you, the case is closed," Detective Piboon said. "I still need to have a few words with Terdsak and inform him about the charges against the motorcycle driver and the pending court case, and then I will be on my way."

I thanked Detective Piboon for visiting again and we said our final farewells. After he left though, I looked at Blackcloud and shook my head slowly in disbelief.

"What do you think of that shit Charlie?" I said.

"Well Bubba, there's not much we can say except, from my point of view, that cocksucker got what he deserved," Charlie said quietly.

I needed to have a few words with Sakda. I told him the reason why Detective Piboon had visited and about the shooting death of California Ken and his lover.

"What did Piboon say about who did the shooting?" Sakda asked.

I told him what Detective Piboon had told me. "I guess the case is closed as far as we're concerned," I added.

"Good," he answered, looking a bit relieved. "Police take the easy way to finish everything about people who try to make problem for you."

"What do you mean Sakda," I asked slowly.

"Mr. Bubba." he said. "I tell you before, I have many friends in Bangkok who know about this business. Is better we believe what Detective Piboon say and forget about California Ken. He make one big mistake when he hurt Terdsak."

I took that to mean the subject was closed, however, I figured Sakda had used the fifty thousand baht bonus he had requested to set the wheels in motion for the payback assassination. In a way, I owed him my life.

There was one thing I had learned about Thailand and Thai people: they do things their way. One of the amazing facts of history regarding the Thais that sets them apart from each and all of their Southeast Asian neighbors is the fact that Thailand has never been colonized. Many nations had tried to do it, and many battles had been fought, but the Thais had never been beaten.

I made a telephone call to Bangkok Bob regarding the California Ken incident. He told me the news was in all the Bangkok newspapers and the cops seemed to have it all figured out. I explained Detective Piboon had visited our workshop and we would discuss it the next time we met at the Hog's Breath.

Two weeks after Detective Piboon's visit, we had wrapped up the contract. The final load out was delivered to the Dredger Committee's storage yard and all documentation had finally been signed-off. I shipped whatever materials were remaining back to the suppliers for credit. Then I contacted Bangkok Bob to let him know the job was officially completed. He arrived at our facilities around noon, along with a bus load of girls from the Hog's Breath and a few other bars in the Nana Plaza. Earlier that morning, Charlie, Sakda, and I had driven into the village to stock up on a truck load of food and booze. We had worked so hard for so long. Now it was party time!

By 6:00 p.m. I had a shop full of drunken Thais and half naked-girls. The distinct odor of Wild Willie Weed and the sound of Thai music floated through the air. The following day we cleaned up the party mess. Then we paid off the labor force, giving each individual a 20 percent bonus. Lastly, we handed the fabrication facility back to the owner. Sakda and Terdsak would receive their final pay-off in Bangkok after the Dredger Committee had sanctioned the final payment and it had been issued to Bangkok Bob.

A few days after we closed up the shop, I received another letter from Weinstein and Weinstein. The California state attorney's office had informed the lawfirm about the demise of California Ken. Additionally, an-out-of court settlement for Donna Johnson and her family of an undisclosed amount in the double-digit millions was about to be accepted. My settlement had been delayed for several weeks, but an out-of-court settlement was being considered in the range of three to five million dollars. At my convenience, I would be required to meet with the law firm and agree upon a final settlement. I responded to Jacob by saying that I would be returning to the United States within several weeks and I would be in contact again then.

The final payment rolled in. I went with Bob and we closed out our joint bank account and then we made arrangements for a farewell dinner at the oldest and grandest hotel in Bangkok, The Oriental. We were seated at an outside table under huge trees that were decorated with small twinkling lights near the Chao Praya River. It was a magnificent location, and the buffet meal was excellent, too. Even better, as I sat among lifelong friends, I realized I hadn't had a single nightmare regarding Don's murder or Kuwait since the death of California Ken. Perhaps I finally had found closure, after all.

Sakda, Terdsak, and Charlie Blackcloud had never visited this grand old hotel before and they all seemed in complete awe of their beautiful surroundings. Bob and I had visited the hotel on several occasions. In fact one evening I had been seated in the main lobby drinking a coffee when I spotted former United States president George Bush enter with the future rogue Thai Prime Minster, Thaksin Shinawatra.

We were all enjoying ourselves immensely, but Sakda seemed to be really having a good time, especially after indulging a few too many whiskies. He decided to give us a little history lesson about the Chao Phraya River that twists and turns its way through Bangkok. He told us that it begins in the forested mountains of Northern Thailand and empties into the Gulf of Thailand. He noted that the river serves as a watery highway for goods traveling in both directions, and barges loaded with teak, rice, tin, fruits of all kinds, and agriculture produce can be seen night and day being pulled by smoking tug-boats. In Thai culture, he added, it is often called the "River of Kings."

Around 11:00 we reluctantly decided to call it quits for the evening. Bangkok Bob, Charlie, and I bid farewell to Terdsak and Sakda. They were good guys and deserved every penny we paid them, which was twice what they had expected. Shit, poor Terdsak had taken a slug meant for me, and there was no doubt in my mind Sakda had set up the equalizer.

Charlie Blackcloud flew out of Bangkok the following day, heading for Florida with his half-million dollars. He promised to take me on an airboat ride through his tribal lands in the Everglades when I visited with him. I wound up putting $650,000 big ones in my ass national. All I had to do now was find that one-of-a-kind bar. Hell I'd probably be able to pay cash if the court case proved profitable down the road. Shit, I thought. When it rains it pours.

Bangkok Bob's final count was around a cool million, and he definitely deserved it. After all, it had been his gig, and he had done a great job of kicking it off and keeping the shit rolling.

It wasn't easy saying adios to those guys. Alaska seemed like such a long time ago. Sumatra had been a buzz. Kuwait had been a real bitch. In the end though, Thailand had made it all worthwhile. I flew out of Bangkok and headed for Houston, Texas. For the first time in a long time, my intentions were clear. I knew exactly what I wanted to do with the rest of my life. I was going to buy a brand new American made crew-cab pick-up truck and head down the Texas Gulf Coast, but I wasn't going to be driving alone. Nope, the little blonde lady from Odessa was also flying into Houston to join me. I could finally focus on making my dreams come true.

THE END

ABOUT THE AUTHOR

Author Tony May spent the early years of his career as a fabricator/ welder in the oil and gas industry working on worldwide offshore and onshore drilling rigs, resulting in his first novel, Rig Pigs. Graduating with a degree in welding engineering in the early 1980s, he then entered the construction industry. Tony spent several years working in Thailand, experiencing a tangled web of deceit which spawned his second novel, titled Codename Dredge. In 1991, he reentered the oil and gas industry managing steel fabrication facilities in several countries including Indonesia, Thailand and Kuwait at the conclusion of 1991's Gulf War, and has now penned Smoke in the Wind. This is fiction based on his oilfield experiences and encompasses Alaska, Sumatra, Indonesia and the Kuwait oil well fires project